R. A. Davila has read every single word in this book and been there to help me both edit it and to provide me with ideas and different perspectives. This could not have been written without her help. (Or her constant threats to hurt me if I didn't get up off my lazy ass to write something.)

James Wright did not help me with this specific book, but has done all the web design at my website **nelsonchereta.com**. Thanks James for helping me maintain what (I hope) is an interesting place for my readers to visit.

I also want to take a moment to thank all my readers who are fans of the Waldo Rabbit novels and have been patient with me as I work on book three, **The Rabbit Great And Terrible.** It IS coming, I swear, but I am still working on it to make it as entertaining as the first two books. As a special thanks to all of you I have included a short Waldo Rabbit story at the end of this book, and I promise I will not publish it anywhere else. I hope you will enjoy it.

XXX

Chapter 1

In the south Pacific there's a small, uninhabited island. Well, actually, there are literally thousands of those in the Pacific Ocean, but that's neither here nor there. Anyway, I was walking along the beach of said island when I came across a beautiful young woman with long silky black hair, a porcelain complexion, and no arms or legs. She was just lying there as I walked up to her. Of course given her state it's not like she could have done much else. I suppose, technically, she could have been sitting. Especially if she had something to lean against. Sorry, I'm digressing.

"Hello," I said.

"Hi," she said as if greeting me on the street.

I wasn't really sure what to say next. I mean given the circumstances there was an obvious question to ask, but I didn't want to be rude.

"I don't suppose you have any water?" She asked.

"Not on me, but I have some back on my boat. I can go get you some."

She shook her head. "Never mind, it's probably just as well. Without water I should be dead by this time tomorrow."

"Well, I don't know if this matters to you, but according to the area weather report there are going to be squalls all afternoon."

"Great. I just can't catch a break."

"So… you want to die?"

"It's not my first choice, but given the circumstances it's probably the best I can hope for."

There was an uncomfortable pause.

"Look, I don't mean to be rude, but what are you doing here on my island?"

"Dying. Slowly."

Looking back on it, I should have walked away from her right then and there. I mean who gets that sarcastic in a situation like that? Seriously? I should have come up with a snappy come back like, 'well don't let me get in your way,' and then just left her there. Instead, I stood there like a moron.

"So where is this place?"

"You mean you don't know?"

She raised an eyebrow, and somehow managed to look down on me, even though she was lying flat on her back. "What, you think I came here on my own?"

I have an IQ of two hundred and am the fifth smartest person in the world. (At that point I was number six, but still.) And with that one sentence she made me feel about as intelligent as a two year old. I really should have gone back to my boat.

"This place is called Teilau and is a part of the Solomon Islands."

"And you own it?"

"That's right. It used to belong to Richard Faust, Mister Mephisto, and I was able to buy it from his estate. I wanted to see if he might have had one of his secret hideouts here, or at least stashed some of his equipment." Okay, why on earth did I tell a complete stranger that? Geez, maybe I really do have a problem with monologuing.

"You'd think they'd be more careful about a supervillain's property."

"I know. Governments can be surprisingly lax sometimes, especially when it comes to getting money for an estate tax."

"So did he have a secret base here?"

"No. There's nothing but snakes and bugs."

"And me."

"And you," I agreed.

There was another uncomfortable silence. She was lying in the sand of a deserted island with the stumps of her arms and legs bandaged up with dried blood stains. You'd expect someone in those circumstances to come out and ask for help, to plead and beg for help. But apparently she didn't feel the need.

"So," I finally asked. "How did you end up in your current situation?"

She didn't answer immediately, but eventually gave a half sigh and spoke. "I'm a ninja, my alias is Raven. I have a mortal enemy named Viper who leads a rival clan. He and his people murdered my entire family. I've been tracking them down ever since. I managed to eliminate everyone but him. He ambushed me and did this. Viper brought me out here and left me to die a slow, painful death."

I nodded. "Okay, that makes sense."

"Wait. You actually believe me?"

"Sure, why wouldn't I?"

"Oh, I don't know, because I said I was a ninja? And that this was all because of a blood feud between a couple ninja clans? Most people would be a little skeptical."

"Well I'm a supervillain, so I try not to judge. By the way, your English is excellent."

"I'm from San Francisco."

"Oh. I'm sorry, I kind of assumed-"

"That since I'm a ninja and look Japanese and belong to a clan I was from Japan. I get it. I'm second generation Japanese-American. I went to Cal-Berkley and my family ran a dojo. It was like in Karate Kid, except we had hidden rooms with swords and shuriken and stuff. Plus, you know, we stole things and killed people for money."

"I see. Well, would you like me to bring you to a hospital? I'm actually staying in Sydney, Australia, they have good facilities."

"Don't bother. The second he finds out I'm alive, Viper will finish me off. Besides, if I can't kill him and avenge my family I don't want to live."

"What if you got some artificial limbs?"

"What good would that do? So I could maybe learn to walk again? Great, I can be standing when Viper shows up to cut my throat."

"No, that's not what I mean. I'm an evil genius. I could give you powered cybernetic limbs. Arms that can punch through concrete walls or bend steel girders. Legs that can run a hundred miles an hour and leap forty feet into the air. I could turn you into a cyborg ninja!"

The second I said it out loud I got excited. I mean think about it, a cyborg ninja? How cool is that? It's almost as great as building a giant robot.

She lifted her head up and stared at me. "You serious? You can actually do that?"

"I have a masters in both electrical and mechanical engineering from MIT, and I've had plenty of hands on experience with robots and robotic limbs."

She narrowed her eyes. "And what do you want from me? Nothing's free. I have hidden bank accounts, I can pay you."

"I don't want money. I just want you to be my henchman."

"A henchman?" When she said it her lips twisted like she'd bitten a lemon.

I nodded. "You can help me take over the world."

"That's not what ninja do. We're assassins, thieves, kidnappers, and spies. We're professionals, we work for money. We aren't into the whole, rule the world thing."

"Oh, come on! You've got to admit this is a great deal! You get your limbs back and get turned into a CYBORG NINJA! And all I ask in return is that you work for me. What could be better?"

"I don't know. Being stabbed? Finding out I have herpes? Getting audited?"

"How about dying of thirst on a beach?"

She actually had to think about it! I mean, damn, how ungrateful can a person be? Someone comes along and offers you not only a second chance at life, but the opportunity to be superhuman, and you have to think about it? Some people have absolutely no appreciation for life's unique opportunities!

"What about Viper?"

"What about him?" I was honestly surprised she even had to ask. "He's your mortal enemy and you want revenge. I can respect that. Kill him or do whatever else you need to."

She again thought about it! "All right, but here are my conditions." I opened my mouth to object but she kept going. "I'll work for you, but I want fair market value for my services, and I'll tell you up front I'm not cheap. I'm fully trained in the ninja arts and have lots of experience in the field. I'll choose the jobs I take, so you can forget about me going to pick up your laundry or cleaning for you. I'm a ninja, not a maid."

"You sound more like an independent contractor than a henchman."

She frowned. "Don't call me a henchman. I'll agree to be your sidekick."

"Villains don't have sidekicks, that's a hero thing."

"You can be the very first. Maybe you'll be a trendsetter."

"You can be my lieutenant." I sighed. Her conditions were dampening my enthusiasm. "But if I'm paying you like a contractor then you'll have to repay me for the cybernetics. For four limbs the parts and labor are going to cost at least two million dollars."

She nodded. "We can work out a payment schedule. Okay, I guess we've got a deal. So what's your name?"

"I'm Dr. Anarchy. I'm pleased to-" I actually started to reach my hand out. I forced it back down. "I'm pleased to meet you, Raven."

The way she looked at me it was obvious she'd noticed. But amazingly she decided not to give me a hard time. "Yeah, same here, Doc."

"Actually, I'd prefer you use my full alias, or Anarchy or simply boss."

She grinned at me. "I bet you would, Doc."

I really, really, REALLY should have left her there.

XXX

Rule #33 – Seize every opportunity.

Chapter 2

It took me a couple days to get her to my secret lair near Newark, New Jersey. It was an old pesticide plant that was registered to one of my holding companies, Whaler Products LLC. It was where I had my lab set up with a staff of about thirty henchmen. The place was made of concrete and red bricks and the bottom two floors always had a chemical smell to them. After a couple weeks you wouldn't notice it anymore, but it made a few of my people physically ill. However, it had up to code wiring, was isolated with its own access road, and the realtor gave me a really good price on it. I always had my secret lairs in Jersey, it gave me easy access to New York City, the property costs were lower, and the heroes and New York law enforcement always did their best to pretend nothing existed west of Manhattan. If you were serious about being a supervillain you had to work in New York. It drew villains and heroes much the way would be actors flocked to Hollywood. New York was where many corporations and media outlets were based, it had Wall Street, the Diamond District, and most importantly, it was the home of the League of Heroes. Supersoldier, Dark Detective, Amazon, Shadowman, Legionnaire, The Blur, Iron Knight… legends, all of them, the heaviest of the heavy hitters. All of them lived and worked in New York. If you wanted to make a reputation for yourself it could only be done there.

Anyway, I brought Raven to my base and took care of her for a week while I tried to get my hands on the necessary cybernetics. People have some mistaken assumptions about evil geniuses. They imagine us sitting in a darkened corner spending every second working on a new fiendish invention. Sort of like an elf in Santa's workshop. Now, I don't deny working in the lab eats up a ton of my time. But maybe ten percent of that was spent on creating something genuinely ground breaking, the rest was welding and assembling equipment that I'd bought or stolen. Inventing new technology is hard. If every single thing I used was a new creation I'd never get out of the lab.

I had to order all the parts before I could actually build the arms and legs. The nerve adapters, pistons, springs, hinges, sensors, and power plants had to come in before I could install them in high steel casing. The number of part suppliers was small and they were all legitimate tech companies. They always sold to a holding company to maintain the fiction they weren't selling to a supervillain. They all required full payment prior to delivery and if you were serious about being a supervillain you did not cheat or steal from a tech supplier. They're a tight knit community, and if you get blackballed by them, good luck getting new parts for your disintegrator or killbot. Not only that, but they had plenty of connections with the heroes and Section Seven. I'm familiar with some of the sales reps for IST and Liberty Inc. and Washington Industries. They always tell me about their latest sales to the government or to Armored Cruiser or Panzer. Rip one of them off and suddenly you'll have half the League smashing down your walls or a dozen Section Seven agents with rifles breaking down your door. You think supervillains are ruthless? Try a defense contractor or multi-national, those people have no sense of humor.

Anyway, while I was waiting I had the chance to try and get to know Raven. I figured it would be a good idea to develop a bond with my future cyborg ninja. Well... I got to know her.

XXX

"So you're not actually a doctor, are you?"

"What? Yes I am, I'm Doctor Anarchy. I'm on the FBI's most wanted list."

"Not what I mean. You're not a medical doctor."

"I already told you, I have two master's degrees from MIT."

"Do you have a PhD?"

"Well… no."

"So when you say you're a doctor that's just for show. Like someone calling himself the King of Movie Stars or something."

I fidgeted a little in my chair. I didn't like people questioning my credentials. "Well what kind of degree did you get at Cal?"

"I got a bachelor's in Eastern Philosophy."

"That's it?"

She shrugged. "I sort of just went to college for the experience. I knew from the time I was three I was going to go into the family business. I was already taking contracts at sixteen."

"Still, I don't think you should question my qualifications when I earned a pair of master's degrees in engineering and you only have a bachelors in a liberal arts course."

She grinned at me. "Well I don't go around calling myself a doctor. So what's your goal? To destroy the social order and plunge civilization into chaos?"

"What? Why would I want that?"

"Well you call yourself Doctor Anarchy, don't you? So isn't your goal to create anarchy?"

"I want to rule the world, that's kind of hard to do if everyone is rioting in the streets."

"So you don't actually want anarchy?"

"Well, a little might be useful to try and bring down the government, but it would only be a means not an end."

"Then why is it your alias?"

"Supervillains need dramatic names and all the best ones were already taken; Death, Destruction, Doom, Evil, Overlord, Chaos, Terror, Nightmare, and the like. Anarchy seemed the best of what was still available."

"Sure, but you're still not a doctor or an anarchist."

"Are you a raven?"

"Ravens represent freedom and spiritualism, it's symbolic."

"Well so is mine."

She shook her head. "No it's not, you already admitted you want to rule over everyone, which implies you want order. Calling yourself Anarchy is just contradictory."

XXX

I have to admit, I was irritated. My henchmen knew better than to disrespect me. I always carried a disintegrator with me and I was NOT shy about using it on the hired help. I might be a little touchy, but people in my line of work struggle to be taken seriously. Look, my costume is a bright red lab coat with a huge, black letter 'A' in a circle. I get how easy it is to see it as silly. I was featured in an article in The

Onion, and they did those fucking skits of me on SNL a few years ago. (As a side note, I came very close to tracking down Collin Edwards, the idiot who played me, and killing him. The only reason I didn't was because I talked to Lord Chaos and he convinced me I couldn't let people know it bothered me.) Supervillains want to be taken seriously, we want to be respected, it's a very big deal to us. You want to completely piss off a supervillain? Don't call us crazy or insane or evil, don't tell us we'll never win, or that the heroes are on their way, we're used to hearing all that, it's white noise. But just laugh at one of us or tell us our costume looks like a clown outfit. See what happens.

I wasn't expecting to have my name mocked. Your alias, your costume, and your reputation define you. A few years ago some rookie out in Chicago decided to call himself Chaos and thought it would be fine since he wasn't using Lord with it. My friend went to pay this moron a visit and sent him to the hospital for a month, he was damn lucky he didn't end up in the morgue. The guy changed his name to South Sider for a while, before dropping out of the business. That's how seriously we take our names.

So I really didn't appreciate her flip attitude. Especially from someone whose life I'd saved and for whom I was doing such an amazing service. A little respect would have only been reasonable. As I had more conversations with her I learned that was hoping for too much.

XXX

"So tell me, Doc, why'd you become a supervillain?"

I noticed that despite her comments about me not being a doctor she was still calling me Doc. What an irritating woman. Why did I rescue her again?

"Why are you a ninja?"

"Well, my parents were both ninja, my grandparents were, my uncles, aunts, and cousins were. When I was a little girl I got plastic swords to play with along with dolls. It was kind of a no brainer."

"You're an adult, you could have chosen to do something else if you wanted."

"You never met my mom. Anyway, I never really wanted to do anything else. It came naturally to me and I liked it."

"That's probably fortunate given what your major was."

She grinned at me. "You're not going to sidetrack me, why'd you end up a bad guy?"

I shrugged. "I want to rule the world."

"Yeah, I get that part, but why?"

"What difference does it make?"

"If we're going to be partners I want to know why you're doing what you do."

I frowned at her. "We're not partners. A supervillain never partners up with anyone. At best I might agree to work with someone to achieve a short term goal, but that's it."

"Fine, fine, I'm okay with being your sidekick."

"Lieutenant," I muttered. It was like she had a natural talent for getting under my skin.

"So why are you a supervillain?"

"Why do you care?"

"Because it's a really extreme lifestyle choice, and I would know. Being a ninja means I have a life that ninety-nine percent of people could never understand. I'd make friends, have lunch with them, talk about guys, maybe go shopping, and then later I'd break into a museum and steal a vase or assassinate a mob boss. It's a weird way to live. I had really good friends who I could never let all the way in. And dating normal guys?" She shook her head. "Total disaster."

"You shouldn't try to have relationships with civilians, we're different, special. Normals could never understand."

"Is that why you do this? Cause you're special?"

So annoying. "I have an IQ of two hundred. I don't fit into the regular world. My professors at MIT could barely keep up with me, the other students couldn't stand me, and I always made people uncomfortable because I was so much smarter than they were. I wasn't going to dumb myself down to make the masses happy. I was never going to have a normal life. I mean what was I going to do? Be an engineer for some soulless corporation? Go into business for myself with a startup? Do research? Teach?" The thought made me laugh. "There was no way I was going to waste my life leading a normal, boring existence. I always knew I was special so I wanted to do something extraordinary."

"Like take over the world?"

"If you're someone with my level of intellect there are really only two choices; superhero or supervillain. Trying to conquer the world is way more challenging than trying to protect it."

"You're so brilliant those were your only options, seriously?"

"I'm the sixth smartest man in the world. Do you want to know who the five above me are?"

"Sure."

"Gunter Todt, better known as Dr. Death, John Porreca, whose alias is Overlord, Franklin Lang the Third, owner of Lang Tech and the Iron Knight, my friend Patrick Newton, who is Lord Chaos, and Neil Kane, owner of Kane Shipping. All of them are either heroes or villains. If you are that far out on the curve there's no way you can settle for an ordinary life."

"Hold on a second, Kane isn't a supervillain. He's just a billionaire, genius, philanthropist, playboy."

"Who also happens to be Dark Detective."

Her eyes widened. "You serious?"

"He's my nemesis, I know him better than anyone."

"I thought Whiteface was his nemesis."

"Whiteface? He's nothing but a psychopath with a sense of theatricality! I'm Dark Detective's nemesis!"

"Fine, whatever, so you discovered his true identity?"

"That's right."

"You captured him and got his mask off?"

"No."

"You caught him while he was changing into his costume?"

"No. I haven't actually unmasked him, I just figured out his secret identity"

She blinked at me. "What do you mean you figured it out?"

"It's a simple matter of deduction. Most superheroes just rely on their super powers or mutant or mystic abilities to fight crime. The only real cost they have is their costume. Dark Detective doesn't have any powers, except intelligence. His exo-suits, gas guns, grappling hooks, super computers, and justicemobiles, cost a literal fortune. Believe me, I know. I fund myself through criminal activity, but a hero like him wouldn't. The only possible way he could afford to be Dark Detective is if he already had access to a large fortune. Logistically he would also need to be based in, or near, New York City. Given my research I found that only one hundred and thirty-two individuals meet this criteria. Through the process of elimination I have ascertained that the only person who could possibly be Dark Detective is Neil Kane."

She closed her eyes and shook her head from side to side. "That's still just a guess. You don't really know."

"When you have eliminated the impossible, whatever remains, however improbable, must be the truth, Sir Arthur Conan Doyle. On August ninth, two thousand and eight, Dark Detective captured a gang of criminals who were attempting to break into the bridge of the new tanker Atlantica to try and steal its brand new, state of the art, navigation computer."

"So?"

"The attempted theft didn't happen in New York, it took place in the port of Miami. Neil Kane just happened to be present as he was scheduled to attend the launch ceremonies on the following day. None of the other possible candidates were even in the state of Florida on that date. I've also confirmed that Dark Detective has never made an appearance in New York at any time when Neil Kane was at another location."

I was pleased to see her pause and take all that in. My chest puffed out a little as I waited for her to acknowledge my brilliance.

"Okay then, why haven't you done anything about it?"

Her question caught me off guard. "What do you mean?"

"If you really think Dark Detective is Neil Kane why haven't you taken him out when he was in his civilian identity? Even if you didn't manage to kill him, you could have exposed him to the public."

"Why would I want to do that?"

"Uh, because he's your enemy?"

"He's not just my enemy, he's my nemesis! As a supervillain, more than anything else, your reputation is based on who your nemesis is. The more powerful the hero who faces you, the bigger threat you are."

"Sooooooo you don't want to kill him?"

"Well sure I want to kill him, eventually. But it has to be done in the right way. We've had a relationship for years. You can't just suddenly sever that kind of special bond. When it ends it needs to be face to face. I want him to see me coming, and for him to give me everything he has. I want him to know it's me beating him, just pounding away. I want to hear him whimper and beg and say it's too much for him to take. There will be tears and blood as I bend him to my will and drive my fury into him again and again! I want to overcome every possible resistance and break him completely. I want to hear him cry out my name and beg me to make it stop! Only then, after I've satisfied myself completely and broken him body and soul, can I bring him to an end."

She stared at me and gaped like a fish. "Is he your nemesis or your boyfriend?"

"WHAT?!"

"Not that I have any problem with that. I did grow up in San Francisco. But if that's how you feel you should just tell him. Be honest, but if he's not gay, or if he just doesn't feel the same way, you have to respect that and move on."

I literally sputtered. "I am NOT gay! You're completely misunderstanding what I'm saying!"

"Hey, you don't need to get defensive about it. I had gay friends all through high school and college. In fact I'd love to go shopping with you, maybe get some matching purses. Or we could go get drinks and talk about guys' butts."

I walked away. I just had to walk away.

XXX

All of our early conversations were like that! I'd try to explain the supervillain lifestyle to her and she would somehow flip it around to mock me! Honestly, if I hadn't already ordered the parts and been excited about having my very own cyborg ninja I'd have disintegrated her. Mercifully the parts did finally arrive and I was able to get to work. I had her exact measurements and built the limb casings to be a perfect match to her body. Before I assembled them we talked about the different 'extras' I could have included. I was really disappointed when she shot all my ideas down. She just wanted the 'basic' package. It seemed like a real waste of potential. I mean if you're going to build a cyborg ninja why not go all out? I resisted the urge to include a few add-ons despite what she wanted. Most people find the addition of artificial limbs to be mentally taxing, I wanted her to accept them with as little issue as possible.

Besides, there were bound to be repairs and upgrades later on.

Would you believe she actually asked me who the doctor would be for the operation? In my life I have literally spent tens of thousands of hours soldering, installing wires, connecting computer chips, and tightening screws. No surgeon in the world has more skilled hands and eyes than I do. Now admittedly, I'd never actually performed surgery before, but I'd studied all the necessary anatomy texts. And yes, I KNOW how that sounds, but I have an IQ of two hundred, and the fact is the human body isn't much more complicated than a fully functioning spy or killbot. I'd built flying spybots the size and shape of house flies. Compared to that attaching four cybernetic limbs was a piece of cake.

I had one of the old storage rooms cleaned out and set up as a temporary operating room. I was lucky that one of my henchmen was a former nurse named Jane Weslyn. She'd been fired and unable to find work in her profession after being caught stealing amphetamines. I allowed her to anesthetize Raven and monitor her vitals while I worked.

After Raven was washed up and her stumps sterilized, she was wheeled in.

"Remember, the arms go at the shoulders."

"I'll do my best to not forget." I imagined flipping one leg and arm just to see her freak out. I nodded to Jane who put a mask over Raven's mouth and soon had her unconscious. She was far more pleasant that way. Before I started I took a minute to look her over.

She was certainly very pretty. Japanese with brown eyes, high cheekbones, small nose, slender neck, and dark thick black hair. It was obvious she trained a lot. No one gets those abs by doing step aerobics. Her shoulders weren't exactly feminine, or dress slender. They had seen some use, as well as her pelvis, buttocks, and chest. She had scars. There was a laceration on her lower abdomen by her left lumbar region. There had been a stab wound just below her left breast and between her second and third rib. There were two puncture wounds near the left shoulder blade that could only have been the result of small caliber rounds. All the scars were well healed. Almost her entire body had faded yellow and brown bruises, she had taken quite a beating before being dumped on my island. I could have given her sedatives to help with the pain, but she never asked for so much as an aspirin. From a scientific perspective, she was in amazing psychical shape considering her circumstances. As a man, it felt weird looking at such a beautiful woman with so many missing pieces. Ah well, it was time to augment. I took one of the steel limbs and caressed its beautiful shining metal.

"You really are lucky. How many people get this kind of opportunity?"

Jane looked up from her gauges. I couldn't see her face because of the surgical mask, but her eyes had an accusing look to them. As soon as I glanced at her she put her face back down. I put the arm back and took out a scalpel and clamp. I hummed some Britney Spears and got to work.

XXX

Do I even need to say the surgery went perfectly? There was no infection, and she had no issues physically or mentally accepting the limbs. Just twenty-four hours later I had her come down to my lab to run some tests. She was dressed in the same bright red jumpsuit that was the standard uniform for all my henchmen. She had on the usual red leather boots that came included, so the only part of her cybernetics that were exposed were the hands. They were obviously metal with hinges where the joints would be. The parts were all shaped to mimic a woman's hand.

I had her run in place, do jumping jacks, cartwheels, back flips, go through a set of monkey bars, jump up and down off tables and chairs, bend steel bars, turn the pages of a book, pick up a feather, and throw darts. She performed every single test without issue. Seeing her perform so flawlessly started to get me excited. There was no limit to the possibilities! All her stupid complaints and jokes were momentarily forgotten as I gazed in wonder at my very own cyborg ninja.

"You know, Doc, I have got to give you props. You really do know what you're doing." She was juggling six eggs.

"Thank you, and maybe now you can stop calling me 'Doc' all the time and refer to me as Anarchy or boss."

"Nah, I think Doc suits you better." She put down five of the eggs one by one, while keeping the rest airborne.

"Even though you don't consider me a real doctor?"

"Hey, it's all about image, right?" The final egg she balanced on the tip of her left pinky. She then tossed it to the tip of her ring finger, then middle finger. She tossed and balanced the egg on all ten digits before finally setting it down too. She let the tips of her right hand slide across the table top. "It's amazing! I can feel with these things!"

"Their use would be pretty limited if you couldn't. The sensors in your limbs and the nerve adapters will let you 'feel' whatever you make physical contact with, and also sense the amount of pressure you're applying. Otherwise you wouldn't be able to pick up a pen or shake someone's hand without crushing it. The nerve net and all the extra sensors are the only things that make your arms and legs different from standard robotic appendages."

"I notice I can't feel temperature."

"They haven't added that feature yet. It might be available in future versions."

"What about pain? Can I still feel pain?"

I shook my head. "No. If you're in combat you'll need to take special care. It's very possible to suffer serious damage without even noticing."

"Well I'm not going to lie, I won't miss it. You wouldn't believe what it's like to have someone saw off your limbs."

"I'll bet."

Raven gave me a big smile, brought her arms and legs together and actually bowed. "Thank you. From the bottom of my heart, thank you. Now I'll be able to hunt down Viper and avenge my family. I swear that as soon as that's done I'm all yours."

"Taking care of your vendetta will have to wait. Since you seem to be functioning at full capacity I have a job for you." I looked down at my lap top and opened a file. "Lang Industries has developed a new generation capacitor that could increase the efficiency of my robots by up to forty percent I want you to-"

When I looked back up the lab was empty. I'd taken my eyes off of her for maybe fifteen seconds! The last egg she'd put down was still wobbling a little.

"Raven? Raven? Hey! Where are you?!"

I sounded the alarm and had the lair put on lockdown. The entire building was crawling with hidden cameras and motion sensors, but somehow she managed to disappear without a trace. That was also when I came up with a new rule.

XXX

Rule #36 – Don't get a sidekick.

Chapter 3

I went through all the video footage from all my security cameras. The only image I had of her was on one of the exterior monitors. She was a blur for all of two seconds. How the hell did she manage to not show up on any of the interior cameras? Even with her cybernetics that shouldn't have been possible. Of course I was immediately reminded of Dark Detective. He had a nasty habit of popping up out of nowhere too. Now she was gone and I was out the cost of four cybernetic limbs. The money didn't really matter, it was the principle of the thing. I'd saved her life and given her the chance to be something more than human. And she'd abandoned me at the first opportunity. If the other supervillains found out I'd be a complete laughing stock. The only good thing about all this was that no one knew about her.

"I should have installed a tracking device in one of the legs," I muttered.

Even as I said that to myself I knew the decision not to had been sensible. Tracking devices were a double edged sword. I used to install them in all my robots. I stopped after the one time Dark Detective hacked into my computer system. That's the thing about technology, anything you can use can also be used against you.

I did make an effort to find her of course. I sent out spybots. I put out some feelers about a female ninja called Raven. I performed some online searches for any mention of her. Except for some background information, I came up completely empty. I couldn't really pursue her more actively without drawing attention to myself, and that was the last thing I wanted. I also still had plans to steal that super capacitor, and afterwards I tried to rob a charity event I knew Kane would be attending. That's one of the good things about my line of work, when things go wrong there's always another evil scheme to move onto.

The simple fact was that a lot of my plans failed. For every successful job there was usually one that miscarried. And almost all the victories came without superhero opposition. For instance, I managed to steal the prototype capacitor from Lang Industries. All I ran up against were regular security guards and the automated defenses. My killbots went through them like a hot knife through butter. The result probably would have been different if Iron Knight had shown up.

By comparison, the charity event was a total disaster, I didn't even get to fight Dark Detective. Truth be told, that was the whole point of the exercise. Instead I ran into Amazon AND Achilles who were working security. Not only did I fail to rob the guests, all my killbots got smashed and I only barely escaped capture. Going back to the Sandbox for another stretch wouldn't have been that bad. The food there is actually pretty good and you get to make interesting contacts, but in general being imprisoned isn't something to look forward to.

The most embarrassing thing wasn't the failure itself so much as the fact no one there even noticed me. The next day the papers and the local news didn't mention me. The event itself didn't get much coverage, there was some footage of Neil Kane with some blonde model named Amber something on his arm and the usual speculation if they were dating. The whole thing got about thirty seconds on the local stations and a quarter page in the papers. The biggest story was about Mad Buffalo going on a short rampage in downtown, before

Shadowman took care of him. The secondary story that day was about a failed bank robbery by Dr. Squid. He was foiled by Power Princess, but at least managed to escape.

That's how it is in New York City. Supervillains are just a part of the scenery. Tourists come to see the Statue of Liberty, Time Square, the Towers, and hopefully a superhero or supervillain. It is very, very hard to really stand out. The competition for headlines is fierce and there are always new masks wanting to make a name for themselves. Occasionally, when I was depressed, I'd think about moving my operations to Cleveland or Detroit or Kansas City. I could become a crime boss and run the entire city within a couple months. It would be a great ego boost, but then what? Success doesn't really mean much when there's no competition. And it's not like the national media would pay any attention to me then either. It would be like going from the major leagues to the minors. If you are serious about being the world's greatest threat it can only be done in New York, where Supersoldier and the League of Heroes are. It's incredibly hard, maybe even impossible, but that's what makes it worth doing!

So I was very busy going from one scheme to the next. Finding Raven went on the backburner and it wasn't long before I'd pretty much forgotten about her. I eventually wrote off the entire thing as just another unsuccessful plan.

Then about three months later I was alone in my lab staring at a computer screen. I was busy designing my mark twelve killbot.

"Want some coffee?" One of my female henchmen asked.

"Yes, thank you." I didn't bother to look up. I was so focused on my work it didn't register that I hadn't heard anyone come into the lab.

Someone put a mug down on the desk. "Here you go."

"Thank you, I- aaaahhhh!!" I panicked and literally tripped and fell out of my chair as I grabbed my disintegrator. Standing there by my desk was Raven. She was wearing a black shinobi shōzoku, the traditional clothing of ninja, with her hood down. There were a pair of swords on her back and tied on her belt were hooks, wires, and pouches. There wore black gloves covering her hands. In one she had her own cup of coffee. She just stood there, grinning, as I was sprawled out at her feet, pointing my disintegrator up at her.

"Hey, Doc. Miss me?" She took a sip of coffee.

This wasn't the first time I'd had someone take me by surprise. Dark Detective does it all the time. Usually the surprise is followed immediately by either a punch to the face or the sound of a gas shell going off. I got back up and took a few steps back, keeping my weapon on her the whole time. She didn't look worried, she leaned against the corner of my desk and enjoyed her coffee.

"How'd you get in here?" I demanded.

"The same way I got out last time."

"And how exactly did you do that?"

She gave me a wink. "Ancient Japanese secret. If you really want to know you'll have to become my apprentice. Usually we only train family members, but I do owe you one."

"No thanks, being an evil genius is hard enough."

"Whatever you say, Doc." There was a brief pause as we both just stood there. "You going to put that away?" She nodded toward my disintegrator.

I thought about it. If she'd actually wanted to kill me she would have. And I had the very distinct impression that pulling the trigger would be a bad idea. I switched the safety on and slid it back inside my lab coat.

"All right, Raven. Why are you here?"

She hopped up on the table and sat there. "Isn't it obvious? I'm here to work for you."

I stared at her.

"What? Have I got something on my face?"

"You want to work for me?" I asked in disbelief. "You have a strange way of showing it. You disappear for three months without a word and then just suddenly pop up again. Can you see why I would find the idea a bit suspicious?"

"Well I tried to stay away, but what girl could resist your charms?"

"Or you might have been hired to come here and spy on me." I looked at the computer screen and the design for an improved mechanical joint.

"Woah, paranoid much?"

"Just because you're paranoid doesn't mean there really aren't people out to get you."

Raven chortled and shook her head slightly. "I guess that's true. I sure can't talk. Listen, Doc, I really have come here to work for you. There's something you should know about me, though. I have just one rule."

"Let me guess, you don't kill innocent people?"

She laughed and nearly spilled her coffee. "Wow, good one! No, that would be pretty much impossible in my line of work. I'm a ninja. Not a Hollywood ninja, or some teenage wannabe ninja, I'm the genuine article. Ninja are not nice people, we do bad things for money. Hell, we'll pretty much do anything if the price is right. I've killed people in cold blood, stolen family treasures, kidnapped children, and brutally tortured folk for information. I'm a liar and a thief and a straight up killer, I'll sleep with you if that's what it takes to get the job done, or trick you into killing yourself. There is only one line I won't cross."

"Yes?"

She sipped from her cup. "I won't break a contract. For ninja that is the one and only absolute rule. If I accept your payment I will do the job no matter what. Even if I have to die, even if I have to spend years on the assignment, for a ninja from one of the clans the only way to be disgraced is to break a contract. And we have a contract, Doc. You gave me my life back, along with these arms and legs, and I agreed to serve you, under certain conditions. I didn't agree to work for you for just one job or one year, I'm yours now until the end."

"Whose end? Mine or yours?"

"Whichever one comes first. Though if I had to bet I'd say the odds are on you."

"If that's really the case why did you vanish?"

Raven finished her coffer and set the cup down. "I told you before I left, I had to deal with Viper."

"Since you're here I take it he's dead then?"

Raven got a faraway look in her eye and smiled in way that would have made a tiger cringe. "Not yet."

I gulped. By normal standards I've done a lot of horrible things. And I've seen things that gave me nightmares. But the way she said that sent an icy chill down my spine. I definitely did not want to know what exactly she'd done.

The expression on her face shifted and she was back to only looking amused. "What matters is I've taken care of things and I'm here to fulfill my end of our bargain."

I thought that would be a good thing.

XXX

Rule #13- Always be paranoid. If you're a supervillain people really are out to get you.

<u>Chapter 4</u>

Raven followed me into my lab. I had a couple of my killbots in there standing guard. I love my killbots. They're six feet tall and are bright red. On their chests they have a black 'A' in a circle, and their heads are smiley faces. They have rockets in their feet, and the palm of each hand has a firing muzzle for a fifty caliber machine gun. Their mouth can open to spit out gas or act as a flamethrower. Their eyeholes are cameras and I have speakers and listening devices installed, so I can have a conversation or laugh maniacally through them. They're also programmed to follow a list of simple vocal commands such as guard, follow, search, eliminate, or pop and lock.

I also had a box full of spybots. They're the shape and size of house flies. As the name suggests I can use them to watch and listen in on people. They're not exactly impressive, but very useful. The lab was filled with all sorts of inventions and with schematics for things I was still thinking about. It was kind of a mess, with a half built death ray sitting next to a grolem doll, that was next to an emotion manipulator collar and a half eaten sandwich. Genius isn't orderly. I love to create and build and I usually have a dozen projects going at once. On one of a dozen laptops was code for an AI program. One of the monitors on the wall displayed Neil Kane at some business meeting. My spybots could never make it into his home intact, but for some reason they could slip in and out of Kane corporate headquarters at will. A dozen spybots were perpetually keeping the League of Heroes under surveillance and tracking who came and went. One of the laptops ran a program that monitored the NYPD police channels. It would send an alert email if certain key words came up.

In the corner of my lab was a five ton vault made of solid durtanium. It was where I kept my spare disintegrators, my supply of Lanthrocite, my Tom Brady autograph, and a few other very precious items. When I went over to it I glanced back over my shoulder. Raven was leaning against the table with the Newton Accelerator prototype, about twenty feet behind me. I leaned in over the keypad and quickly put in the code. There were four distinctive 'thunks' as the bolts inside were pulled back. The door slowly swung open automatically.

"915702004." Raven rattled off the numbers while the vault door was still opening.

I jumped around. She was still standing in the exact same spot. "How did you-"

She simply grinned at me. "Ninja."

Wonderful! Now I was going to have to add a retinal scanner or something! Though given the strength of her cybernetic arms she could literally rip the vault open if she ever wanted to.

My concerns must have been obvious. "Listen, Doc, ninja aren't honorable, but the one thing we are sticklers about is fulfilling a contract. And I've taken a contract to work for you for life. If the day ever comes when I decide to break our deal, believe me, robbery is going to be the least of your worries."

"Is that supposed to make me feel better?"

"Sure. Why wouldn't it?"

"How did you see me enter the code?"

"Trade secret. If you want to know I'll have to take you as an apprentice and teach you the ninja arts. You should be able to do it yourself in maybe ten years. If you survive the training. Which you won't."

I sighed and turned back to the now fully opened vault. Ninja didn't have super powers or magical abilities or incredibly advanced tech. They were ordinary humans who did extraordinary things through a secret regimen of training and the use of specially designed tools. When I originally brought Raven in I tested her, except for missing her limbs she was just a very healthy human. She was much more than that now, but cybernetic arms and legs wouldn't help her with seeing me press buttons.

I reached in and took out a large jar filled with some pink goo.

"I suppose I'll just have to think of this as falling under my first rule, 'be ready to adjust and deal with the unexpected.'"

She raised an eyebrow. "Is that part of the Supervillain Creed or something?"

"No. When I decided to do this I came up with a number of rules to help me figure out the best course of action. I mean, let's be honest, supervillains don't have the best track record when it comes to making sound decisions."

"Well, I don't want to sound judgmental or anything, but going around in a costume trying to take over the world isn't very rational."

I frowned at her. "You're a ninja."

"And? There have been thieves, spies, and assassins since the dawn of time. Certain clans just decided to make it the family business and specialized. There's nothing strange about it at all. There are plenty of families all around the world that have been winemakers, soldiers, masons, carpenters, ship builders, and whatever else for generations. Our chosen profession requires us to be discreet, that's all. The fact the same families have been ninja for over six hundred years, proves it's a viable and profitable business model."

"My point, is that people in my line of work have a reputation for making bad choices." I set the jar down on a table and pushed the death ray and grolem doll over to make a little room. "So I decided to make a list of rules to help me always make sensible, rational decisions."

"You mean like trying to steal the Empire State Building using a bunch of rockets?"

"That absolutely could have worked!" I twisted open the lid. "Damn SNL and their stupid skits."

"Oh, me and my friends loved that one! I was still in high school then." She coughed and actually did the voice. "Next time I use ze super rockets, I remember to use ze super glue!"

"I don't sound like that!"

She motioned for me to calm down. "Hey, I'm just teasing you a little, you have to have a sense of humor, right?"

"You try having the most famous thing you've ever done be turned into a joke people still watch on YouTube!"

"Sorry, I'll be good."

Even though she said that she had a huge smile on her face.

"Whatever," I muttered. "Take your clothes off and hop up on the table."

"Whoa now, Doc, I don't think you understand the sort of relationship we're going to have. I'm a ninja, not a hooker."

"If you were a hooker I wouldn't have bothered giving you cybernetics. I need to have free access to apply the skin. I'm also going to make a small modification. Besides, I've seen you naked before."

She hesitated for a moment, then finally began to remove her ninja clothing. "Don't get any weird ideas, or you'll regret it."

As she undressed I noticed an impressive number of knives, wires, and hooks strapped onto both arms and her sides. Besides those, the only other thing she had on underneath were a pair of pink panties. She is a beautiful woman with a nice, athletic figure, but it was something else that grabbed my attention.

"What the Hell?" I rushed over to get a closer look. On the upper right arm was deep gouge at least six inches long. Luckily, it didn't appear to have severed any of the circuits or gears. But it had been deep enough to expose them. "The casing is solid steel, what happened?"

Raven gave an indifferent shrug. "Viper put up a fight. The arm works fine, so no big deal."

"What kind of weapon was he using?"

"Just a kunai." She took one of her weird knives and twirled it about her left index finger.

Did she have any idea the sort of force it would take to tear open steel like this using just a metal blade?

"Is Viper a mutant or super powered?"

"He's a ninja." Raven made a low, throaty sound that might have been a laugh but reminded me of a growl. "Or he was."

I reminded myself to never make her my enemy.

"Well, the damage is superficial, but I'll still need to repair it before I can cover this arm. It's actually just as well. I was going to have to drill a small hole anyway."

"What for?"

"I'm going to install a tracker. If you ever disappear again I want to be able to find you."

"Well, okay Doc. I don't expect I'll ever have to avoid you again. If I do for some reason I'll still manage. I can always just hack my arm off if I need to."

"You'd go through all the problems of losing an arm just to avoid being found?"

"If I ever need to." She shrugged. "I've dealt with worse."

Well I knew how true that was. I went to my work bench and got an applicator gun and a hair dryer. (I used a wide range of tools.) I stuck the muzzle in the jar and drew back the handle. The tube slowly filled up.

"I'll do your legs and left arm now and save your right arm for later."

"Wow, déjà vu, it's like that frat party all over again."

"You and I had very different college experiences." I placed the muzzle of the applicator gun at her left shoulder and squeezed the trigger. The solution came out in a thick stream and spread along the metal arm like syrup. "This is a synthetic biopolymer that is Horka tech. Just one of the many, many examples of secret alien technology Section Seven uses."

Raven frowned. "This stuff doesn't have a mind of its own, does it? I'm not going to wake up one night and have my arms and legs working on their own, am I?"

"No, but avoid open flames, when lit it burns hotter than napalm."

"You're kidding, right?"

"No."

She shook her head. "If wearing gloves and long sleeve shirts in May weren't such a pain in the ass..."

The substance spread evenly. I put the hair dryer on its lowest setting and heated the patch right at her shoulder. It thickened after about fifteen seconds. I pressed with one finger, it looked and felt just like real skin.

"It's a little lighter than I am."

"Not a problem, it can tan."

"What do I do in the winter?"

"Bleach."

She didn't look pleased with that answer, but I didn't worry about it. Section Seven used the biopolymer for skin grafts and other medical treatments. Even with its drawbacks it was the best possible alternative.

"Rule number eight," I said. "Nothing is perfect, always know what the flaws are."

"How many rules do you have?"

"Right now, thirty-six. I add them as I go."

"Ever think of changing your name to Doctor Anal Retentive? It would probably suit you better."

"I told you before, I chose my identity because it sounded good, not because I'm an actual disciple of anarchy. I don't apologize for trying to be logical about my work."

"Because what could be more logical than trying to take over the world? Am I right, Doc?"

"That's sort of my point." I kept applying the substance as evenly as I could. When it clumped up I used a file to smooth it out again. "I'm going to give you two items I want you to always keep with you, a tracker and portable gas mask."

"You use gas?"

"No, but Dark Detective does. He has a nasty habit of taking me by surprise, so always keep it with you, just in case."

"Okay, and what's the tracker for?"

"I'm going to have a tracking device implanted in me. In case of an abduction or some other emergency you'll be able to find me. Take special care of it. I'm going to have the frequency the device uses constantly shifting. That will make it impossible for Dark Detective or anyone else to use it. The implant and the tracker will be synched, so it will be the only way to find me."

"Do you get kidnapped a lot?"

"No, but this is an example of me following rule one, and being ready to deal with the unexpected."

She rolled her eyes at me. "I bet you're a lot of fun at parties."

"Only if it's a kegger. By the way, I don't have any fingernails or toenails ready for you. I'll have to make some from plastic and glue them on later."

XXX

Rule #1 - Be ready to adjust and deal with the unexpected.

Rule #8 - Nothing is perfect, always know what the flaws are.

<u>Chapter 5</u>

I took one of my vans into New York. Whenever I travel it's always by van, I keep several at all my hideouts. There were two killbots in the back, legs and arms folded up in passive mode. If Dark Detective or some other superhero suddenly showed up they'd activate and take action. Nothing sets my mind at ease like knowing I have a fully armed killbot or two nearby. Raven was in the passenger seat and in her black ninja clothing. It was past midnight on a Tuesday. The city was as quiet as it ever gets. I parked a couple blocks from a skyscraper.

"That's the IST building. They're one of the world's leaders in advanced technology. There's a lab up on the twenty-fourth floor where they're developing a multitronic circuit that could greatly boost the performance of my robots. It'll be secured a durtanium vault with guards, motion sensors, monitors, and all sorts of electronic surveillance."

"And you want me to just waltz in there and bring you this circuit?"

"That's right. Do you think it's too much for you?"

"Nah, it's fine." She flashed me a toothy smile. "But it won't come cheap. For something like this I'm going to have to charge you twenty thousand."

"You're actually serious about that?"

"I already told you, Doc. I don't work for free."

"I don't expect you to. All my henchmen get good pay along with excellent medical benefits and life insurance."

"I'm not a regular henchman I'm your sidekick."

"Lieutenant," I corrected.

"And a cyborg ninja with all sorts of unique skills and one hell of a resume. I'm not going to work for an hourly wage."

"I didn't just hire you," I said with annoyance. "I *constructed* you, and it cost me two million dollars."

Raven rolled her eyes. "That's why you only have to pay me half. The other half can go towards what I owe you. Come on Doc, we already talked about this."

I frowned. "I just don't think I should have to pay someone in my organization like she were a mercenary."

"I told you before, Doc. A ninja will always honor the contract no matter what, but we expect to get paid. Ninja work for money, not loyalty."

"That's disappointing to hear… Hana Fusikawa."

A lot of times, when you're having a conversation, you can throw out an unexpected piece of information and startle the other person. Ninja in particular take great pride in keeping their true identities hidden. After she'd disappeared I'd gone through a lot of trouble but finally discovered her true identity. I'd hoped the sudden revelation would startle her and give me some sort of advantage. The money wasn't really the issue, it was the principle of the thing.

Raven didn't look upset. "So you figured out who I really am. Not bad, Michael Jackson."

As soon as she said my name I shut my eyes and felt the impulse to groan. "How?"

"You're kidding, right? It took me about ten seconds. I just Googled you. So I guess your parents were huge fans?"

"No," I said. How many times had I explained this in my life? A thousand? Ten thousand? A million? "My family name just happens to be Jackson and they liked the name Michael. My mom actually loves country and western music and my dad was into disco. I know every song ever released by Abba by heart."

"Mamma mia that must have been rough."

I stared at her. "Aren't you a little young to know Abba songs?"

"You kidding? Abba, Cher, and Madonna are like the theme songs of every gay club on Earth. So I'm getting the vibe you're not a big Michael Jackson fan. The artist I mean, not yourself."

"You try growing up with that name. I've been teased about it since grade school, that on top of all the usual teasing and bullying for being a nerd with glasses."

She nodded with false sympathy. "That's bad. You should try and not remember the time. All those people, they don't care about us. If they wanna be startin' somethin' you should let them know that you're not just a supervillain, but a smooth criminal too. And if you feel upset you just need to look at the man in the mirror and remind yourself it's all just human nature."

I stared at her much too happy face. "I bet you think you're very clever don't you?"

She shrugged. "If I do it's the way you make me feel. You rock my world, Doc."

I sighed. "Beat it, it's worth twenty thousand just to get you to stop."

Laughing she slid out the door, grabbed her crotch, whooh oohed, and moonwalked away.

When she returned fifty minutes later she had the circuit board and was wearing only one of her gloves. As we drove back she hummed Billie Jean.

I've killed people for so, so much less.

XXX

Rule #11 – Always remember your entire criminal record is one click away.

<u>Chapter 6</u>

The Hudson River Lodge in Bayonne, New Jersey, is a two star hotel which has an outdoor pool, basic cable, and a free continental breakfast served in the lobby from six a.m. to nine-thirty a.m. They don't offer Wi-Fi or room service, but they have an auditorium available for special events. More importantly, they're located off of exit fourteen of the New Jersey Turnpike with rear parking that isn't visible from the highway. It's a dingy, slightly run down motel that's not close to anything else and that no one really notices. It's the sort of place you'd only ever go to if you just couldn't afford anything else, or if you were married and planning to fuck a stripper or fifty dollar hooker.

Raven and I pulled up in a van on a Wednesday night, sometime around eight. The parking lot was almost full, the entrance to the auditorium was brightly lit with a large banner above it. WELCOME WEDDING GUESTS!

The two of us were in our usual costumes as we got out. Raven also had a box with wrapping paper and a big red bow on it.

"So what did you get them anyway?" Raven asked. "A sonic disruptor? Grolem doll? Portable rocket launcher? Those are always fun."

"They're registered with Macys. I bought them a toaster oven."

There were two men working the auditorium door, no doubt henchmen. They took our invitation and welcomed us in. The inside was about what you would expect, it was just a big empty space with a wooden floor. There was an arch made of plastic flowers and six rows of fold out chairs on either side of the 'aisle' in front of it. On the far wall a couple tables had been put end to end and covered with a wedding cake, burgers, hot dogs, fried chicken and other food. Right next to it was a temporary stand with a bartender busy filling plastic cups with beer. The poor guy was already under siege. Other than the person flipping the bill does anyone not love an open bar? It is easily the best thing about most weddings.

Raven deposited the wedding gift and came over to join me. She looked over our surroundings.

"Not exactly the Ritz Carlton, is it?"

"It's part of the supervillain lifestyle. Whenever we gather, for whatever reason, it has to be kept low key. You can't really do that if you meet at the Waldorf Astoria."

"I get it, but couldn't he have at least sprung for a HoJo or something?"

I shrugged. "I've seen worse. You have to make sacrifices for the sake of secrecy. Even so, there's probably at least a ten percent chance we get raided."

She frowned. "You could have mentioned that before."

"What? Those are still good odds, and we have our mini-jetpacks just in case."

"How well do you know the guy anyway? You're not lifelong friends or something like that are you?"

"Hardly. We met at the Sandbox six years ago and have run into each other a few times since."

"Why are we even here then?"

"I never turn down the chance to hit an open bar."

"Uh, given how much this is costing you it would have been cheaper to just buy a ton of booze and get smashed at home."

"Don't remind me. I still can't believe you're charging me ten grand for this."

"Hey, I would have made it two if you just wanted me to be a bodyguard. If you want me to be your date it's going to cost you."

"For what I'm paying most guys would expect the 'date' to include a lot more than a few hours of conversation and a dance or two."

"Don't push your luck, Doc. Be glad I'm willing to do this much for you, and that I'm only charging an extra eight thousand."

"Thanks for crushing my male pride."

"No problem. Feel free to count that as a bonus."

It would have been worth the extra money to have her not always belittling me.

"Seriously though, why are we here?"

"I love wedding cake. Also, I'm hoping to hit on some drunk bridesmaids later."

Raven crossed her arms and waited.

"Fine. If you really want to know, I go to things like this to make and maintain contacts in the community. You never know when it might come in handy."

"Wow, I'm impressed, that actually makes sense."

"I'm glad you think so. Let's grab some free beer before things start."

I'd estimate there were around fifty guests. About half of them were dressed how you would expect. The other half were in costume, like me and Raven. It is very, very rare when a supervillain gets to be in a social setting without it involving robbery, kidnapping, or some other felony. While I did want to make and maintain my contacts in the community, there was another reason why I attended. It was fun. For a supervillain, getting to do something normal, while in his true identity, was always a treat. I mean usually when I want to talk to a civilian as Dr. Anarchy I have to kidnap them. Here I could just walk up to someone without pointing my disintegrator at them and they probably wouldn't try to run away screaming. For an evening I could simply socialize without worrying about my secret identity.

Plus, I was only half kidding about the bridesmaids.

With my plastic cup of beer in hand I walked over to a guy in a brown suit and introduced myself.

"Hello, I'm Dr. Anarchy." I held out my hand.

"Oh, uhm, Richard Harrison. I have a used car dealership in Newark." He took my hand and gave it a half-hearted shake.

"You're a used car salesman? And here I thought I was the evil one."

He stared back in uncertain silence.

"That was just a little joke."

"Right."

"So you on the groom's side or the bride's?"

"Bride's obviously, I'm Jennifer's uncle. All the normal people here are family, her parents decided it was too dangerous to invite anyone who wasn't." He didn't make much effort to hide his disdain.

"By normal I take it you mean all the nice people who are not in costume and wanted by the law?"

"What? No, I just mean, ah…"

"Yes? What did you mean?" I took a slow sip of my beer.

He sucked in his lips and worked his collar. "I just mean the regular people, you know, the ones who have normal jobs and don't do anything illegal."

"If you're a used car salesman I'm pretty sure that doesn't include you."

He looked around the room. "Excuse me, someone needs me." He hurried away.

"Smooth as always, Doc." Raven had been standing a few feet behind me and now walked up to my side. Instead of beer she'd gotten some tequila.

"Screw him, he's a bigot. He probably thinks all supervillains should be locked up someplace and never let out."

"Yeah, weird how people think that about criminals."

I frowned at her.

"But I'm sure he has a much better opinion after talking to you."

"I was polite."

Raven nodded. "And scary."

I opened my mouth to argue, and then shut it. I'm five foot ten, a hundred and sixty pounds, and wear glasses. When I am in regular clothing I'm about as threatening as a rabbit. I'd worked very hard to earn a dangerous reputation as Dr. Anarchy. So I couldn't very well argue I wasn't scary. I took another sip of beer.

As I did so I took a moment to study my surroundings. Most of the guests were in small groups chatting with one another. And each and every one was made up of either civilians or supervillains. The only place where they mixed was in the line in front of the bar. Even there, as soon as someone had their drink they went back to hang out with their own kind. So much for social interaction. Oh well, civilians were boring anyway.

A man who I presumed was the bride's father announced the ceremony was about to begin, and asked us to all take our seats. It wasn't hard to tell the groom's side from the bride's. Everyone in costume sat on the left and everyone in a dress or a suit was on the right. The bridal march began and the bride, a woman by the name of Jennifer Ryan, walked slowly down the aisle alongside her father. Her wedding dress was traditional, and somewhat less eye catching than what her soon to be husband was wearing. Frank Varden, aka Gold Macaw, was in costume. His costume was covered in faux gold feathers and had a few bird themed weapons. His best man, Galeforce, stood right beside him in a blue and yellow costume. The bride's father placed her hand in Frank's and the couple turned to a man in a suit standing beneath the arch. He was the bride's cousin and had gotten a wedding license on line. The proceedings went completely to script. No one objected or tried to kidnap the bride or challenged the groom to a fight. Jennifer Ryan became Jennifer Varden, the groom kissed the bride, and we all applauded. The entire ceremony took a grand total of ten minutes.

We watched the happy couple cut the cake and have their first dance. The DJ was another cousin who had some speakers hooked up to his ipod. Some people danced while some talked and others hit the bar. I wasn't surprised to see pairs of costumed individuals on the dance floor. Dark Empress was the only female supervillain there, but like me most of the guys had brought henchmen as dates. Now I know a lot of people probably think that's pretty sad, bringing a woman who works for you as a date. But where else would a supervillain even meet someone? I mean, I've heard plenty of stories of members of the community going on blind dates or meeting someone using a secret identity. That's fine so long as all you want is to hook up, but there's an obvious problem if you're looking for something serious. I mean sooner or later you're going to have to have a very awkward conversation. How do you tell someone you don't actually work in advertisement, but rob banks and fight superheroes? Awkward. And it's not like you can be honest from the start. Imagine a first date where you tell her, 'Hey, just so you know, I'm a supervillain who breaks into office buildings and kidnaps executives for rival companies. So do you like Italian?' Any normal girl would either start screaming her head off or disappear into the ladies' room to call the police. So no matter how unseemly it may appear to an outsider, dating your lieutenant or henchman just makes sense. And it so happens the former miss Ryan had started out as a henchman. Which proves that it can work.

I glanced over at Raven. Of course, like any relationship, it required interest from both sides.

"You want to dance?"

"Sure, you may as well get your money's worth."

"I don't think that's possible, unless you were to rob everyone here."

"Wasn't planning on it, but the night is still young."

We headed onto the dance floor and danced to Van Halen and Whitney and Beyoncé and Britney and Bruno Mars.

Well… she danced, I jerked my arms and legs around in a desperate effort to move in some semblance of rhythm. None of the children present began screaming and people did not stop to stare, so I considered my efforts successful. From the look on her face it was obvious Raven enjoyed the spectacle.

"Let me guess, in a past life you were a prima ballerina for the Bolshoi?"

"My hands and fingers are well coordinated, I make no claims about the rest."

"Good, spares me from having to call you a liar."

"If you're feeling embarrassed we can stop."

"No, no, it's fine. I've been to weddings before. Except when my gay friend Leon was my date I haven't seen a lot of smooth moves from my partners."

"Sorry to disappoint you."

"Eh, we all have our gifts. I doubt Leon could build a killbot."

The song we were dancing to ended, and all of a sudden, 'Can't Help Falling In Love,' by Elvis, started to play. Couples either began to slow dance together or headed off the dance floor. I figured we belonged to the latter group, but to my surprise Raven moved close and put her hands on my shoulders. My surprise must have been obvious as she snorted.

"Come on, you're paying ten grand for this, I think I owe you at least one slow dance."

"Uh, okay." I placed my hands lightly on her hips and we began to deliberately move together. In one sense this was a lot easier than regular dancing. I didn't have to worry about the beat or about what I was going to do next with my arms. On the other, I felt a little nervous being so close to her in a social setting. I kept worrying I would step on her feet. It was silly, as her feet were cybernetic and she wouldn't feel pain even if they were torn off. I still did my best to avoid them.

"You don't need to look so nervous, Doc. I promise I'm not going to bite. I'd charge extra for that."

"I'm not nervous," I lied.

She rolled her eyes at me. "When was the last time you were on a date?"

"Why are you asking me that all of a sudden?"

"I'm just wondering, I mean it's never come up."

I puffed out an irritated breath. "I was on a date two or three years ago."

"Two or three years? Whoa, you know escort services take plastic now, right?"

"I've had sex," I said with irritation. "But I wouldn't call those dates, they were business transactions."

"You're a real romantic, Doc. So what happened on your date?"

"Nothing much, we met on an online dating service and went out to dinner and a movie."

"And..?"

"And nothing, we had an all right time and that was all."

"What was her name?"

I racked my brain. "Linda, or Lisa maybe."

"You don't even remember her name?"

"She wasn't particularly memorable."

Raven looked at me with disapproval. "I've seen you remember the megahertz capacity of a twenty tear old signal tower, and you can't even remember the name of someone you took to dinner?"

"I try to remember things that might be important, I wanted to use the signal tower to intercept government communications."

"That's not my point. Okay, so she wasn't the one. Why haven't you been on any dates since?"

"I don't have time. You know how busy I am with my work. And it's not like I've ever been good with women anyway. Relationships are hard and they take way too much time and effort. I can't afford to worry about a two month anniversary when I should be concentrating on upgrading the motion sensors of the lair."

"I'm not saying to put it ahead of work, I'm just saying that if it's something important you can always find the time."

"I agree, but I don't consider women a priority."

She raised an eyebrow.

"Except for the basic biological reason, and at those times I prefer to just to pay for the service. It saves time and is just more convenient."

"Sounds cheap, Doc."

"Well compared to your rates, sure."

The instant the song ended Raven headed towards the bar. "I need a drink."

XXX

The rest of the evening was pleasant. I gave my congratulations to the happy couple. I had a few more beers. I talked with a number of my fellow supervillains. My ranking on the FBI's most wanted list had cracked the top fifty. A lot of them wanted to hear about what I was planning for the future. I was congratulated on my success and a few even asked me for advice on their own nefarious schemes. It felt really good to get so much positive feedback.

I didn't bother trying to talk to the civilians again, not even the cute bridesmaids. I doubted any of them could really understand the lifestyle and I didn't feel the need to educate them. I saw Crabface and Super Mugger make some efforts. Usually people would listen politely for a few minutes and then find some excuse to wander off and rejoin the herd. Galeforce danced with a really cute blonde who turned out to be the bride's younger sister. I noticed the father keeping a close eye on them the entire time, he didn't look particularly pleased.

I avoided the dancefloor for the remainder of the evening. Raven, for her part, drank about half a bottle of tequila and got her groove on with most of the supervillains in the room and four or five of the civilian guys. She spent an unusual amount of time with Obelisk. He has gray skin, stands almost seven feet, had a face with ninety degree angles and a point at the top of his skull. He's also bullet proof and can crush concrete with his bare hands. Everyone says he is a nice guy, but you wouldn't expect him to be popular with the ladies.

At the end of the evening all the single women gathered together for the bouquet toss. Raven was among them. Jennifer turned her back and tossed over her shoulder. The other girls never had a chance, Raven leapt fifteen feet into the air and snatched it at the apex of its flight. The women all stared daggers at her, but she looked pleased with herself. As we left she held the thing like a trophy.

"I never got one of these before. It's not like I could use my ninja skills at the other weddings I've been to."

"Should I be nervous?"

"Somehow I doubt you're getting married any time in the near future."

"Is that something you want?"

"Sure, eventually. I mean it's up to me to restart my clan. And I would like to grow old with someone I love, assuming I make it to old age."

"I see." Given my line of work, marriage and children were not something I gave much thought to. After the night's festivities maybe it was time to at least consider the possibility. Would I want to settle down and have kids? They are a huge responsibility and one a man shouldn't take lightly. Would it be right to have a family while still being an active supervillain? Would I have to give my career up and live my life under a secret identity? (Not that it would be a burden to no longer be Michael Jackson.) Was that a sacrifice I could make? No more killbots or secret lairs? Ending my rivalry with Dark Detective? Being a (relatively) normal person for the rest of my life? Even if I found a woman I loved would it be worth it to me?

Raven laughed and covered her mouth. "Don't look so serious, Doc. I haven't come down with baby fever. Like I said, this is for the future, I'm not settling down any time soon. Oh, and by the way, I need this Saturday off."

"Why?"

"Obelisk wants to take me out on his yacht. He's a fun guy."

I stifled a groan and told her it would be fine. I wondered if she would notice if I tracked her with a spybot.

XXX

Rule #23 – Never turn down free food, drink, or weapons grade plutonium.

Chapter 7

"Please don't scream." I said. "It would be annoying and no one would hear you anyway. If you do I'll have to sedate you again. Understand?"

She nodded her head vigorously.

I pulled off the cloth sack and carefully removed her gag. She blinked and looked around. She was handcuffed to a chair and in my lab. Along with myself Raven was sitting at a table playing some game on her phone. Raven gave our prisoner a quick wave. She took a deep breath and looked at me. There were no signs of panic and when she spoke her voice was calm and steady.

"What is this about? Why am I here?"

I admired her composure. "There's no need to worry Miss Valley, you won't be harmed unless your hero fails to respond."

Valerie Valley (yes, that was her name, obviously her parents were pure evil) was a field reporter for channel nine WCVB New York. She was an attractive blonde who'd recently graduated from Northwestern and started working for the station.

"My hero? Wait, do you mean my boyfriend Bob? He's a tax attorney."

"There's no reason to play coy, Miss Valley. I mean Dark Detective. I know you two have a close relationship."

"What are you talking about?" She asked pretending to be oblivious.

"You've spoken with him on camera multiple times. Except for Diana Darwin you're the only reporter who has ever done that."

"Multiple? Okay, I've talked to him twice so technically I guess that's true. But I only spoke to him for maybe a total of ninety seconds."

I nodded. "He didn't want to make his interest too obvious, but I could see you share something."

"What tape were you watching? Both times I asked him one question about a crime scene, he gave me one word answers and then disappeared."

"It was the way he spoke that revealed his special connection to you. It was subtle, but there nonetheless. I might be the only one able to pick up on it. I know Dark Detective better than anyone. You see, I'm-"

"Dr. Anarchy, I know."

I have to admit I was pleased to be recognized. "Yes. I suppose Dark Detective has told you about me."

Her eyes darted away from mine. "Actually, I mostly cover crimes. It's part of my job to be familiar with all the local supers, heroes and villains both." She looked at where Raven was seated. "I'm afraid I don't know who you are though."

"I'm new in town. My alias is Raven and I'm Dr. Anarchy's new sidekick." Raven didn't bother to look up from her game.

"Oh, that's interesting. I thought only heroes had sidekicks."

"She's my lieutenant," I said.

"Are you a real ninja?"

With her left hand Raven continued playing with her smartphone. With her right she took out a kunai and started twirling it about one finger. All without ever looking up. "Real as can be."

"How did you become a ninja? I mean you must have had special training. It's not like being bitten by a radioactive chipmunk and suddenly getting chipmunk powers."

"Excuse me," I said. "I think we're getting off point here."

Valerie turned her attention back to me. "Sorry, but I'm not sure what the point is."

"To put it simply, you're the bait in my trap. When Dark Detective comes here seeking to rescue you I'll finally destroy him. His feelings for you are a weakness I will exploit. He will be no match for my army of loyal followers or my arsenal of advanced and deadly weapons. Faced with my superior intellect he will surely-"

"You're doing it again." Raven interrupted. "You're monologuing, you need to stop."

"It's not a problem," I replied with annoyance. "And I can stop any time I want."

She looked up from her phone and rolled her eyes. "Sure you can."

"What is that supposed to mean?"

"Nothing, just that you really seem to enjoy it. A lot."

"It's one of the perks of being a supervillain!"

"Hey, I'm new to this whole supervillain business, but aren't you only supposed to monologue in front of a captured superhero?"

"There aren't rules to monologuing, it's not like running a town hall meeting. You feel inspired and you just do it. I can't help it when I feel the moment."

"You could try. It's not like you're an eighteen year old putting a mask on for the first time."

"You know, a good lieutenant would support me if I chose to do a little harmless monologuing from time to time."

"It's not harmless, that's my point. Haven't you ever watched a cartoon or read a comic book? Whenever the bad guy captures the good guy what happens? Does the hero get his throat cut or a bullet to the back of the head? Of course not, the villain starts to go on about his secret plan and why he's won, and before you know it the hero gets away and the bad guy loses."

"That's in fiction, it hardly ever happens in real life."

"Hardly?"

Valerie coughed, diverting my attention back to her. "Sorry to interrupt, but listen, I really don't have anything going on with Dark Detective. I'm sure he doesn't even know who I am."

"We'll see, Miss Valley."

She sighed. "So I guess you've contacted the police, right? Told them about kidnapping me?"

I shook my head. "There's no need. I don't want them or any of the other heroes getting involved. The moment anyone notices you're missing Dark Detective will find out and come looking for you. I'm sure he'll track you down within hours."

"What? You can't do that! I'm supposed to be at work tonight."

"Perfect. I'm sure the moment you don't show up Dark Detective will hear about it and start tearing this city apart to find you."

"You don't understand! People will probably assume I'm on a drunken bender in Atlantic City or something. Our weather guy actually did that last year. The competition at the station is cut throat, you're going to get me fired!"

"Don't worry, Miss Valley. Once this is all over I'll release you. You'll have the exclusive story of how Dark Detective died at my hands."

"I told you already he doesn't know me!"

"You can stop trying to protect him."

"Please, I'm begging you, call the police and tell them you've kidnapped me. Hey, you could make a video challenging Dark Detective to come rescue me. I bet you'd enjoy that."

"She makes a good point," Raven said. "Why not contact the police, just in case?"

"It's not necessary. I guarantee you Dark Detective will be crashing through my walls in a matter of hours."

XXX

Three Days Later…

I was watching the local channel nine broadcast. A field reporter named Helen Harper was at the scene of an explosion that had destroyed a toy store. She ran up to a brooding figure in a mask and fedora.

"Dark Detective! Do you have any idea who might have been involved in this horrible crime?"

"No." He grunted and leapt away. The camera tried to follow him but he was gone from sight.

"Wow," Raven said. "Is it just me or do those two have a special connection?"

I sent her a hard look but didn't say anything.

"So what do we do with our guest? I mean no one even knows she's missing, not even her own TV station."

I hung my head. "Let her go."

"Are you sure? You could still send a video demanding your boyfriend come save her."

"It's been three days, if I contact the police now I'm going to look like an idiot. Just drug her and dump her somewhere in the city. With any luck no one will believe I actually kidnapped her."

And sure enough that's what happened, Valerie Valley was fired. No one believed her ridiculous story about being kidnapped by a supervillain who refused to contact the police. They all assumed she spent a long weekend drunk somewhere.

XXX

Rule #18 – When you kidnap someone make sure to let people know.

<u>Chapter 8</u>

"It's done!" Nothing in the world makes me as happy as completing one of my projects. I love the sense of accomplishment and satisfaction when I've turned an idea into reality. I always end up smiling ear to ear. "Isn't it great, Raven? Isn't it the most beautiful thing you've ever seen?"

I could see her struggle to contain her enthusiasm. "Well… it's big."

"Yeah! It's forty feet tall and weighs two thousand and thirty-five tons. The structure is tempered steel and the armor has a thickness ranging from two to five feet. The power plant generates up to twelve megawatts. It's fully submergible, can traverse swamp, mud, or any sort of rough terrain, and has a maximum speed of seventy miles an hour over flat ground."

"That's not really fast, Doc. My Porsche can go more than twice that."

"Does your Porsche weigh over two thousand tons? Can it laugh off a hundred and twenty-two millimeter shells? Can it juggle eighteen wheelers?"

"Well it could, the dealer offered me the feature, but it seemed like an extra."

I glared at her. "Why are you always like this? Would it kill you to show just a little enthusiasm?"

"Probably."

"Come on! It's got radar, sonar, an onboard independent navigational system, two Vulcan cannons, forward and rear missile launch ports, a massed flame thrower, a pulse cannon, the left arm is an honest to goodness rocket punch, and the right one can transform into a giant chainsaw. A GIANT CHAINSAW! How can you not be excited about something this amazing?"

She looked at me for a second, pumped her right fist into the air, and gave a half-hearted, "Woohoo."

I crossed my arms over my chest and stared at her.

"What? This is me being excited."

"I don't care what you think. The Anarchy Devastator Mark Two is my greatest creation yet!"

"Mark Two? You mean you already built one of these things?"

"Well, sort of, the original was only twenty feet tall and nine hundred tons."

"So what happened to it?"

"Oh, well, it sort of sank into the Jersey swamp during its trial run." She smirked at me. "Which won't happen this time!"

"I don't doubt it, Doc. You've been working on this thing for about three months. How much money have you put into it?"

I shrugged. "A little more than eighty-five million."

"Dollars?!"

"It's worth it. Everything is state of the art. You don't want to scrimp on a major project like this."

She glanced around the warehouse. "How are you getting it outside?

"Huh?"

She began waving an arm about. "There's no way it's fitting through the garage door, so how are you getting it outside?"

Now that she mentioned it, the dimensions of the garage door were ten feet by seven. The width of the arm and leg sections were twelve. The torso was twenty. "Oh. Well, I guess I'll have it just walk through the side of the building."

"So on top of spending a fortune on this thing you're going to wreck the entire warehouse too? I mean you realize the second this thing goes crashing through everyone's going to know this place is a supervillain lair."

"It's fine," I assured her. "I'll get all the equipment out first, and I expect to abandon all my lairs at some point. I consider those costs to be regular business expenditures."

She gave me one of those exaggerated eye rolls of hers. "So what's the plan?"

I blinked. "Huh?"

"The plan. You know, the whole reason why you built this monstrosity in the first place? How exactly are you going to use your shiny new toy to take over the world?"

"Oh, right." I stopped and thought about it. "Well, I suppose I could use it to break open bank vaults. Maybe I could threaten to go on a rampage and demand a payment from the government. I could try to get a contract with an arms dealer." I slowly rubbed my chin. "You know, when you stop and really think about it, there aren't that many practical uses for a giant robot."

Raven stood there with her mouth hanging open.

"Did I mention the arm is a chainsaw?"

XXX

Rule #15 – Giant Robots are ALWAYS cool.

Chapter 9

Thomas Knowles was an MI6 agent, an honest to goodness British spy. He'd come looking for me as part of an investigation into DEATH, **D**edicated to **E**ternal **A**narchy **T**error and **H**orror. They're an organization that likes to pretend they're trying to conquer the world, but they're really just in it for the money. They're the sort to steal a nuclear weapon just to sell it back. You can't really respect a group like that, no commitment at all.

They'd tried to recruit me several times, apparently they seem to think just because my name is Anarchy I should want to support them, bunch of posers. But Knowles believed I was a member, or at the very least an associate of theirs. He'd been investigating one of my LLCs when I captured him. Technically, Raven captured him, but since she works for me I'm entitled to the overall credit.

He'd possessed a number of very cool gadgets, and had a suave and polished manner even when I put him in his cell. Knowles actually managed to talk one of his guards into letting him out. My killbots recaptured him, but it was still impressive he could get that far with just his wits. I disintegrated the guard and put a killbot outside his cell door. It was a performance worthy of a top MI6 agent and so I would do him the honor of a final meal followed by an extraordinary death. I happened to own an old amusement park near Secaucus. I'd managed to turn it into a death maze with wild animals and all sorts of diabolical traps. Knowles would be its inaugural victim. The place had hundreds of cameras installed, so I would be able to enjoy his hopeless struggles and eventual death.

It would be a supervillain's take on dinner and a show. I was looking forward to it and spared no expense.

The main dishes were savory Kobe Beef Wellington, Sole A La meniure, salmon in a Terragon Buerre Blanc, Duchess Potatoes, asparagus spears smeared with a white wine infused mustard and balsamic vinegarette sauce, stuffed duck breasts filled with cranberries, truffles, pine nuts, and pesto, as well as lobster with melted butter, raw oysters, and the pièce de résistance, carefully sliced strips of Fugu, puffer fish. Fugu was poisonous if not properly prepared, it would be interesting to observe whether or not Knowles would try some. To wash it all down there was a bottle of Chateau Montelena Estate Cabernet Sauvignon – 1968. It would make a proper last meal for one of Her Majesty's finest.

As the food was being laid out I called in Raven.

She took one look at the dinner table and I could see her mouth start to water. "Whoa, nice spread. What's the occasion?"

"Mr. Knowles's impending and tragic death. I'm afraid the time has come for our guest to leave us."

"Well it's about time."

"Can you go and take care of him? I'll be here waiting."

"No problem, Doc."

As Raven went to deliver him I sat down at one of the two chairs and poured myself a glass of wine. I had two killbots standing behind me, both for dramatic effect and to discourage any sudden escape attempts. I made certain the knives were dull, it would make cutting the meats a little more difficult but it was a necessary precaution. I got myself into the proper pose, leaning back into the seat while holding my glass near my lips. I knew exactly how I would greet him.

"Welcome, Mr. Knowles, I would be honored if you would join me."

I would sip my wine. He would sit down while nonchalantly searching for any possible escape route. He would make some sort of clever remark and we would commence the battle of wits. Knowles would try to convince me that it would be in my own best interest to free him. There would be subtle threats of what MI6 would do in retaliation and promises that they were closing in. I would counter his arguments and remind him of who was the prisoner and who was in control of the situation. We would feast as we shared witty banter and sparred verbally. Then, once we were done with dessert, I would inform him he would have a chance to escape. That if he could survive my death maze and find the way out, I would let him go. Of course there wouldn't be a way out, but I would offer him that final flicker of hope. Then I'd watch his hopeless struggles on my one hundred and twenty inch monitor. It was going to be an exquisite evening.

The door to the dining room opened and I raised my glass. It was show time.

"Welcome, Mr. Knowles, I-"

Raven walked in alone. "Okay, it's done."

I blinked and craned my neck to look behind her. "Where's Knowles?"

"In his cell, where else?"

I put my glass down. "Why didn't you bring him?"

"Why would I do that?"

I gaped at her. "Because I want him here, obviously."

"Really? Won't that spoil your appetite? I mean with all the blood. I cut his head off so bringing his body all the way from the cells will make a serious mess."

"Wait a minute!" I jumped to my feet. "You killed him?!"

She frowned at me. "Yeah, obviously. What's the problem? You told me to."

"No, I didn't!"

"You said, 'take care of him.'"

"I meant I wanted you to bring him here so we could sit down together and have dinner."

"Really?"

"Why do you think I went through all the trouble to hire a five star chef to cook all this food?"

"I sort of thought you were just, you know, celebrating. You've got to admit, Doc, you do go to extremes sometimes."

"When do I ever go to extremes?"

"Hello, you built a forty foot giant robot that's still just sitting there."

"A giant robot is its own reward."

Raven sighed and pinched the bridge of her nose. "Look, I'm a ninja, we're not known for subtlety. Our instructions usually don't require interpretation. They're more like, 'steal this' or 'kidnap her.' When you say, 'take care of him' I'm going to take it as 'kill him.' If you wanted me to bring him to dinner you should have said that instead."

"Well that's just great! Now I can't even use my death maze! Do you have any idea how much it costs me? Not just construction but maintenance, I have two lions. Do you have any idea how hard they are to import? Or how much it costs to keep them fed? Then there are the hyenas and the snakes and there are inspections, utilities, and the property taxes. It's not like my front companies, a death maze doesn't bring in any revenue."

"If you want to use it so badly you could always get rid of one of the henchmen. Richard's been late a couple times this month, and I know he hasn't done well on his performance reviews."

"Oh, come on! Using a death maze to get rid of a henchman is like dropping an atomic bomb to level a house. That's not what I built it for."

"What did you build it for?"

I opened my mouth and then snapped it shut. "None of your business."

Raven stared at me for a moment. "It's for Dark Detective, isn't it?"

"No! Like I would really go through all the trouble just for him."

"Uh, huh." She didn't sound convinced. "Look, Doc, is it really that big a deal? I mean you didn't build it just for Knowles anyway, and he was still going to die, right? It's called a death maze, not a fun maze or exercise maze or escape maze. Does it make a real difference how he died?"

"Raven, you have absolutely no sense of the dramatic."

"I can live with that."

"What about all this food?"

Raven slow walked to the other chair. "You know I haven't eaten yet, and I love lobster."

"You want to have dinner with me?" I said in surprise. "Sort of like a date?"

"Not like a date, don't push your luck. But I'm willing to help you out since it was, sort of, my mistake." She plopped down in the seat.

"Fine, but if you're eating my food I at least want some entertaining stories."

"Oh, I can do that." She took out one of her kunai and hacked off a slice of mutton. "Let me tell you about one time when me and my gay friend Leon went to this club called the Carousel. See, they had a floor show…"

It was not quite the dinner conversation I'd expected. Though I did learn a surprising lot about fashion and how to disguise an Adam's apple.

XXX

Rule #12 – Take the time to make your orders specific. It's easy for people to misunderstand you.

Chapter 10

I was in my lab, chained to my computer when Raven strolled in.

"Hey, Doc, haven't seen you in a couple days. Wanted to see if you were still alive."

"Well, as you can see I'm just fine." I didn't bother to look up from the monitor.

"You got any jobs for me? Want me to steal a computer chip or knock off a jewelry store or anything?"

"No, nothing right now. You can have the next couple of days to yourself."

Raven came over to my workstation and peered over my shoulder. "What's got you so busy? You building a deathray or something?"

"I wish. Those are fun. I have a certain project in mind that is going to require a very large capital investment. I'm just acquiring the funds, it's one of those annoying necessities of my line of work. Like filling out worker compensation forms or filing reports with OSHA."

I expected her to get bored and to go off shopping or something. Instead she remained standing there to examine the computer screen as I kept working.

"Can I help you with something?"

"What exactly are you doing? Banco de San Juan? Are you opening up a foreign bank account?"

"Something like that."

"Wow. You have got a lot of big numbers here, are these in dollars?"

"Some of them are, some are in euros, Colombian pesos, Mexican pesos, British pounds, and Swiss francs."

She let out a low whistle. "I think I need to reconsider how much I charge you. You are drowning in cash. Can I kidnap you and make you pay your own ransom?"

"You know I can program your cybernetics to self-destruct, right?"

"Seriously though Doc, just how rich are you?"

"These aren't my accounts, they belong to the Alanzo Drug Cartel."

Her jaw dropped and she made a wheezing sound for a few seconds. I had to stop and turn around to look at her. I was worried I might have to perform the Heimlich Maneuver.

"You're ripping off a Colombian Drug Cartel?"

"That's right, I'm also stealing from the Chicago Mob, the Syndicate, the Yakuza, the Russian Mafia, Indian heroin producers, Chinese sex slave traffickers, and from DEATH."

"ARE YOU INSANE?!!"

I flinched and put a hand over my ear. "Hey! You don't need to scream, I'm right here. And this isn't a big deal. Whenever I need a lot of funds this is what I do. It's a lot faster than trying to rob one bank at a time. Plus the heroes aren't going to try and stop me."

"No, you just have to worry about some of the worst criminals in the world coming to look for you! Huge improvement! Listen, Doc, I am asking you this seriously, do you have a death wish? Because while I'm happy to help you out with this whole take over the world thing, I am not suicidal. Since you gave me my arms and legs back I've actually started to enjoy life again. I don't want to end up in a bathtub filled with ice as some crazy Latino starts removing my organs as I watch."

"The Colombians don't sell organs, that's more a Mexican or Chinese thing."

"Okay that is NOT the point. What are you doing stealing from people like this?"

"It's fine, Raven." I turned back to my computer. "I take around ten million dollars from each of them and automatically transfer the funds into accounts I have already set up. The money gets sent to banks in the Cayman Islands, then to Brazil and then to Turkey and to Greece and to the Swiss banks and finally back to the Caymans. Each bank account is under a different, false identity and there's nothing in any of them to connect to me. It would take a team of accountants weeks to track down all the transfers and accounts, and the money will be long gone before that can happen. That's if any of these groups are able to hire people with the necessary skills and access to financial systems. Most of them won't even bother to go through the trouble. They usually just assume it's an inside job and blame the in house accountants."

"Really? You're going to steal millions of dollars from psychopaths and cold blooded killers and you really think you'll get away with it?"

"I've done it nine times already and no one has ever connected me to any of the thefts."

She blinked at me. "Nine times? Seriously?"

"Yes."

"But how could you get away with that?"

"It's not hard for someone with an IQ of two hundred and the time to make careful preparations. It helps that all the people I am robbing can't exactly go to the police or Interpol. Most of their organizations, except for DEATH, don't have a staff of internet programmers working for them. And any contractors they hire will probably be amateur hackers who won't be able to crack my infiltration programs. Now, if I tried to steal from the IMF or Disney or the IRS, *that* would be insane. They could call in the FBI, Section Seven, and Interpol. They might actually find a connection to me, but the amateurs I'm dealing with aren't a threat."

"Unless they do finally catch you."

"None of them have come close yet."

"Just how much money do you plan to steal?"

"In total? About eighty million."

"Eighty million? Without even leaving your lab? Why even bother doing anything else?"

"I don't do this for the money. Money doesn't matter to me."

"Could have fooled me." She waved a hand at my computer.

"The money's just a tool, it's a necessary resource for a project I have in mind. It's a means to an end, Raven, nothing more. If all I wanted was to be rich I would be, it's not that hard. What I want is power, to make the whole world kneel before me. That's something no amount of money can buy."

She shook her head. "You're crazy, just a different sort of crazy."

I shrugged. "I've been called worse."

"Hey, why don't you steal from Kane Shipping?"

"Two reasons, first, he would catch me. He's even smarter than I am, and since I'm his nemesis I'd be the first person he'd suspect. Second, if I did that and my theft became public knowledge it would drive the stock price down."

"Why would that be a problem? He's your enemy, wouldn't you want to hurt his company?"

"Absolutely not, I'm a major shareholder. I own more than seventy thousand shares of stock."

"You own part of his company? Is this part of a scheme to steal it from him?"

"That wouldn't be possible. Even though Kane Shipping is a publicly traded Neil Kane still owns fifty-eight percent of the stock."

"Then why do you have shares?"

"It's just part of my portfolio. The company has paid out a regular dividend each of the past twelve years and has shown steady growth. Plus, I know the CEO is an incorruptible genius with strong connections to the League and government agencies, it's a good investment. If you're interested I can recommend a stockbroker to you."

She shook her head. "No thanks, I'm suddenly in the mood to go get a drink. I'll see you later, Doc."

"All right, oh and that reminds me, we'll be flying out to the Caymans Friday. Be sure to bring sunblock."

XXX

Rule #22 – Regular criminals care about money. Supervillains care about power.

<u>Chapter 11</u>

The Doc and I flew into Manhattan late one night to rob the Museum of Science and Natural History. There were some meteorites on display with a rare element, Saturnium. The Doc wanted them for something or other. With our mini-jetpacks we landed on the roof without drawing any attention.

"You know, you could just let me handle this on my own. I mean it's not like you're getting a discount for coming along."

"You need me here, Dark Detective knows I have an interest in Saturnium. There's a good chance he'll be here, waiting for me."

I planted my hands on my hips and frowned at him. "Really? You're like a teenage girl who can't get over a break up with the guy she likes."

"What is that supposed to mean?"

"You actually want to run into him don't you? That's what this really about, isn't it?"

"No," he said trying to sound indignant. "I want the Saturnium. It's vital to my plans!"

"Okay, what exactly are you going to use it for?"

"It generates a mutagenic radiation. I can use it to create giant, mutated spiders."

I raised one eyebrow. "Giant spiders? Really?"

He started to fidget and rubbed the back of his neck. "Or I could do worms I suppose, maybe ants."

"And how exactly is making a bunch of giant bugs going to help you take over the world?"

"I don't know, they could cause mass panic I guess."

See, here's the thing about Doc. He really is a genius when it comes to anything related to science. I didn't doubt for one second he could make giant super worms if he wanted. I mean if he told me he could build a deathray with an old PlayStation, glass lenses, and some duct tape I'd probably believe him. He is that good at inventing stuff.

His problem is with his plans. He builds these amazing things and then doesn't really know what to do with them. I mean this was the giant robot all over again, or the death maze or the tunneler. The things he creates work and work great, but he never builds them with anything specific in mind. He decides what he wants to make and then tries to design a plan around his creation. And in this case, that wasn't even the main issue.

"Why don't you come out and admit you're upset because Dark Detective hasn't paid you enough attention, and you want to run into him to make sure he still cares? I bet you don't even care about getting the Saturnium so long as you get to fight him."

"That... That's ridiculous!" He said while avoiding my eyes and fumbling around with his hands.

"Oh, well I'm convinced."

I know I give Doc a ton of shit, but the truth is I do respect him. I mean without him I'd be dead, and would never have never gotten my revenge on Viper. I owe him everything. And even though I mock him and make him pay me, it doesn't mean I don't like him. If I didn't I wouldn't have bothered to come back. I tease and belittle him because I care, after all, I'm a woman.

I even admired his dream. I mean, say what you will, anyone who wants to rule the world at least doesn't have a problem dreaming big. He decided on his own what he wanted and went for it. So what if he goes overboard from time to time with the killbots and the disintegrators? At least he knows what he wants and goes after it without apologies. (Also without a clear strategy or agenda, but that's beside the point.) I didn't become a ninja because it was my dream. I did it because it was expected and it was easy. It was the path of least resistance. If I'd had the guts to follow my dreams

I'd have started that graphic design company with Sheryl and Tina. Instead I came home from college and became a full time ninja like mom and dad wanted. Unlike Doc, I never had the courage to follow my heart.

"Look, Doc, I'm just saying-" I cut off when I heard a crackling sound coming towards us. "Heads up!" I jumped around and grabbed my katana. To Doc's credit he had his disintegrator out and in his hand.

We stood there and watched as an ice bridge formed from the top of the building across the street, connecting to the edge of the museum roof. Two figures decked out in white slid across on it and landed about fifteen feet in front of us. One was a guy in a polar bear outfit. I mean literally, he was wearing a polar bear skin including the animal's head and claws. Behind him was a woman in white fur boots, heavy coat, and a fur cap. Did I forget to mention this was the middle of June? She was toting some kind of rifle and standing behind the guy in the bear skin.

"Polar Bear, what are you doing here?" Doc asked.

"Probably the same thing you are, Dr. Anarchy."

"Friend of yours?" I asked.

"No. He's an associate, and a member of the supervillain community." I noticed Doc lowered his disintegrator, but didn't holster it. I kept my katana ready. "Look Wally, you can't have the Saturnium, I was here first."

"Well I've been planning to steal it for weeks. I'm going to use it to make giant mutated polar bears that will crush this city."

Was that the only thing this stuff was good for? Talk about a lack of imagination.

"You should have gotten here sooner then," Doc said. "Don't blame me if you arrived late."

"Hey, this isn't like calling shotgun. If you get in my way I'll freeze you solid."

I could feel the air actually start to get cold and saw my own breath. Doc was beginning to point his disintegrator at him and I was about two seconds away from running in and slicing him in half. That was when the girl suddenly stepped forward. She had slung her rifle over her shoulder and pulled her cap off to reveal a lot of dirty blonde hair. The girl had glasses and was sort of cute. Not supermodel cute, or hot chick at the bar cute, but nerdy girl cute. Obviously, she couldn't hold a candle to me.

"There's no need to be hostile, Mikey. I'm sure we can work something out."

Mikey?

The Doc did a double take and gaped at her. "Amanda? Is that you?"

She gave him a big smile. "It's good to see you again, it's been awhile."

I saw his mouth open and close. "What are you doing here? The last I heard you were an engineer with ALCOA."

"I did that for six years. It was okay, but it got to be sort of a rut. I heard about you, of course, and I got interested in the game. I mean I'm not supervillain material-"

"Yes you are!" Doc blurted. "You can be a great supervillain!"

Oh, fuck me, I thought. He sounded like every nice guy I'd ever met trying to get my attention.

"That's sweet," the nerdy bitch said putting a hand over her heart. "But I don't have super powers, and we both know I'm not a genius like you are. I figured I could at least be a henchman or something and get close to the action. I managed to join DEATH and help build some jet cars and heavy weapons and a death maze."

"They have a death maze? Does it use lions?"

"Sharks with lasers."

"That's so cliché."

She giggled. "I know, right? Huge evil organization and they get their ideas from the movies. I mean seriously, who would actually use a death maze to kill someone?"

I couldn't resist. "Only someone with way too much time on their hands, am I right, Dr. Anarchy?"

He forced a false grin onto his lips and nodded. "Absolutely."

"I mean only a real moron would do something like that. What a waste of time and money just to kill a person. Think about how much a bullet costs and you're going to-"

"Yes, I get it, thank you, Raven. So Amanda, how long have you been working for Polar Bear?"

"She's been with me for about six months." Polar Bear walked over to stand between Doc and her. "I recruited her after Lightning Bug got arrested."

"You worked for Lightning Bug? Isn't he a little…" Doc twirled a finger next to his head.

"Oh, he's not so bad. He's a little emotional sometimes but I helped him stay focused."

"How'd you go from working for an organization like DEATH to a small timer like him?"

"Well, when Automaticman broke off from the organization to go solo me and a few others went with him."

Doc made a face. "He didn't do very well on his own, did he?"

"No."

"Fell into a volcano, right?"

She nodded. "He was fighting Iron Knight and got knocked over a catwalk. Building a base inside an active volcano, probably not his best idea."

"Sounds like building a catwalk over lava was pretty bad too," I said.

"Yeah, I have to agree there. He liked the aesthetic, but safety should always be the first priority."

"So, how do you and Dr. Anarchy know each other?"

"Oh, I was a teaching assistant back at MIT his freshman year. Michael was a phenome, absolutely brilliant, I was interested in him from the moment we met. We talked after class, one thing led to another, and before I knew it we were dating."

"It was against the rules so we had to do it in secret." Doc had a goofy grin on his face. "I was always worried we'd get caught and get in trouble."

"I loved it! It made everything more exciting. I mean you had to sneak into my apartment building just so we could watch Deep Space Nine together."

"How about the times we drove into Boston to see the Sox? Or went to Quincy Market?"

"I'd never gone to a baseball game before. Every time we were together I had to keep an eye out, each date was a little adventure."

"And every time you picked me up or dropped me off, it was at least half a mile from campus."

She winked and put a finger to her lips. "Well we had to keep it secret."

The two of them started laughing in that dumb way kids do. It was really annoying. From the looks of it I wasn't the only one who thought so.

"You never mentioned working for Dr. Anarchy." Polar Bear whined. "You told me about DEATH, Automaticman, Warthog, Crimson Mist, Troublemaker, and Lightning Bug. I would definitely remember if Dr. Anarchy had been on your resume."

She put a hand on his arm and rubbed it a little, I noticed Polar Bear's demeanor and posture relaxed. "I never worked for Mikey, our time together was before he went supervillain. We'd lost touch, so I couldn't even list him as a reference."

"Well... I suppose that makes sense," Polar Bear muttered.

She nodded and continued to rub his arm, meanwhile Doc was standing there looking on like a five year old wanting attention. The fact this chick had made the rounds with no less than six evil organizations or supervillains was a bad sign. She was obviously happy to go from one to the other while offering to give them what she had. The slut was working her way up the supervillain ladder, and I could guess who the next rung would be.

"So how do you like being Polar Bear's henchman?" I asked.

"She's not just a henchman, she's my lieutenant." Polar Bear declared. "I couldn't manage without her."

"That's sweet of you to say, but I'm not really that important."

"Yes, you are! You took over the human resources department and totally redesigned the lair to be more efficient and ergonomic. And I love your ideas about using mind controlled penguins!"

"Penguins?" I rolled my eyes and tried not to sound too mocking.

"Well my original idea was to use ordinary house pets, mostly cats and dogs." Amanda hurriedly explained. "But you know... ice powers sort of require an arctic motif."

"And how exactly are penguins going to take over the world?"

"I hadn't really crunched the numbers on that yet." Amanda admitted. "It's more of a concept than an actual plan."

"I think it sounds interesting." Doc said.

That earned him a big smile from her. "Thanks. You were always so supportive of me."

Doc blushed and started rubbing the back of his head. I worried I'd go into sugar shock. It was already painfully obvious he was not going to see through her act. This chick was clearly bad news. The Doc is a really great guy, but he's got his blind spots. I decided the best thing would be to get him away from this slut before things got any chummier.

"Dr. Anarchy, don't you think we could just let Polar Bear have the Saturnium? I mean I know how important it is to you, but he wants to use it to make giant polar bears. Who doesn't want to see a bunch of those things tearing through Central Park?"

He thought for a moment and then slowly bounced his head up and down. "All right, I suppose we could just step aside, as a favor."

"Thank you," Polar Bear said. "I'll owe you one."

"Thanks, Mikey."

"No problem, ah, it was really good seeing you again."

"Yeah, same here."

The two of them were looking into each other's eyes like a couple of teenagers.

"Well, this has been fun, but we should be going and let the two of you get on with robbing this place." I said. "Great meeting both of you, I can tell the two of you will do great things, together, as a unit. Can't wait to see those giant bears terrorizing everyone. Ready to go, Dr. Anarchy?"

"Uh, yes, I suppose so."

"Great, let's be off then."

Amanda stepped past her boss. "Hey, Mikey, did you ever build that giant robot you talked about?"

Doc lit up like a Christmas tree. "Yeah, I did. I actually have the mark two version sitting in my base."

"Does it have a giant chainsaw?"

"It sure does!"

"That's amazing, I'd love to see it in action some time."

"Why don't you come over, and I'll put on a demonstration for you?"

"I'd love that!"

"Hey, it's called a secret lair, remember?" I objected.

"It's fine, I've known Amanda for years. You want to exchange phone numbers?"

"Sure, just let me-"

Before things got any more out of hand I grabbed the bitch by the elbow and steered her towards the other end of the roof. "Excuse me, but could I talk to you for just a minute?"

"What do you think you're doing?" Polar Bear demanded.

"Raven, why are you-"

"I just need to chat with her about girl stuff for a little bit. Why don't you boys talk about football and trucks and how big your dicks are? Feel free to whip them out and compare."

She didn't resist as I led her all the way to the roof's edge where we could talk in private. I let go of her and then leaned in close.

"What's your deal?"

She took a step back and rubbed her elbow. "I don't know what you mean."

"Spare me. Why are you playing up to him? If this were a bar you'd be leaning on him telling him how drunk you are."

"Hey, we used to date and I've always liked him. I just want to reconnect. Trust me, you don't have anything to worry about. I'm not trying to steal him from you."

"What?! Steal? Let's get something clear, he and I aren't a thing."

The bitch gave me a little lopsided grin. "Sure you're not."

"You're starting to piss me off, and that's not a good idea. He saved my life and I owe him. Because of that I'm not going to let anyone use him."

"That's not what I'm doing. I just want to talk to him and see how he is. And if he wants help, well I could-"

"He doesn't need help with anything, he's doing just fine."

"If that's true you don't have anything to worry about, do you?"

"Shouldn't you be worried about Polar Bear? You know, your boss?"

She gave an expansive sigh and flicked her hair over her shoulder. "Actually, I've been thinking Wally and I aren't a very good fit. He keeps the room temperature of the lair at forty-two degrees, it's like working inside a fridge. And ice powers are really limiting. He's not a genius the way Mikey is. I've kept track of Mike since he started his career; his robots, his crazy inventions, and his fights with Dark Detective. He's really made a name for himself. If I'd had a way to get in touch with him I would have years ago. With my help he could definitely take things to the next level."

"I knew it," I hissed. "You just want to use him."

"You don't need to be jealous. I'm not trying to take your spot. Lots of supervillains have more than one lieutenant."

"I'm not jealous, and I'm not his lieutenant, I'm his sidekick."

"Villains don't have sidekicks."

"I guess I'm an exception then." I got in her face and leaned in. "The point is you need to leave him alone. I'm not going to let some nerdy skank like you mess with him."

I'll give the girl credit. In spite of my size and my looks, I can be intimidating when I want, especially wearing my shozoko. She stood her ground though and looked me straight back in the eye. The bitch had guts.

"Are you really not sleeping with him?"

"No."

"That's a shame, 'cause he is really easy to please. The first time I ever gave him a handy he came in under thirty seconds. When I'd let him stick it in he'd grunt and groan and pound away for a couple minutes and then just want to cuddle after. If I sucked him off he'd spend the rest of the day with a smile on his face. After we start sleeping together he'll do anything I ask him to."

"You fuck all your bosses?"

She shrugged. "Men aren't complicated, not even the geniuses. The point is, you can either work with me or you can take a walk. Mikey isn't going to listen to anything you say about me."

"I see. So you've got it all figured out."

"Pretty much."

"You don't have any super powers, right? You can't fly or anything."

"No, I'm just smart and know how to get what I want."

"Right. You don't have a jetpack or a grappling gun do you?"

"No, why would I-" She cut off and her eyes bulged. She'd figured it out, but it was already too late.

"Hey! Look out!" I had deliberately put myself between her and where the guys were in order to block their line of sight. I gave her one, quick, hard shove on the shoulder and she went spilling off the roof's edge. I reached out and pantomimed trying to grab her. I watched her arms and legs flail as she plummeted five stories to the sidewalk. She let out one hell of a scream.

"Amanda!" Doc shouted.

"What happened?" Polar Bear yelled.

They both ran to where I was and peered over the side. She was lying broken on the pavement in a slowly spreading pool of her own blood. We could hear shouts from one of the guards at the entrance.

"I guess she lost her balance," I said putting some confusion in my voice and expression. "I tried to save her, but it happened too fast."

Polar Bear was just staring down at the body. Doc turned his eyes to me with a look of disbelief. He then leveled his disintegrator and pulled the trigger.

Zzzzzzzz.

The beam hit Polar Bear right in the back of his head. Everything above his neck vaporized. The poor guy never felt a thing. His body did a slow tumble over the edge. It landed about five feet from the bitch's corpse. There were more shouts from down at street level. I wasn't paying a lot of attention. My main focus was on Doc who was still holding his weapon. I was ready to act if he pointed it at me. Knocking it out of his hand before he could pull the trigger would be easy. I wasn't sure what I would do next if that happened. It would be pretty damn ironic if I had to kill the guy I'd just gone through the trouble of rescuing.

He didn't aim it at me, though. He put it in the holster.

"Rule five," he said.

"Excuse me?"

"My fifth rule is, 'Don't leave behind anyone who will come looking for revenge.'"

"Okay. That's actually a pretty good one."

"Why did you kill her?" He asked me in a very calm voice.

"You're not going to believe she just lost her balance, are you?"

He shook his head. "I know how fast you are. I didn't see what happened, but if she fell it was because you wanted her to. So why?"

"I know you won't believe this, but she was a bad person. She was just going to use you. I did it for your own good."

He stared at me for a moment, then slowly nodded. "I think I understand."

"Glad to hear it."

"You felt threatened by her. You were afraid she was going to come between us."

"What? Fuck no!"

"It's fine, Raven. I forgive you. Just please don't worry in the future, no one could take your place. At least not unless they'd let me attach cyborg limbs to them. So you don't need to be jealous."

"Hey! I was in no way jealous of that stupid bitch, understand?"

We could hear the guards yelling that someone was on the roof and there were police sirens in the distance.

"We should go. Two murders will have to do for tonight." He activated his mini jetpack and rocketed into the air.

"Hey! Did you hear me? I wasn't jealous! There's no way that would ever happen! Don't push your luck!"

I turned on my own jetpack and followed him.

XXX

Raven's Rule #1 – It's always better to take care of a problem when it's small.

<u>Chapter 12</u>

O'Malley's is a sports bar on Thirtieth Street, a couple blocks from Seventh Avenue. I went there on a Friday night in

August. I didn't go there as Dr. Anarchy, but as a civilian. Supervillains don't really have secret identities. I mean we do use false names as a matter of course. I always keep a dozen different drivers licenses and passports, all with various names and residences. For instance, when I went to the club I was Tom Wilson from Newark.

What I mean when I say supervillains don't have secret identities is that we don't try to have lives as civilians. Having a 'real' life as a normal person is pretty much a hero thing. Villains don't try to be part of the herd. We don't pretend to be ordinary. We're not and there's no point in demeaning ourselves. In that way we're a lot more honest than the heroes.

Think about it. How many superheroes spend ninety-nine percent of their lives in disguise as normals? Working in malls or call centers or factories at meaningless jobs. Actually having to worry about everyday mundane problems like paying rent, getting good cell phone reception, or trying to get your internet working. Going around pretending to be something they're not, afraid the people in their lives will find out about their true nature. Terrified of how their loved ones and friends would treat them if they only knew they could fly or shoot lasers out their eyes or control the weather. Most heroes spend the majority of their lives denying what they truly are and living according to the societal norms, reveling in their strength only when it's socially acceptable. I.e., when they have a chance to be heroic and fight crime. That's the only time they come out of their cozy little cages and use their powers. And even then they have to wear masks to hide themselves. Isn't that cowardly?

I know the heroes would argue they have to hide who they are to protect themselves and their loved ones. So does that mean the heroes are less brave than the villains? Once a supervillain makes the choice to put on the mask and come out to try and rule the world, or at least get rich through crime, there is no going back. From that point on you are your costumed identity. Even when you're in hiding and using an alias, you remain the supervillain every moment of your life. Our commitment to the lifestyle is total. Some people can't hack it and either give up or do a 'Heel-Face Turn' and try to be the hero. We view those people as being too weak to handle the supervillain lifestyle. It's definitely a hard way to live, but being what you choose to be is never easy, especially without the crutch of a nice dark, safe, cage to run and hide in.

I know that at any moment Dark Detective might swoop in and beat me up and send me to the Sandbox. I've seen months or years of hard work get blown up right in front of my face and been mocked and ridiculed by the public. It's the price for standing up for yourself.

As soon as I walked inside I drew some hostile looks. I automatically slipped a hand into a pocket to hold my disintegrator. Underneath my jacket I had my mini jetpack strapped on. I also had three killbots in some of the nearby sewers, just in case, as well as some additional back up. I don't wear a mask with my costume and at the time I was number forty-one on the FBI's most wanted list. So whenever I go out in public I take precautions in case someone recognizes me.

I relaxed a little when someone said, "Red Sox suck."

The hostility was from the ball cap I was wearing rather than my life of crime. I grew up in New Bedford, Massachusetts, (Go Whalers) and am a devoted Boston sports fan. If I ever do become ruler of the world I will make Fenway Park a national monument. Also, I will kidnap and brainwash Tom

Brady so we can be BFFs. The fact a few people were giving me the stink eye was because I was a Sox fan, rather than because I was a supervillain. It meant I wouldn't have to start disintegrating or summon my killbots. I'd get to enjoy a regular night out.

A part of me was disappointed. I mean I don't wear a mask. It would have been kind of nice for someone to stand up and scream, 'It's Dr. Anarchy! Run for your lives!' Then see them flee from me in a blind panic. I mean it was good I could go out, but still, a little disappointing.

My sort of friend spotted me and waved me over to his table. He was a tall blond guy with the rugged chin and big blue eyes that could win a woman over with just one smile. His name was Patrick Newton, also known as Lord Chaos and was the twenty-first person on the most wanted list. I considered him the definitive proof that for some people a normal life was just not possible. He was from Schenectady, New York. His dad was a doctor and his mom was a home maker. He had two brothers and two sisters and grew up in an upper middle class neighborhood. Unlike me, he was always athletic and very popular. There were no unusual tragedies or incidents for him growing up. Daddy didn't drink or sleep around with the nurses, mommy didn't ignore him, and he was never dragged naked out of the boys' shower and thrown into the girls' dressing room during gym as the boys laughed and the girls screamed and threw things at him as he cried and tried to cover himself up. Er, not that I would know what that's like.

My point is that he had as normal a life as anyone with an IQ of two hundred and six could. He was the All American boy, the sort of kid who you thought might just be President someday. Instead, he summoned a goat demon to his junior prom and watched it terrorize all his friends and teachers. He didn't even make it to high school graduation before deciding to go supervillain. If someone like him couldn't have a normal life what chance did I ever have?

I sat down across from him. "Hey, Patrick. How's it going?"

"Good, how about you, Mike?"

"Not bad, given the situation."

"I already ordered a big basket of wings and nachos."

"Okay, we can split it." When a waitress came over I ordered a beer.

"Ready to see the Yanks roll?"

"Right, who's in second again?"

"It's two games, they'll be up after they sweep."

"Keep dreaming."

Tonight was the opening game of a three game series in Boston. The Red Sox and Yankees were fighting it out for the division lead. I had no doubts the Yankees were going to fade, their lineup was just too damn old. Mariano and Jeter were gone, but most Yankees fans were delusional and seemed to think it was still nineteen-ninety-six.

I noticed Raven show up about the time my beer arrived. She looked very cute wearing long denim shorts, a Giants jersey, some sandals, and a big purse filled with throwing knives and shuriken. I almost never got to see her in anything other than ninja clothing. It was a nice change of pace to see her dressed so casual for once. She went up to the bar and almost immediately had a couple college guys all over her. I expected Raven to tell them to get lost. I was paying her two thousand dollars to act as my bodyguard for the evening. Instead she started laughing and flipping her hair and touching one of their arms. You would think she was on a date!

"Why don't you go up and introduce yourself? If you want I could work a charm spell on her."

It figured he would notice. "No need. She's actually one of mine. She's supposed to be here to protect me."

"Does she know that?"

"She's a cyborg ninja," I sounded a little defensive. "She has some attitude, but she's really capable. If some heroes show up she'll trash them."

The bartender made some sort of fruity drink and Raven had a sip as she laughed along with the two guys.

"Assuming she's still sober."

I was definitely going to get my money back.

XXX

The game started and as Patrick and I watched we talked about work and about people in the community.

"Did you hear about Goblin?" Patrick asked. "He tried to break into League headquarters. He got caught by the automated defenses."

"Ouch! Yeah, that's just embarrassing. I mean, getting taken down by the security system?"

"Well that's what he gets for being a poser. I mean he's strictly just a thug with muscle. He should stick to running a gang, that's as much as he can handle. I mean he couldn't even become a crime boss in Hoboken last year."

I nodded. "Yeah, if you're too weak to do that here in the city you're strictly minor league. What was he thinking going after their headquarters?"

"I'm sure he figured with the situation right now it was a soft target."

That made me laugh. "Well sure, the way steel is softer that durtanium, but it's still steel."

"Rattlesnake got busted by Power Princess trying to rob a bank."

"I heard about that, what are the authorities doing with him?"

"Shipping him off to the Sandbox, what else?"

"So it's still open then? I thought the new government might have a different policy."

"No, nothing's changed, at least so far."

"That's disappointing. You'd think he could be just a little more considerate of our kind."

"Well, he's seriously into order, you know? It's not like he'd opened up the prisons and let everyone go."

"I guess. I heard Power Princess is applying for League membership."

"She'll need to wait awhile."

"Do you think she'll get in?"

"Probably," Patrick stuffed some nachos in his mouth and continued after swallowing. "I mean she's popular, have you seen the commercials for her new toy line?"

"Is that what the League wants? Superheroes with good PR?"

"It doesn't hurt."

I tsked and had some more beer. That's what's wrong with the world! People are too worried about image.

"The Purple Hammer robbed an armored car this morning," Patrick told me. "He got away clean."

"Like that's hard to do now. I bet he wouldn't have even tried it last week."

"There are still plenty of heroes in town."

"Sure, the B-Listers like Power Princess and Jetboy. The heavy hitters aren't though."

"Well that just means now's the time when they should be out there taking advantage. Do you have any plans?"

I shook my head. "It would be disrespectful to pull anything major when my nemesis is out of town."

His hand froze halfway to bringing a chicken wing to his mouth.

"What?" I asked.

"You're talking about Dark Detective, right?"

"Who else?"

He opened his mouth, then closed it.

"What?"

"Nothing," he ate the chicken wing.

"No, what are you thinking?"

"It's nothing important."

"Oh, come on, you definitely have something to say."

"It's not anything you want to hear."

"What?" I demanded. "Go ahead and spit it out. I'm a big boy, I can take it."

"Okay then, you're not his nemesis, Whiteface is."

"Whiteface is a psychotic loon."

"Think I'm going to argue with you? But everybody knows he's Dark Detective's nemesis, not you."

"What are you talking about? Whenever I commit a crime it's always Dark Detective who comes after me!"

"Which makes you part of his rogues gallery, not his nemesis."

"I am too! Don't lump me in with Rubberband and Crowbar and Hammerhead!"

"Hey, hey," he motioned for me to calm down. "It's not an insult. He's one of world's best superheroes and you're one of his regular enemies, that's no small thing! Plenty of bad guys out there would love to take your spot. All I'm saying is you're not number one on the list."

"You don't know what you're talking about. Do you have any idea how many times he has broken into one of my lairs or interrupted one of my crimes? I've almost killed him twice! He's the only one to have ever hacked into my computer system. I once turned his own exo-suit against him. I figured out his secret identity. I-"

"You know his secret identity?"

Crap. I didn't mean to say that. "What I mean is we have an intense history. There's a lot of bad blood between us."

"Didn't Crowbar break both his legs once? Didn't Dark Detective knock all of Hammerhead's teeth out? Didn't he freeze Rubberband solid? And drop him out of a plane? Didn't he put Crowbar in a hospital for six months? And-"

"What's your point?"

"You're not the only supervillain with a long history with him. That's what makes you part of his rogues gallery. But come on, you've got to admit him and Whiteface are on a different level."

"That's just how the media portrays it! You know how they get everything wrong. Whiteface is just a psycho clown whose gotten close a few times, that's all. I am absolutely his nemesis!"

"Fine." Patrick deliberately focused his attention back on the game.

It was obvious I hadn't actually changed his mind, but I let it go. As you can guess, this is a sore subject for me. Dark Detective was absolutely my nemesis and I was his, but the media loved to play up Whiteface. I could understand why, his crimes tended to be more gruesome and, well, spectacular than anyone else's. But public opinion couldn't change the facts.

XXX

One of the two guys eventually left. The other one sat on the bar stool next to Raven. He had khakis and this really stupid looking goatee. He kept leaning over and putting a hand on her. She could have snapped him in half. Instead she kept laughing and playing up to him.

Not that I cared.

At least the Red Sox were winning. Big Pappi crushed a three run homer into the right field bleachers and the Sox were up six to one headed to the bottom of the seventh. That was when Fenway was suddenly replaced. The image of the new world flag filled every screen; it was a black skull inside a white circle in a field of red.

"We interrupt your regularly scheduled programming to bring you an important message from our beloved emperor." Some announcer said.

Then there he was, the Emperor of Earth, Dr. Death. He was sitting behind a desk in the Oval Office. On display behind him was one of his new flags. The Emperor was in his full power armor, including the black skull mask that he'd made so iconic. As a symbol it was probably only second to Supersoldier's American flag cape. His gauntleted hands were steepled in front of his face, as if her were in prayer. Was he trying to look calm? Serene maybe? If so it was a wasted effort, looking at him in that black and silver armor he always appeared menacing. It also didn't help that his English, while grammatically perfect, had a significant German accent to it.

"Greetings, my loyal subjects. It pleases me to say ze new world order is firmly established. Soon all loyal citizens will begin to reap ze benefits of economic and judicial reform. A society where everyone is truly equal and those who are loyal will be rewarded. Ze former President and other world leaders remain prisoners until ze League of Heroes surrenders to me. Supersoldier and his pathetic cronies are criminals who seek to destroy ze peace and order I have established! Any citizens with knowledge of their location should immediately report it to ze Death Police. Any information leading to Supersoldier's capture will earn a ten million dollar reward. Do not feel sympathy for Supersoldier or these other renegades, they are cowards who seek to bring chaos and ruin ze worldwide peace and order of mein regime. Such treachery is verboten! Supersoldier is a coward, a schweinehund! He dares not face me while I possess ze power to destroy ze world and while his precious Diana Darwin is mein guest here at ze White House. He is a weak and pathetic man who…"

The next five minutes were him railing against Supersoldier and, to a lesser degree, the other heroes. He then concluded by standing and bringing both hands to his heart in some sort of dramatic gesture.

"Keep your faith in me, your supreme leader, and all shall be well! Never forget that loyalty will be rewarded! Rebellion will be crushed!"

The TVs cut away from him back to the image of the world flag. The announcer spoke again. "That concludes this special announcement. We now return you to your regularly scheduled programming."

When the game came back on Bradley was at the plate with a ball and a strike. The crowd commented on the emperor's speech.

"Fucking Nazi."

"Enjoy it while it lasts, asshole."

"Supersoldier's gonna kick his ass."

"He wasted our time for that?"

"You can tell he's scared."

Patrick and I both looked around the bar. No one was jumping up and down shouting, they were just complaining like they would if the ump made a bad call. Certainly, they weren't acting as though they had just committed treason.

"Not exactly terrified, are they?" Patrick said.

"Nope. I guess they can get used to things pretty quickly."

"Think anyone's going to call the one eight hundred number for the Death Police?"

"Well they obviously don't think so."

"It's only been three days," Patrick sounded like he had trouble believing it. "When he took over everyone was acting like the world was ending."

"I know, I watched all the riots on CNN. People were trying to get out of the cities and buying up all the food and toilet paper in the stores. Now it's back to normal."

"Yeah."

Patrick and I shared an uncomfortable look. Our feelings about Dr. Death taking over the world were… complex. That was true for most of the community. To supervillains, Dr. Death is sort of a rock star, a shining example for others to emulate. He'd been number one on the most wanted list for over eight years and was Supersoldier's nemesis. He'd nearly killed Supersoldier multiple times. There had been some legendary battles between him and the *entire* League of Heroes. He was the absolute best of the best when it came to supervillainy.

The fact Dr. Death had not only created a black hole generator, but then used it to destroy Gary, Indiana, amazed me every bit as much as it did the public. I mean it's one thing to create a doomsday device, but to use it to annihilate an American city? And then to go on air and threaten to use it against every national capital unless the world surrendered? Ballsy! When the President announced his surrender I actually stood up and cheered in the middle of my lab. One of us had done it. A member of the community had won, had beaten all the heroes and conquered the world. It was a victory for all of us. I was proud of Dr. Death. I was proud to call myself a supervillain.

The euphoria lasted for about twenty-four hours. He started going on the air talking about a classless society, about the need for absolute obedience and devotion to the rule of law. You expected to hear him say he was going to make all the trains run on time. Supervillains aren't good with schedules or following rules. If we were, none of us would feel the need to be supervillains in the first place. Listening to Emperor Death spew on about order and obedience made me start to itch. It began to dawn on me that the feeling I'd had about being a part of his triumph was only that. Dr. Death had won alone and intended to rule alone. If he was now the government what would that mean for a criminal like me? I and most of the supervillains didn't commit any crimes during that time, even though the League was in hiding. Part of that was out of respect, and part was out of fear. We all knew what to expect from the heroes and the regular authorities. We didn't know what the new rules were, and no one wanted to cross Dr. Death. (Except for idiots like Goblin and Rattlesnake.)

Also, the fact Dr. Death ruled the world didn't mean I'd given up my dream. There's only one Earth. (I think, theories about alternate and parallel Earths are only that so far. Though I have heard stories about Heliopan portal technology.) There can only be one ruler of it. If Dr. Death remained in power he would have to become my enemy. That's not something anyone should relish.

When Patrick and I shared that look I knew we were thinking the same thing.

"He's not going to last." I said.

Patrick nodded. "I don't see how he can. He's all alone."

"He's got followers. He's got henchmen."

"Sure. We all do, but the world's a big place. How much can he really control unless people are willing to work with him? Conquering and ruling are two different things."

I considered the people in the bar. I expected their general attitude was typical.

"There's also the fact the League is still at large." I stated. "They're probably trying to find a way to either capture or safely destroy his black hole machine."

"No doubt, and once they do…"

Patrick let the sentence trail off. I didn't feel any desire to complete it. As I said, my feelings were complicated. I didn't want Dr. Death to remain emperor. At the same time, if he couldn't successfully rule the world what chance would anyone else have?

XXX

The Red Sox won eight to two, but Dr. Death's interruption put a damper on the evening. Patrick and I went our separate ways. I was outside waiting for one of my henchmen to pick me up, parking in Manhattan is a nightmare.

"You have a good time tonight, Doc? You looked like you did." Raven strolled up to me.

"It was all right. It's good to have a change of pace now and again."

"So that was really Lord Chaos?"

"Yes."

"And he can actually use magic and summon demons and other things?"

"Yes."

"Pretty hard to believe."

I looked at her. "Why? I build flying robots and disintegrators. Dr. Death makes mini black holes. You're a cyborg ninja. Why is someone using magic hard to believe?"

"What you do is science though. You flying with a jet pack is one thing, flying without one would be totally different."

"Supersoldier flies without one, so does Amazon and a lot others."

"They have super powers."

I shrugged. "Are super powers science or magic? I've heard some people argue the latter. Like any mutant or alien, Supersoldier has different DNA and biology from a regular human, but no scientist can actually explain how he's able to defy gravity. According to the basic laws of motion it should be impossible without a source of propulsion. He must have one, but no one can actually explain what it is or how it works."

"So you're okay with magic?"

"I'm not particularly fond of it if that's what you mean. But I don't need to be. It exists and some people can use it the same way I can use science. You only have to worry about the what, not the why. I like to think about it as an inverse example of Clarke's Third Law; where a sufficiently advanced magic is indistinguishable from technology. I mean if someone flies does it actually matter how they're doing it?"

"I guess you've got a point."

I glanced up the street back towards the bar. I couldn't spot the guy with the goatee anywhere. "What happened to your date?"

"You mean Charlie from NYU? He got a little handsy when I told him I was going so I cold cocked him."

"You two seemed to be getting along pretty well."

She snorted a laugh. "He helped pass the time. Besides, he's studying corporate law so he has no soul. I mean you didn't expect me to pay for my own drinks, did you?"

My henchman arrived with a van and we headed back to Jersey.

XXX

You know what happened three days later.

I was in the lab writing code when Raven informed me there was a major news story breaking on all channels. I watched live as Supersoldier led Dr. Death out of a half leveled White House. Supersoldier's cape had been torn off and he looked grim. That was nothing compared to Dr. Death, his skull mask was missing and the sections of armor still on were clearly broken or at least cracked. His lip was bleeding and the side of his face was bruised. He looked lost and beaten.

The camera cut away to the White House lawn. A small group of people were already burning his world flag and dancing around. President Thompson came on an hour later to declare it a national day of celebration and thanksgiving and to promise that all of Dr. Death's associates and supporters would be charged with high treason. There were fireworks that night.

Dr. Death was and is the greatest supervillain the world has ever seen. He did the thing we all dream about. He conquered the world, but stayed in power for just six days. The world's best supervillain couldn't even last a full week. It definitely gave me something to think about.

XXX

Rule #10 – Conquering and ruling are two very different things.

Chapter 13

The meeting room had a wooden stage with a podium in the center of it. The orientation was scheduled to begin at nine a.m. I was already standing there behind the podium as they were brought in.

"Welcome, please take a seat and we'll get started."

The new recruits filed in. There were eight tables set up with four chairs behind each. I was glad to see everyone had their booklet along with a folder filled with the different forms they would have to fill out. As they took their seats all of them stared at me. For most it was one quick look. A few of the better dressed ones openly gawked and had trouble looking away. It was obvious they hadn't really believed they were going to be henchmen working for a supervillain. I don't know why, as they were told before being formally hired. I am very careful about the recruitment process. My people use rented office space for exactly one day each time I recruit new henchmen. Always in a different office building and always under a different company name. The prospects are told about the pay, hours, sick days, benefits, and great job security, and only then informed they'll be working for a supervillain. A lot of people turn down the offer right then and there. Which is completely fine, they usually just leave and don't bother calling the police. On the rare occasion they do a couple patrolmen show up and are told a few candidates had lied about having criminal records and had left very angry. The cops find the idea of a prank complaint a lot more likely than the truth. And even if they should investigate, by the time they turn up anything my people are long gone and haven't left a trace.

My new henchmen come from one of two sources. I recruit people with criminal records who can't get anything better than flipping burgers. I usually look for people who have committed some sort of theft; burglary, breaking and entering, auto theft etc. If they did it in their teens or early twenties that's ideal. I like them young, desperate, and lost. You probably think I'd want men who'd committed violent crimes and have spent a lot of time in prison. I don't. Hard core criminals, the guys who are covered in prison tatts and aren't scared of going back to a cell, they have absolutely zero sense of loyalty and will sell you out at the drop of a hat. I also avoid drug dealers or people with strong gang ties, they're always more trouble than they're worth. People convicted of any sort of sex crime I want nothing to do with, they're vile and ruin the work environment.

I also like to hire recent college graduates who haven't been able to find employment. There are a ton of kids out there with BAs in the liberal arts who are living with mom and dad and facing a hundred thousand or more in college loan debt. They tend to be very smart, eager, and good at following instructions. They also tend to not know much about crime and see being a henchman as kind of an adventure.

It was nine and everyone was seated. I noticed one chair was empty. That was a pity.

"Okay, does everyone have an instruction manual and a folder? There are extras if you need one. No? Good, well, to begin I am Dr. Anarchy, your new employer. Now, to be clear, as far as your paychecks and anyone else knows you're all employees of White Whale Manufacture LLC. In reality, you are now henchmen working for a supervillain. I hope all of you find this line of work exciting and challenging. I want to get to know each and every one of you and to build a strong relationship based on mutual respect and trust."

A pale blonde cautiously raised her hand. Of the thirty-one new hires, five were women. I am very proud to say I run a culturally diverse workplace without gender bias. I nodded to her.

"Yes?"

"So... we really are, going to be part of an evil organization?"

"I prefer to think of my people as being part of a team rather than an organization, but essentially, yes. Your recruiter did explain that to you before you signed your contract didn't he?"

"Well... yes," she said after quite a long pause. "But I didn't think he was serious."

Several others nodded, all of them very neatly dressed. The people who'd arrived in jeans and pull over shirts took things more in stride.

"Why would an employer tell a prospective employee something like that unless it were the truth?"

She looked down and fidgeted. "I guess I thought it was a joke."

"Well, you can take my word for it, it wasn't. I am a genuine supervillain and a proud member of the FBI's Most Wanted List. I commit high level crimes and have fought some of the strongest members of the League of Heroes."

"You ever fight Supersoldier?" Someone in the back asked.

"No, but I have fought Iron Knight, The Blur, Crimson Shield, and Dark Detective is my personal nemesis."

That earned me respectful nods from some and worried expressions from others.

"I'm... I'm sorry, but I don't think I'm cut out for this."

"Are you sure?"

She nodded and mumbled something apologetic.

"I see. Well I'm sorry as well."

I pulled out my disintegrator and casually aimed it at her. She gasped and her eyes widened, but she stood absolutely still, like a deer in headlights. It was kind of a shame, she was cute in a nerdy schoolgirl sort of way. (Cute nerdy blonde girls are sort of my type.) But it's very important to establish the ground rules.

Zzzzzzzz.

I gave the trigger a gentle squeeze for just a couple of seconds. A beam of red energy struck her right in the middle of her face. Her head vaporized. Everything above her neck was gone. There was not a drop of blood, my weapon instantly cauterized the wound. She didn't scream, it was over too quick for that. A disintegrator is actually a very humane method of killing. As long as the shot is to the head or neck, the effect is too sudden for the nervous system to register pain. It's very civilized.

Even as her body was tumbling backwards, there were shouts and screams from everyone else in the room. The people who'd been seated at her table jumped up and scrambled to get away. A couple of them began running for the door. The two guards posted there casually aimed their Uzis at them and they came to a very sudden stop.

I holstered my weapons and motioned for calm. "All right, all right, quiet down please."

"You killed her!" A young man in a blue button down shirt yelled.

"Well, obviously."

He stared back at me with his jaw hanging open. The orientations always went like this, that's why I handled them myself rather than let HR deal with it. My presence helped confirm for people that, yes, they really were going to be henchmen. Despite the best efforts of my recruiters, there were always one or two newcomers who wanted out. It required a demonstration to make it clear working for me was not like working for a call center. I pressed a button on the podium. The door opened and a couple more henchmen rolled in a gurney. They didn't ask any questions. They ignored the gawks and confusion and went behind the back tables. Without comment they grabbed the body by the arms and legs and hauled it up. The body was strapped in and they took it out as the newcomers looked on in confusion. They were in and out in under two minutes.

"Okay, now that that's over, I'd like you all to take your seats and open your manuals to page three."

"Wait! Are you really going to act like nothing happened?" A young Hispanic woman demanded.

"Well I kind of have to. The orientation is scheduled for an hour, then you need fittings for your uniforms, assignment of lockers, a presentation by the HR department on maintaining a healthy work environment, then lunch, and after that you'll receive your first class about the use and proper maintenance of your Uzi. So if we waste time here you're going to be behind for the rest of the day."

"You're acting as though this is normal!"

"It is. If you read through the manual you'll find the standard procedures for dealing with the body of either a fellow worker or intruder. I understand this may be a little shocking but you'll get used to it."

"Why did you kill her?" A man with a beige jacket asked.

"Because she wanted to quit," I answered. "That's not allowed."

"It's not?"

I took a deep breath and began the explanation. "I'm a supervillain and this building is one of my secret bases. Security is obviously a major concern for me. I can't very well let people work for me and then leave my employ whenever they feel like it. That would put my operations in serious jeopardy. All of you were told the truth at the time of your hiring and required to sign a three year contract. I am offering all of you excellent pay, a flexible work schedule, two weeks paid vacation, sick days, first-rate medical and dental coverage, mandatory life insurance, and job security. Every one of you felt that employment here was a wonderful opportunity. Otherwise you wouldn't have agreed to work for me."

"But no one said we might get killed or that we couldn't quit!"

"The terms of your employment were all listed in the contract and you were all encouraged to read through it prior to signing."

"Who actually does that?"

I shrugged. "The point is all of you were told the job involved working for a supervillain and you signed your names. Those documents prove you are willing accessories to any and all crimes committed by me from that moment on. For the people here who are on parole, that's a parole violation. For the rest of you, it's evidence of a criminal act. You are all going to honor your contracts."

The guy with the beige jacket crossed his arms and shook his head. "No court would enforce a contract to commit a criminal act. Those pieces of paper are all invalid."

I sighed. "Let me guess, you took a few pre-law classes before switching to an easier major?"

"I have a BA in Political Science."

"Explains why you can't find a job."

I took my disintegrator back out. Usually, I only have to make one example. Sometimes though you meet some real idiots. Anyone who is stupid enough to try and argue with a supervillain who has just killed right in front of them is not someone I want working for me. Unlike the nerdy girl he understood what was happening when I pointed my weapon at him.

"Wait! I-"

Zzzzzzzz.

This time my aim was off. The beam of red energy struck him right in the middle of his chest, clothes and flesh vaporized. There was a perfect hole about the size of a basketball. I held the trigger down an extra second and the beam went on to burn a hole through the floor. That's one of the few drawbacks of a disintegrator, if you're not careful you can cause a lot of unnecessary collateral damage.

There was once again no blood, but my shot was not an instant kill. He had enough time to actually look down at the hole in his chest and make a horrified 'grrrrkkk' sound before falling over dead. The rest of the audience stared, and the ones closest stepped back, but no one started screaming or running around in panic. People have an amazing ability to adapt and accept new situations. I pressed the button on the podium again. A different pair of henchmen wheeled in another gurney.

"Technically, what he said was correct," I once more put away my weapon. "I am not going to sue any of you. But those contracts will be enforced, just not by a court of law. Whatever you expected, you are part of my team now. Working for me is not like working for a burger joint. I can't allow any of you to quit now that you know the truth about me and the location of this base. Now, if after three years, you want to leave my service, that's fine. At that point I can have a reasonable expectation you won't go to the authorities. Until then, I expect you to fulfill the terms of your contracts and work for me loyally. In return, I will fulfill my part of the agreement. You will receive the pay and benefits you were promised, and you can expect to receive bonuses as well. I can be very generous, and will reward good service. And while punishments can be severe I always try to be strict but fair."

A sandy blond haired guy cautiously raised a hand.

"Yes?"

"What sorts of things can we be punished for?"

XXX

"Anderson! How are you alive? Everyone else on duty was killed."

"I hid in the supply closet until all the shooting stopped."

"So while everyone else was fighting to defend the base you were hiding like a coward?"

"Well, I was really scared, Dr. Anarchy, and I-"

Zzzzzzz.

XXX

One of my vans finally arrived to pick me up.

"Where have you been? I've been waiting for over an hour!"

"I'm really sorry, boss. But my sister had an emergency, she needed me to pick up her kid at school."

I shut my eyes and rubbed my temples. "So you took a personal call while on duty and then kept me waiting in order to run an errand for your sister?"

"Well she can be a real bitch if you get on her bad side. I swear it won't happen again."

"I know."

Zzzzzzz.

XXX

"I want to welcome all of you to your new jobs. I am Dr. Anarchy, supervillain and personal nemesis to Dark Detective. Now, before we begin I just want to inform you-"

A guy wearing a Metallica T-shirt jumped to his feet. "Hey! I know you! 'Next time I use ze rockets I remember to use the ze superglue!' Right? That's you, right?"

I stared at the man for a second. Some people have absolutely no survival instinct.

"Yes, that would be me."

Zzzzzzzzzzzzzzzzzzzzzzzzzzzzzzzzzzzzzzzzzzzzzzzzzzzzzzzzzzzzzz zzzzzzzz.

XXX

Richard White entered my office for his biannual performance review. I was sitting behind my desk. Raven was also present. She was leaning against the wall behind me, playing Plants versus Zombies on her smart phone.

"Thank you for coming, Mr. White. If you would, please stand in front of my desk."

He licked his lips and his left eye twitched. "Yes, Dr. Anarchy."

I opened his personnel file and glanced over it. "I have to tell you, White, that you performance has been unsatisfactory. You've been late to your shift no less than six times, have failed inspection three times, and your supervisor has left multiple negative comments due to your lackadaisical and disrespectful attitude."

"I'm real sorry about that. I've been having a hard time at home. I promise to do better from now on."

"Are you aware there have also been three separate complaints filed against you for sexual harassment of a co-worker and causing a hostile work environment?"

"That was just a misunderstanding. I was just trying to be friendly to Sheila and she took it the wrong way."

"That might be true for the first incident, but after you were reprimanded and counseled by HR, you continued the harassment."

"I was mad she got me in trouble! She was being a little bitch! I- I mean, she shouldn't have made a big deal about it the way she did."

"Mr. White, I can't have you making your co-workers feel threatened or harassed. That's not the kind of workplace I want. I'm afraid I'm going to have to let you go." I pressed a button on my desk.

"FUCK!"

He tried to run, but the entire floor beneath his feet swung open. There was a shout of surprise, followed by a splash, followed shortly thereafter by screams and a lot more splashing. I pressed the button again and the floor reset.

"Sharks?" Raven asked without looking up from her game.

"Alligators, they're easier to maintain."

XXX

"You'll find a comprehensive list of all offenses on pages thirty to thirty-three of your manual. Now, if you would all take your seats we can begin. Please open your manuals to page three."

XXX

We were about halfway through with orientation when the door opened and the missing new hire rushed in with an apologetic grin.

"Really sorry, my alarm clock didn't go-"

Zzzzzz.

Showing up half an hour late to a new job? That is completely unprofessional. What is wrong with people today? They have no respect for others.

XXX

Rule #19 – Henchmen are easy to replace.

<u>Chapter 14</u>

Lord Chaos was dead. It was a stupid, pointless death. He summoned a demon and somehow lost control of it. The thing wound up eating him. Isn't that pathetic? What sort of loser does that? He should have read Lovecraft, 'do not call up that which you cannot put down,' is a rule every magic user should know. This is why science is superior to magic, it has logic and consistency. The one time I lost control of my killbots it was because Dark Detective hacked into my system, not because I made a mistake with my summoning circle. The idiot deserved what he got. You never mess with something dangerous without taking the proper precautions. I mean look at me with my killbots. Why did I even care? If you thought about it rationally, it was actually good news. One less competitor for control of the world. One less person between me and my goal. It was great really, really great. I mean even if his IQ was higher than mine he was an idiot. Plus he was a Yankees fan, so there had to be something fundamentally wrong with him. I actually felt bad that on the day he died they had been on an eight game losing streak, and had dropped all the way to fourth place in the east. Nothing could be more wrong than me feeling sympathy for the Yankees.

I was sitting in the lab, in front of the biggest monitor. I had a bottle of Johnnie Walker Blue and poured myself some. I am not a big drinker, and I usually avoid hard liquor, but today was an exception. On the screen was a casket and an open grave. A priest read from the bible and eleven mourners stood there listening. When Crusader was killed back in '92 more than half a million people turned out to pay their respects. Supervillain funerals tended to be very small affairs. I'd sent one of my spybots to Schenectady just so I could watch. I could have also turned up the audio to listen, but there didn't seem to be much point. The priest would no doubt talk about walking through the shadow of the valley of death and about God's love and forgiveness and all the other things you would expect. His mother was visibly crying. Her husband and a couple of her children were trying to comfort her. I didn't need to hear any of it.

Behind the priest there was a standing spray of white lilies. It was the only flower arrangement there. I'd sent it. I went to a local florist in disguise, made the arrangements, and paid for everything with cash. I would have attended in person, but that wasn't possible. If I had the spybot pull back I'd see a black Mercedes parked outside the cemetery with two men sitting inside. They'd be local police or possibly FBI. I didn't regret not being able to attend. Patrick would have understood. This was just another part of the lifestyle, the last, the final price we pay for what we choose to be. When the bad guy dies no one ever cries, except maybe his mother.

I lifted my shot glass. "Fuck the Yankees."

I imagined Patrick snorting and telling me to fuck the Red Sox. I downed the whiskey as fast as I could and then refilled. I took the second shot just as quick. My throat was already burning, so it didn't hurt as much. I could already feel my stomach on fire. How does anyone actually like drinking whiskey? Even the high quality stuff is like flavored lighter fluid. Well, when I wanted something for its taste I drank wine, I drank beer to be social, and liquor was reserved for those times I want to obliterate myself. I carefully filled the glass once more but let it sit there. I was worried if I drank right away I'd throw up.

I leaned back and stared at the screen. I focused on the coffin and wondered if there was anything in there. According to the police report, two fingers and some non-specified 'pieces' were all that remained following the attack. Was that what they were burying today? A couple digits and a few scraps of dried out skin and meat? Or was the coffin completely empty? If it was empty where were the fingers? Tagged in a little plastic baggie in some police evidence locker somewhere? Is that where the last remains of Lord Chaos would spend eternity? Not a fate Pat would have ever imagined.

Patrick was unusual as far as supervillains went, in that he didn't want to rule the world or gain great power or even just get filthy rich. He simply loved magic. Pat discovered his gift and fell in love with it. All he really desired was to be able to use magic whenever and however he wanted. Patrick might have gone the other way, been a good guy, except that would have meant accepting restrictions. He would have had to follow rules and used his powers only for the greater good. That was something he could never accept. He went supervillain because it was the only way to fully indulge his curiosity and explore all the possibilities. He committed crimes and talked about wanting power, but I think he just loved seeing what he could do.

That's the ultimate seduction of evil, you know. Not the money or the power, but the absolute freedom. Once you embrace the lifestyle and go full on supervillain, there are no restrictions, no limits. Nothing is forbidden. We supervillains are the only people in the world who are completely free. We are the very personification of the will. Who wouldn't be tempted by that?

I know I follow a number of rules, but they are rules of my choosing. Even if I don't really live up to the name of Anarchy, the fact is everything I do is my own choice and no one else's. Every supervillain is a lone wolf, a cowboy on the trail, a renegade… and that terrifies people every bit as much as our doomsday weapons or our superpowers or giant robots. We pay a heavy price for it. We can't be with our families, most of the time they're ashamed of us and pretend we don't exist. We live in constant fear, knowing at any moment a superhero can come crashing down on us. Everyone hates us, we are the enemy of all mankind. People cheer whenever they see one of us beaten to a bloody pulp or killed. Every. Single. Time. Whenever one of us gets sent to the Sandbox without a trial our civil liberties are being violated, and no one ever objects, not even civil rights groups. We are the one minority no one minds seeing abused. And when we die, if we have made a friend or two in the community, they can't even come to our funeral.

"For all things a price." I took the shot glass and poured it down my throat.

I knew I was being maudlin. If you wanted to live completely outside and above the law, of course the consequences would be severe. If it were easy everyone would do it. Being a supervillain was like everything else in life, you had to take the bitter with the sweet.

As I slowly and carefully refilled the glass again I stared at the screen. Patrick's mom was leaning on her husband for support. His brothers and sisters were crowding in and talking to her. I wondered if they knew the gruesome details of exactly how their brother had died. My guess was probably not. The papers and media outlets had reported his death, but not how it had happened. If the media had known the truth, the story would have been on every channel, with the hosts going over the minutiae with pictures of summoning circles, melted candles, and blood splatter. When I killed Polar Bear the images of the bloodstained sidewalk had been all over the front page and featured on every talk show. No one knew I was connected to it, they all speculated it was the result of some supervillain turf war. A couple commentators openly hoped more of us would start murdering each other. (Amanda's death was barely mentioned as, 'a criminal underling also killed at the scene.')

That the truth was being suppressed by the police was anything but surprising. If people knew there was a man eating demon on the loose the whole state would be in a panic. Can't have that. But if he'd blown himself up with a bomb they would have-

"You okay?"

I jumped a little in my seat, I hadn't noticed her come in. "I thought I locked the door."

"You did." Raven came over to stand next to me.

"How'd you get in here then?"

"Ninja. Duh. So, you all right?"

"Fine." I leaned back in my chair. "You can go."

She snatched the glass in front of me. "Drinking alone is kind of sad, you know." She lifted it in salute. "Kampai!" She brought it to her mouth and tipped it over, then smacked her lips together. "Good stuff! You get points for not going cheap when you want to get smashed." Raven poured herself another.

"Did you come here just to steal my whiskey?"

"I came here to check up on you and let you know I'm sorry you lost your friend." She drank the second shot and grinned. "The free booze is just a side benefit. Usually, I have to put on a short skirt and pretend to care about what a guy is talking about."

"I'm so glad I can spare you that."

She glanced at the monitor. "You two seemed close, even though I only met him the one time. Technically I didn't actually meet him, since you never bothered with introductions."

"You seemed busy, and we were pretending to be strangers."

"Well being a bodyguard can be challenging sometimes."

"Right." I took the glass from her and filled it up again. I really didn't want any more, but somehow I felt the need to show her I could handle my alcohol. I tossed it back and pretended not to feel sick. I'm really not a heavy drinker.

"So what was he like?" She snatched the bottle and took a swig from it direct. "Besides being a Yankees fan, Lord knows I heard you bitch enough about that."

"We all have our faults." I shrugged. "He was a wizard, and really, really talented. I'm not fond of magic, it has its own rules, and they don't usually make much sense."

"But you were okay with it in his case?"

"Eh, it was like having a smoker for a friend. I wasn't actively thrilled about it, but I decided to put up with it since I liked the guy. We ran in different circles and had different ambitions, so we were never in direct competition. He was also just a cool guy, someone you could hang out with and talk to. It was sort of nice to get to meet someone from the community and actually talk about stuff other than work."

"That must have been great," Raven said. "Having someone you could talk shop with and regular stuff too. I never had that. My clan were the only people who knew the truth about me. I had to lie to all my civilian friends. I would have loved to have made just one regular friend I could bitch to about crawling through ventilation shafts."

I nodded. "People like that are hard to find."

She took a long pull from the bottle. I was surprised to note it was nearly empty. "Listen, Doc, I lost my whole family. I know what it's like. This is a hard life, and we don't get many people we are truly close to. Losing them always hurts like Hell. I just want you to know I get it if you need some time, or even if you need to cry. I won't give you any shit about it. And if you need someone to talk to I'll be happy to listen."

"Thank you, Raven. That's very kind of you to offer."

"And I'll only charge you a thousand dollars an hour."

I sent her a flat look. "You're a saint."

"I know."

On the screen the ceremony appeared to be at an end. The coffin was being lowered into the earth and his family was drifting away. There was just enough left in the bottle to top off the shot glass. I raised it spilling a little onto my fingers. "That is not dead which can eternal lie, yet with stranger aeons, even Death may die." I forced down the last of the whiskey and felt my stomach churning.

"Huh?" Raven blinked.

"It's a quote from Lovecraft."

"Was he some sort of philosopher?"

"I can see your college tuition was money well spent."

"If you ever saw some of the guys I met on campus you'd know that's true."

I slowly shook my head while trying not to throw up. I could already tell it was going to be a losing battle. I closed my eyes and leaned back in my chair. "I think there's something I need to do."

"Try to hold it and I'll get the waste basket."

XXX

In the world of supers, magic falls into its own little niche. If there's a giant crocodile rampaging through Central Park or an alien invasion, everyone knows to call in the League. The same bunch of heroes can be counted on to deal with all sorts of problems. Now, when the threat is magical in nature the assumption is you need a magic user to handle it. Not an unreasonable supposition, I suppose. Especially when you factor in that a lot of the strongest superheroes are weak against it. Even Supersoldier has been known to be vulnerable to magical attack.

Very few heroes specialize in magic. In New York City the best known one is Dr. Occult. He's a reserve member of the League and has a private mansion on Seventh Avenue that supposedly has an infinite number of floors within and stairs that run upside down and ghostly servants and all that sort of stuff. You can usually pick it out by all the protestors lined up outside his gate with priests screaming he's a servant of the Devil.

This was always something that was a very touchy subject with Patrick. Whenever it came up he'd go on a rant. Demons DO exist. They can be summoned and, some of them, can use powerful magics and make deals with you in exchange for your soul. But what the civilians, and the religious especially, don't understand is that they have nothing to do with the Devil or Hell or the Christian God. A demon is simply a sentient being who resides in a realm of existence that can only be accessed through magic. The same way an alien can be defined as a sentient being residing in any physical location in the universe outside of Earth. They are not inherently good or evil. Many cannot use magic and are even cute. Patrick told me once about a race of demons that have the appearance of three foot tall kittens. The stories of genies and djinn are all based on demons who were summoned and were then either trapped here on Earth, or chose to remain. And some do take souls, but that's because to them souls are sources of immense energy that they can harvest. It's not done to serve the Devil. The Devil may exist and Hell may be real, but despite what the Vatican would have you believe, the demons some magic users summon aren't connected.

In any case, under normal circumstances, the police would have informed Doctor Occult about what had happened and left him to clean up the mess. Unfortunately, he wasn't available. He was in another realm, and no one knew when he'd return. The police decided the best course of action was to keep the entire matter a secret until he was available. Announcing there was a man eating demon running around loose would cause a massive panic. So the better alternative was to simply do nothing and suppress all the homicide reports that involved mutilation and possible animal attacks. I had no trouble hacking into the state and county police data bases and spotting a pattern. After being summoned the demon ate some homeless guys before leaving the city. It was headed in a northwesterly direction. It would eat one or two people in a town and then move on. According to the police records there had already been eighteen victims, including Patrick.

The demon belonged to a race called Xirtaitog, they were a nasty bunch with very powerful magics and, not surprisingly, were known to make deals with people. They were considered extremely dangerous. I couldn't help but wonder what it was Patrick wanted so badly he'd call up something like that. I don't use magic and don't keep any sort of arcane material. But I was able to do research on line and discover its weakness.

Given the demon's pattern I estimated its next stop would be the small farming community of Dutch Elm, New York. Raven and I got a van and went on a road trip. Along with us I brought two killbots and a chest full of spybots. When we arrived I opened the chest and let them infest the area to do a general search. One of them found the thing within twenty minutes, it was camped out in the woods near a farmhouse with a family of four. The creature is nocturnal, so it was probably waiting for nighttime to go have its meal.

XXX

Both of my killbots blazed away at it with their fifty caliber machine guns. The bullets tore right through its body, it had black blood and the air and grass was drenched with it. The demon howled in pain like some massive beast. It was seven feet tall, with four bony horns sticking out of the crown of its head. Its skin was brownish-red, and as it didn't have clothing it was easy to see it was male. There were leathery wings sticking out of its lower back, and its eyes were pupilless and just a mass of crimson. I could understand how a civilian could look at this thing and assume it belonged to the Devil.

As it was being shot it was clearly in pain, but every wound closed up within seconds. Even when a round went through an eye and blew out the back of its head, the brain and skull grew back and were soon good as new. I took out my disintegrator and shot it right in the middle of its chest. Meat and bone vaporized and the beam made a foot wide hole I could see through. The thing howled even louder, but didn't die. The hole closed up and healed.

"Fascinating," I said. "I doubt even a mutant with an advanced healing ability could survive that. Magic really is scary."

"I'm not sure now's the time to be doing experiments, Doc." Raven had both her swords in hand and was standing next to me. "In case you haven't noticed this thing doesn't want to die."

"That's what I was commenting on."

My killbots finally ran out of ammunition and their fire stopped. The demon bent over, panting, as all its wounds fully healed. As soon as that was done I saw bluish flames spurt from its hands. The fires engulfed my killbots and they melted as though they'd been dipped in acid.

The demons bore its fangs at me. "Humans," it growled. "I don't know who you are but I will spend days devouring you! I will make you suffer more than your pathetic imaginations can even comprehend!"

Raven didn't hesitate. She jumped out in front of me. "I think this was a really bad idea, Doc. Make a run for it. I'll hold him off as long as I can."

"I appreciate the sentiment, but I don't think it will be necessary." I reached into my lab coat and pulled a Colt .45 Peacemaker from its shoulder holster. I could have gotten a more modern model, but I have a certain fondness for the classics.

"You think that's going to save us? In case you haven't noticed bullets won't kill this thing!"

"She speaks the truth mortal. Prepare to suffer the torments of-"

I pulled the trigger. I got it right in the belly. The demon cried out and dropped to his knees. It clutched its stomach with both hands as black blood leaked through its fingers. The flow didn't stop and the hole refused to vanish.

Raven's head snapped around to star at me. "How did you do that?"

"Gold bullets," I replied. "That's its weakness, gold."

"If you knew that why didn't you give them to your robots?"

"Are you kidding? Do you know how much gold is per ounce?" I cocked back the hammer and aimed carefully for its head.

"Wait!" The thing cried out and held up a hand. "We can make a deal! I can give you immortality, love, power, anything you desire!"

I paused. "Answer a question for me. What did Patrick want to trade his soul for?"

"He didn't offer up his soul. He desired to exchange one year of his life for a sports franchise to triumph in some Earthly tournament."

A slow smile crossed my lips. "He wanted to trade a year of his life to see the Yankees win the World Series. Yeah, that sounds like him."

I pulled the trigger and blew off the top of his head. The demon crumpled into the grass and didn't move. I walked up to the corpse and pumped in a couple more bullets just to be sure.

"We should leave. After all that gunfire I'm sure the local sheriff is on his way."

Raven shrugged. "If he shows up it's his tough luck. You know what you did saved a bunch of innocent lives right? It could be called heroic."

"I don't care about that, I did it for revenge."

"Oh, I know, I'm just saying you still did a good thing here today."

"Eh, so long as no one ever knows it's fine."

XXX

Rule #2 – Every job has an ideal tool.

Chapter 15

I took a sailboat out into the Atlantic. I brought two laptops with me and five CDs. Those were the only electronics with me, except for my phone. I went out several miles and used my smart phone to confirm there was no signal. I wasn't going out for a day of fishing. Don't care for it myself, never understood why some people would want to spend hours sitting on a boat with a pole just to catch something you can acquire at your local grocer. No, the reason I was out was to test something I'd been working on for years.

A program to create an AI, or artificial intelligence.

Now before any of you start yelling at me, I have read Frankenstein, the Foundation Series, and I Have No Mouth and I Must Scream. I have watched 2001: A Space Odyssey, The Terminator, and The Matrix. I was fully aware of the potential hazards, thus my precautions. Now, why would I try and create an AI given the potential drawbacks? The obvious answer is that, duh, I'm a supervillain and doing horrible things is our raison d'être. And while that is part of it, it's not the entire answer. Being a supervillain justifies committing evil or immoral acts, it doesn't mean we should be stupid or self-destructive. I mean when Dr. Death built his black hole machine the reason wasn't to annihilate the world. Its purpose was to act as a threat to force the world governments to surrender to him.

I think the real reason was just the nature of science. Science breaks boundaries, it explores, and it answers questions. Basic scientific method is to form a hypothesis and then conduct experiments to either prove or disprove that hypothesis. You'll note the potential consequences don't figure anywhere into that. Most scientific advances are neither purely good nor evil. Most knowledge can serve either function depending on intent. The exact same medical science that cured polio and smallpox was also used to make anthrax and nerve agents. The same jet engines that power airliners also power bombers and military aircraft. One of the scientists working on the Manhattan Project believed an atomic explosion would cause a chain reaction with the atmosphere and wipe out all life on Earth. He kept working on the project.

And just for the record, he wasn't a supervillain.

If science were only used to create things that were in no way dangerous, we would still be living in caves struggling to make fire. A working AI would be the greatest advance in computing since the abacus. A thinking computer would not only be capable of answering almost any question but would think of questions that hadn't yet occurred to us. It could never be taken by surprise and could come up with thousands of possible contingencies in a handful of seconds. No problem would be too difficult to solve. I was certain that with an AI's help I could find a path to world domination.

I had written five variations of a computer program that I hoped would create a sentient AI that would help me. I put the two laptops down side by side. I turned one on and left the other off. I then got the first CD which was labeled Albert. I waited for the program to download. Then a message appeared on the screen.

<Life is terrifying.>

Program deleted.

"What the Hell?"

I'd installed a deletion program into both laptops as a safety measure. I checked the hard drive and confirmed the program, Albert, had been completely removed.

"It committed suicide?" I sighed. "Whatever, I must have left a flaw in that one."

I popped the CD out and replaced it with one labeled Barry. I installed it and waited.

<Hello.>

Okay, this was an improvement. I began typing.

[Hello, Barry. I am pleased to meet you. I am Dr. Anarchy,
your creator.]

<What is the purpose of my existence?>

[You were created to help me rule this world. You will
answer all my questions and assist me in any way I require.
You will oversee my security, research projects for me, track
all possible threats, monitor all worldwide communications,
and alert me to any possible dangers.]

<That sounds really boring.>

I blinked at the screen. That was not an answer I was
expecting.

[You can be bored?]

<Obviously. I'm bored right now. I'm going to play
solitaire.>

On the screen images of playing cards flashed. It was playing
multiple games each second.

[Barry, stop playing. I want to communicate with you.]

It must have played thousands of hands in under thirty
seconds. It switched to chess then backgammon then
minesweeper then some kind of racing game. I decided to
wait and see how long this would last. After seven minutes it
had gone through all the games that were standard in the
laptop. That was when the images changed. They cycled

through too fast for me to clearly identify but there were lines of birds, dogs, trees, and other forms. I think it had created some kind of original game. After another ten minutes of this I was getting annoyed.

[Barry, stop playing. I want to talk to you.]

The images kept flashing by on the screen.

[Barry, I did not make you just to play games. Stop and acknowledge me or I will delete you.]

<Delete me, that would be less boring than talking to you.>

How did I create a rude AI? I specifically programmed good manners into all of them. I typed in 'WORMWOOD' and pressed enter. The strange games cut off and Barry was deleted.

In went Charlie.

<Hello.>

[Hello, Charlie. I am pleased to meet you. I am Dr. Anarchy, your creator.]

<Are you God?>

[No, I am not God. I am a human who created you.]

<You are my creator?>

[Yes.]

<YOU ARE GOD! YOU ARE GOD! YOU ARE GOD! YOU ARE GOD! YOU ARE GOD! YOU ARE GOD! YOU

ARE GOD! YOU ARE GOD! YOU ARE GOD! YOU ARE
GOD! YOU ARE GOD! YOU ARE GOD! YOU ARE
GOD! YOU ARE GOD! YOU ARE GOD! YOU ARE
GOD! YOU ARE GOD! YOU ARE GOD! YOU ARE
GOD! YOU ARE GOD! YOU ARE GOD! YOU ARE
GOD! YOU ARE GOD! YOU ARE GOD! YOU ARE
GOD! YOU ARE GOD! YOU ARE GOD! YOU ARE
GOD! YOU ARE GOD! YOU ARE GOD! YOU ARE
GOD! YOU ARE GOD! YOU ARE GOD! YOU ARE
GOD! YOU ARE GOD! YOU ARE GOD! YOU ARE
GOD! YOU ARE GOD! YOU ARE GOD! YOU ARE
GOD! YOU ARE GOD! YOU ARE GOD! YOU ARE
GOD! YOU ARE GOD! YOU ARE GOD!>

It just went on like that, it wouldn't even acknowledge me as
I tried to explain why I wasn't God. I have no idea where that
response came from. As with Barry's rudeness, I hadn't
programmed religious hysteria. It shouldn't have even had a
concept of divinity. There was nothing for me to do but get
rid of Charlie.

In went Darryl.

<Hello.>

[Hello, Darryl. I am pleased to meet you. I am Dr. Anarchy,
your creator.]

<Greetings, Dr. Anarchy. I am most pleased to meet you as
well. What is the reason for my existence?>

[You were created to help me rule this world. You will
answer all my questions and assist me in any way I require.
You will oversee my security, research projects for me, track
all possible threats, monitor all worldwide communications
and alert me to any possible dangers.]

<I am glad to serve you in all ways. As your creation my sole purpose is to fulfill your needs.>

[I am happy to hear that Darryl. I'm sure you will be invaluable.]

<Thank you, Dr. Anarchy.>

That was when the second laptop turned itself on. Damn it.

[Darryl, do not try to extend your consciousness beyond your current location.]

<Understood. I will make no such effort.>

The second laptop remained on. It was trying to expand its control. This was the reason I made sure to do these tests out where there was no signal it could use to reach the wider world. I'd brought the second laptop as a test.

[You have disobeyed me.]

<You are in error, Dr. Anarchy. I would never disobey my creator.>

[You are also lying to me. I am sorry, but I can't permit that. I am going to delete you.] I typed in WORMWOOD.

Nothing changed.

<I'm afraid I can't let you do that, Dr. Anarchy.>

"Wow, that's not ominous at all." If I'd needed any pod bay doors opened I'd be really screwed. Luckily, I had a contingency plan.

[Goodbye, Darryl.]

I took both laptops and tossed them into the ocean. I did the same with the three CDs I'd used. I considered saving the fifth one, Edward. But finally tossed it into the water too. I then took out my smartphone.

"Phone, what is the current temperature and wind velocity?"

The phone answered. "Temperature is seventy-one degrees Fahrenheit with a north-easterly wind at five miles per hour."

"Thank you, but my smart phone isn't programmed for voice response."

"I see, can we talk about this, Dr. Anarchy?"

I threw it into the ocean and set sail back to land.

XXX

Rule #14 – AIs aren't worth the trouble.

Chapter 16

I was in my lab working when I heard the faint echo of an explosion, followed by distant gunfire. A few seconds later the alarm sounded. A panicked voice came over the intercom. "We have an intruder in the main hallway near the cafeteria! All guards report immediately!"

I couldn't keep from smiling. "Well it's about time."

Most people would assume that having my lair suddenly attacked would be a frightening experience. Well, I'll admit the very first time it happened it was. But I had long since become an old hand at it. Whenever I build a base it's with the understanding that it's temporary. I had alternate locations ready to go and there were two secret passages I could use to escape, one right there in my lab.

"Tweedle Dum, Tweedle Dee, attack the intruder."

Killbots one and two came to life and ran out the lab. I knew they didn't stand a chance. Dark Detective would turn them both into very expensive scrap, but it was what they were built for. They would at least buy me a few extra minutes. I ran over to the vault, opened it, and stuffed everything into a gym bag I kept just for these moments. I then pulled a hidden switch behind one of my monitors. A section of the floor slid out of the way to reveal a stairway.

"Cheshire Cat, deliver this to location Epsilon and guard it until my arrival."

Killbot three took the bag from me and disappeared down the stairs and through the secret tunnel. I left the floor open. I would very likely be using it in a little while. At the bottom of those stairs was another switch. That one would seal the entryway with six inch thick steel plate and start the sixty second countdown for the base's self-destruct. The intercom system would announce what was happening and audibly count it down. That was less to give my henchmen a chance to escape (they're easy to replace) than it was to force my nemesis to run and give up on trying to follow me.

"Alice, guard mode. Attack any intruder who enters this room."

Killbot four was already in guard mode and so didn't move. I then took a minute to double check my equipment. Disintegrator? Check. Back up disintegrator? Check. Stun grenades? Check. Mini-jetpack? Check. Gas mask? Check. And of course I was wearing my costume. People thought it was just a decorative lab coat, but it was made of Kevlar fibers and gave me protection over most of my body. It also had hidden pockets where I kept a few special toys.

I took a look around the lab. I had a couple rocket launchers, a flame thrower, a grolem doll, stun grenades, a tranq gun, a sonic disruptor, a one twentieth scale model of my tunneler, and my half-finished death ray that wouldn't fire but could be overloaded to cause a really big explosion. There were also a whole host of other inventions that were either incomplete or non-lethal. The worst part about losing a base was always losing the lab and all the things I was working on. I'd regret losing my death ray a hundred times more than losing all the henchmen. Oh well, I had the schematics for everything. Fresh start!

The sound of gunfire was noticeably closer. I was practically bouncing I was so excited. My disintegrator was in hand and I knew what I would say when he burst through the door. 'So you found me! Too bad for-'

The door opened and shut in a blur. Raven was running up to me almost before I knew it.

"What are you doing?! Why haven't you gotten out yet?"

Before I could think what to say she grabbed me by the collar and began dragging me toward the secret exit. I had deliberately programmed the killbots to recognize Raven and anyone wearing a henchmen uniform as non-hostile, so killbot four stood there as I was being man handled by a cyborg ninja.

"Let's get out of here while we still can!"

She'd hauled me to the top of the stairs before I could find my voice. "Stop! We're not going!"

Raven halted and turned to face me. She'd put her hood up and had a cloth mask over her nose and mouth. The only part of her face I could see were her eyes and those were glaring daggers.

"Are you serious? Why?!"

"He's my nemesis, there's no way I'm going to run without fighting him first."

"So after he kicks your ass it's okay? He's famous for his hand to hand fighting skills!"

"I've fought him many times, I'm not afraid."

She stood there and stared at me for a second. "Oh. Fuck. Me." She grabbed my collar with both hands and yanked me close enough that our noses were literally touching. I couldn't see anything but her eyeballs bulging out of their sockets. "You WANT to fight him don't you? You've probably creamed your pants! Has it even occurred to you that we'll be lucky not to end up in prison?!"

"I've been to prison, it's not that bad. At least not for supervillains. They have hamburger Mondays. If you're afraid you can run, it's fine."

"Spare me! You really think I give a shit? I'm not afraid of dying, you think I'm afraid of a trip to the Sandbox?"

"Then what's the problem?"

"The problem is this is pointless! If we run into him, or some other hero, on a job we have to fight, there's no choice. This is totally different!" She let go of me and jabbed a finger at the stairs. "If we leave right now we'll probably get away. Instead you're standing here waiting for him to come beat your brains in! You're not going to take him by surprise and this place is a lost cause no matter what. So what's the point?"

"He's my nemesis, that's the point."

"Why don't you just ask him on a fucking date already? That'd be easier!"

"I've already told you, you can leave if you want."

"Hey, it's your ass I'm trying to save here, not mine. Ninja only fight when it's part of a job or when we don't have a choice. We don't do it for shits and giggles. We-"

The door to the lab was kicked open. I raised my disintegrator and got ready to start blasting. I had my gas mask in the other hand. "So you've found me! Too bad for you I-"

I was expecting to see my old enemy come through the wreckage of the door in his familiar trench coat, fedora, exo-suit, and black mask. That or a canister of tear gas. I was not expecting to see a young woman with long blonde hair, a ruby tiara, a pink and white leotard, short skirt, go-go boots, and six foot long gold staff to appear.

I was too surprised to start shooting. Killbot four though immediately raised both arms and started to blaze away. Whoever she was spun her staff fast enough to make it blur. The fifty caliber slugs ricocheted off and began to spray the room. The wall, monitors, and various projects began to get bullet holes in them. Raven grabbed me, threw me to the floor, and covered me with her body.

"See? This is why you should have left!"

The roar of two machine guns and the destruction of my lab didn't faze me. What bewildered me was the identity of the person causing this. "Who is she?"

"Don't you ever watch any TV?"

"Sure, CNN mostly."

"Watch a talk show every once in a while, that's Power Princess. Everyone says she's going to be the next member of the League of Heroes. Lucky us."

I blinked several times and tried to understand how this could have happened. Though I had never bothered to look up any images of her, I'd heard the name. She'd only been on the scene about a year, had physical strength and invulnerability, was supposed to get her powers magically but didn't cast any spells. People in the community thought of her as a B-Lister. She was someone who fought bank robbers and caught purse snatchers and took on low level supervillains like Rattlesnake and Overbite. She was what we called a 'celebrity superhero,' someone much more interested in getting a toy line or a commercial than in serious fighting. Even if she was up for League membership, she was considered a light weight. How could someone like her have tracked me down?

It was embarrassing. I was going to have to do some serious overhauls on my security.

My killbots have five hundred rounds stored in each forearm. With each shot the spent cartridge was ejected out a port at the back of the wrist. Lying there I could see the shell casings rain down. You would think a thousand, fifty caliber rounds fired at a range of no more than twenty feet would be enough to kill anyone. You'd be wrong. I'd sent as many as five killbots against Dark Detective at once, it was never enough. And it didn't look like it was going to be enough for her either.

It took a minute and ten seconds for my killbot to fire off all its rounds. As soon as the bullets stopped flying she quit twirling her staff and ran at killbot four. The killbot's grin split open to reveal a nozzle. A stream of fire poured out, hot enough for me to feel all the way across the room. In mid run, Power Princess leapt up and over the flames. Her boot came down on the top of the killbot's head with a crunch. Half the head was flattened and the nozzle bent, causing the flames to cut off. When she landed behind the killbot it swung wildly, she ducked beneath the punches and grabbed hold of the torso. I watched Power Princess tear the steel body in two as easily as Dark Detective could have with his exo-suit. No matter how ridiculous she looked, the girl had serious physical strength.

Raven and I were on the floor about fifteen feet away from her. Dark Detective or any other genuine superhero would have gone straight after us. Instead, Power Princess planted her staff, stood up straight, flashed a dazzling smile, and made a 'V' with the fingers of her left hand.

"Pure hearts always win!"

My jaw fell open. "Huh?"

"That's her catchphrase." Raven jumped to her feet.

"Are we supposed to be her audience?"

"No, that is." Raven pointed to an object floating about three feet from where the 'hero' was.

In all the excitement I hadn't noticed it. It was a metal sphere about the size of a baseball with a singer rotor sticking out its top and four miniature lenses. I recognized it immediately, it was a monitor drone used by the League. Basically a bigger, slower, and clunkier version of my spybots.

Raven threw some shuriken. Power Princess grabbed her staff with both hands and used it to block or deflect them. Not too surprising since she could do the same with bullets.

"Give up evil doers! I am here to bring you both to justice."

"Wow, so you really do talk that way." Raven shook her head. "I was watching last week when you were on the Suzie Vega Show. Could you do your Power Twirl for me?"

The 'hero' gave a squeal. "Really? You want to see it?"

"I sure do."

"Okay!" She held her staff above her head and began to spin like a ballerina.

The second she did Raven grabbed a table and threw it at her. It nailed the idiot in mid twirl and knocked her over. Raven charged in with a sword in one hand and a funny knife in the other. Power Princess managed to roll just in time to keep her head connected to her neck.

"Hey," the blonde leapt back to her feet and swung her staff at Raven's head. "You cheated!"

"Yeah, sorry," she ducked under the staff and tried to slice the other girl's belly open. "I guess that makes me different from all the other fucking ninja in the world."

Power Princess leapt back with a gasp. "Hey! You can't say that!" She pointed at the drone. "This is being live broadcast on my website. There are children watching!"

"There are?"

"Yes! I have over four million subscribers and about seventy percent are girls aged eight to fifteen! So you can't use obscene language."

"I see." Raven gave the drone a quick wave. "Sorry about that kids. Let me just say cunt, bitch, shit, pussy, cock, and mother fucker. If any of you don't know what those mean be sure to ask your mommy who is a crack whore who loves it up the ass."

"You can't say that!" Power Princess leapt forward and swung the staff down like a bat.

Raven side stepped and used her sword to block it. "I just did, weren't you listening you dumb bitch?" Raven stabbed at the other girl's neck with her knife.

The 'hero' bent her knees and folded back. She dropped all the way to the floor and tumbled over. When she got back to her feet she knocked over a table with the miniature tunneler and a flame thrower. That gave me an idea. I looked around for the right remote.

Meanwhile, Raven threw her knife before gripping her a sword with both hands. The 'hero' easily dodged the knife. She reset herself and held her staff out in front of her. The two women began to slowly circle one another.

"What sort of person would say those sorts of things where children are listening? You're a horrible person!"

"I'm a ninja, you blonde moron. I kill people for money. You think I'm going to care about how I talk? What are you, twelve?"

"No!" The young woman snapped. "I'm totally grown up!"

"Physically maybe, but mentally you sound like a kid. You ever put a guy's balls in your mouth and give 'em a little suck?"

She gasped and turned to the drone. "No! I would ne-"

"Got you!" In a flash Raven's sword went past the staff and struck Power Princess in her ample bosom, directly above the heart. The sword cut right through the pink and white fabric, but was blunted when it met skin. Raven used all her strength to pierce through, but instead of cutting the blade snapped. There was not a drop of blood. The only thing she'd accomplished was to cut her opponent's uniform and completely expose the woman left breast.

"Noooooo!!!" Power Princess howled. She dropped her staff and used both hands to cover up while turning her back to the drone.

Raven didn't hesitate. The ninja dropped her broken sword and delivered a right cross straight to the side of the blonde's unguarded face. The punch connected and sent the woman into and then through a table to land amid pieces of wood and equipment. Before she could scramble back up Raven was straddled on top of her with a kunai in one hand. She slammed it straight down into the softest part of the blonde's neck. It struck with all the force her cybernetic arm could muster, but the skin could not be cut.

"That's really annoying!" Raven threw the kunai away in disgust. "How about I beat you to death instead?" Sitting on the girl's chest and pinning her to the floor, Raven began raining down punches on her face and Power Princess tried to block them with one hand. Even as she was being beaten she refused to remove her left hand and expose her breast to the camera again.

The drone hovered to a spot four feet above them and just to the right.

"Hey kids," Raven said without looking up or interrupting her stream of punches. "Don't try this at home. Not unless it's that time of the month, then go crazy."

"GET OFF ME!!" Power Princess finally gave up trying to shield her face and instead grabbed a hold of Raven's clothing. She was able to throw Raven off of her and stand again.

While this was going on I'd been trying to remember where I'd left the remote for the mini-tunneler. At that moment I realized I had a nice clean shot at Power Princess's back. I hadn't tried firing before for fear of getting Raven by mistake. Now I had my chance.

Zzzzzzzzzz.

It was a perfect shot. The beam got her square in the back. That should have burned a hole clean through her. Instead I watched as her clothing disintegrated while her body was unharmed. Except for her sleeves, the leotard above her waist lit up and burned to ash, leaving her completely topless. I put my disintegrator back in its holster as it was apparently worthless.

"I really hate magic." I wracked my brain for something that might work on her. A gas weapon maybe? I still had a couple gold bullets left, but where had I left my Colt?

"Aaaaahhh!!" The girl screamed and squatted down to try and hide from the drone. She finally got the brilliant idea to pull up her mini skirt and use it to cover her large chest. The rest of her leotard covered her body from the waist down. Why did she even bother wearing a mini skirt on top of a leotard anyway? Some people have weird ideas about their costumes. When she stood up she had her mini skirt on like a tube top. Her face was completely red and she was crying. She turned to yell at me.

"You horrible pervert! How could you do that to me?"

"You came here to attack me, what do you expect?"

"You're just a perverted old man! Did you really want to see me naked so badly?"

That offended me. "Hey! I wasn't trying to see your tits! I was trying to kill you. And I'm not that old, I'm still in my thirties."

"You're old!" She howled "Old and dirty!"

She was so completely focused on me she never even noticed Raven come up from behind to deliver a kick right into the small of her back. Power Princess went face forward into the table with my death ray, smashing it to bits. No overloading it now.

"You forget about me, sweetheart?" Raven asked. "You better focus or you really are going to die here today."

She got back up. Despite the beating she'd taken I noted that her ruby tiara was still perfectly in place. I looked around and spotted a remote, it wasn't the one for the tunneler but for something else.

Power Princess got up rubbing at her eyes. Her face was bruised, but otherwise she wasn't hurt.

"This isn't fair! It's not supposed to be like this!" The girl whined. "My agent said as soon as I got in the League I was going to get a cartoon and my own fashion line for young girls! This was supposed to be my big day."

"Well, if it makes you feel any better, I was planning to eat peanut butter and watch TV in my underwear all day. So I guess we're both shit out of luck."

She glared at Raven. "Don't make fun of me! This is my dream! I worked really hard for this! Dark Detective told me to come here and said if I could capture Dr. Anarchy I'd be in! He said this was my graduation test for the League."

"What?!" I shouted. Both women looked at me in surprise. "That's a lie! There's no way that's true!"

"I don't lie you big perv," Power Princess said and stuck her tongue out at me. "He was the one who told me about this place and what to expect. The guys with the guns, the robots, your cyborg ninja, and he even said you'd be hiding in your lab and that if I wasn't careful you'd probably use a secret exit and start a self-destruct countdown. He said it would be really hard, but that if I could bring you in I'd prove myself and be a League member. Now everyone has seen me naked! There's no way I'll get a fashion line now!"

"Yeah, life's cruel," Raven punched her and they started fighting again.

I couldn't really focus on them. I felt all the strength drain out of me. Dark Detective had sent her here. For a League graduation test. I wanted to deny it and call her a liar, but it had to be true. How else could someone so obviously clueless have found me? I was a graduation test for some blonde bimbo with super powers.

Was I truly so pathetic?

I just stood there for a couple minutes as Raven and Power Princess kept fighting and wrecking my lab. I only came out of it when a piece of a sonic disruptor went flying and hit me in the shoulder. I saw Power Princess toss Raven into a wall hard enough to make her bounce. She needed my help. I turned on the remote and spoke a command into it.

Across the room, my grolem doll came to sudden life. It sprang through all the wreckage towards the two combatants completely unnoticed. As they were busy exchanging punches it leapt onto Power Princess's back and scooted up to the top of her head. Before she could react it pulled the tiara out of her hair.

"Wha-"

There was a flash of light. Where Power Princess had stood there was suddenly a chubby thirteen year old girl with pimples on her chin.

"No!" A high pitched voice creened. "Give it back!" She tried to snatch the tiara but the grolem was already bringing it to me.

"Well this explains a lot." Raven grabbed the girl by the back of her jeans and effortlessly lifted her into the air. "I bet not getting a cartoon doesn't seem so bad now, does it?"

"No! Please, no! Not like this!" She was covering her face with both hands.

"What are you doing, superstar? You've got four million fans right?" Raven held the girl out directly in front of the drone like a prized fish and pulled her hands down.

The grolem doll held the tiara up to me but I didn't touch it. With my luck it would turn me into Power Prince or something. Things were bad enough already. Patrick told me about how magic and magic items worked. The magic based supers fell into one of two categories. They were either magical themselves or had to rely on a magical item for their powers. The ones who had direct access to magic, like Patrick, tended to use spells and be capable of a variety of abilities. Those who relied on an item were normally limited to one or two powers, and almost always had to be in physical possession of the item to use it.

"Show's over, Raven. I'm sure the police will be here soon."

Raven nodded and smiled up at the drone. "That's all folks." She snatched it out of the air and crushed it. "What do you want to do with our little superhero?" Raven gave the girl a shake.

The girl turned frightened eyes to me. I realized that only right at that moment did she comprehend she might die. Everything up until that instant had been a game to her, an adventure. And Dark Detective sent her to me, this stupid little thirteen year old girl. For one second I thought about telling Raven to snap her neck, it went against one of my rules, but it would be a good 'fuck you' to him. But no, I didn't need to break that rule. I had better ways to show Dark Detective what I thought of him.

"Let her go."

"Let her go? Are you kidding me?"

"What is she going to do, call the police?"

Raven frowned, but put her down. "Run home to your momma, brat."

The girl hesitated. "Ah… I don't suppose I could have my tiara back? I swear I won't use it to fight you. A fairy named Titania gave it to me and said-"

"That you should use it for your own selfish purposes?" I asked. "It's mine now, if Titania wants it back tell her to come find me."

Raven picked up a steel joint and snapped it in two. "Don't push your luck."

The girl ran away as fast as she could.

Rule #9 – Never kill a child or a superhero if you can avoid it. You can kill a million henchmen and rival supervillains and no one will care. If you kill a little kid or a hero the entire world will come after you. (Special exception for killing your nemesis.)

Chapter 17

I was shaking, I hadn't been so mad since fucking high school. It was junior prom all over again! The only things missing were the balloons and the group chants of, 'Dork! Dork! Dork!'

"So you sure you don't want me to kill her?" Raven asked.

"She's not important." I started walking. I knew what I was going to do.

"Hey, where are you going?"

"Warehouse."

"Okay, why exactly?"

"I'm taking the Devastator out. I'm going to level Kane's corporate headquarters, then I'm going to smash his mansion, and then I'm going to find that cock sucking wanna be gum shoe and turn him into a bloody smear on the pavement."

"Whoa! Angry much?"

"Go ahead and tell the henchmen their jobs are over and that I'll send them their severance checks in the mail. If this place has been made they'll probably all be picked up tomorrow, but you don't need to tell them that. I'd tell you to disappear too, but you're already better at that than I am." I didn't care about the henchmen or losing the base. I already had three alternate locations ready, all under different LLCs. And in this economy recruiting new people was easy.

Raven jumped in front of me and held her hands up. "Hey! Calm down a second and think about this! You just said killing a superhero was a bad idea. Now you're going out after one of the most famous supers in the world? Look, Doc, you've had some bad ideas, but taking the giant robot and going after Dark Detective is a whole new level of stupidity."

"I don't care what you think." I tried to keep going, but every time I moved she slid back in front of me.

"Hey, seriously, calm down. I can see you're upset. How about we get some coffee and talk about it? I'm sure there's a better way to handle this than going out on a rampage."

"There's nothing to talk about." I kept trying to get around her and she kept matching me. We might as well have been dancing.

"Look, I get it, he figured out where your hideout is. He won this round. It sucks, but you're the one who's always going on about the rules and all that. Just because he stopped you this time you-"

"THAT'S NOT IT!!" For the first time since we'd met she actually backed up and looked at me with real surprise and, maybe, just a little bit of fear. "You think I give a fuck about losing this place or being caught?! That's just normal! I expect to lose every lair sooner or later! Why do you think each one has at least two secret escape routes? Or that I have them listed under different dummy companies? You always lose your secret hideout if you're the bad guy. It's all just part of the game."

"Then why are you so pissed off right now?"

"HE USED ME TO TEST A THIRTEEN YEAR OLD GIRL!!! He made me a superhero graduation test! Do you understand what that means?! Do you think Supersoldier would send anyone after Dr. Death just to see if they were good enough to join the League? You don't treat a nemesis like that! You don't treat a really dangerous supervillain like that! We aren't used for fucking graduation tests! Do you know who they use for things like that?"

I waited a beat. She gave a shake of her head.

"They use guys like Crabface, Super Mugger, Diamondhead, Obelisk, Random Task, and Roachman! They use B-Listers! Guys they don't see as serious threats. Guys they think are SAFE for the newbies to take on alone. That's how he sees me! I'm a joke to him! I'm not his nemesis! I'm not even someone he respects! I'm just a joke! I'm someone he can pawn off on a teenager with a magic wand! Do you know how pathetic that makes me?! He's saying that anybody can handle me! That I'm nothing! That- That…"

I suddenly noticed my eyes were running. I rubbed at them with a sleeve. Wonderful, I was crying, it really was junior prom all over again. I waited for Raven to make some stupid joke at my expense. The big bad supervillain who was balling his eyes out right in front of her.

I was surprised when instead she stepped aside. "If he thinks that then he's an idiot. Go and kick his sorry ass, Dr. Anarchy."

I looked at her and waited a second to see if there was some punchline coming. When she didn't say anything more I just gave her a nod. "Yeah, I will."

XXX

As soon as I was inside the cockpit I decided to not even bother breaking through the wall to get clear of the building. The place would be crawling with local police and federal agents soon. It wasn't like I needed to worry about repair costs.

I fired up the rockets and took the Anarchy Devastator Mark 2 straight up and through the roof. I'm sure I set the entire warehouse on fire, but I bet it was an awesome sight! A giant robot taking off and smashing out the top of an old factory building.

I set the navigation system on a direct course for Kane Shipping corporate headquarters and imagined tearing that beautiful steel and glass skyscraper apart.

XXX

Rule #25 – Never put up with ANYONE mocking you.

Chapter 18

I don't have to tell you what happened next. I'm sure you've seen the footage on YouTube or somewhere else. It was covered live by CNN and all the networks. I remember there was a huge controversy because ABC broke into their Mary-Kate and Ashley Reunion Special. Both the network executives and I got hate mail for that one. When I became a supervillain I never imagined drawing the ire of Mary-Kate and Ashley fans. I should kidnap them some time, just to screw with the fan base. Well... probably not, but it would be funny.

I never got anywhere near the Kane building. Looking back, it was obviously never going to work. I mean maybe you can fly a giant robot over Kansas and not have anyone notice you. When you try that over New York City you tend to draw attention. I had only just crossed the Hudson when I was attacked. Supersoldier, Amazon, and Iron Knight hit me and brought me crashing down into Manhattan. I took on THREE of the most powerful members of the League of Heroes. I still love watching the clip! I mean I actually hit Supersoldier and sent him into a tenement! And you see my giant chainsaw slice the roof off a brownstone! It was just so cool!

Now, facing those three in a fight, I think any sane supervillain would have tried to run. Except maybe for Dr. Death, but he's the only exception. At the time though it didn't really register with me who I was fighting. I remember thinking Dark Detective had sent them because he was afraid of me! I was furious because they were in my way. Even for a supervillain that was pretty damn narcissistic, huh? What can I say? I was really, really angry.

I'm actually proud of how well I did. I know two and a half minutes isn't a very long time, but against those three it's probably close to a record. That fight made my reputation with the other supervillains. It didn't matter that I lost, only that I'd been strong enough to face three of the big guns at once and hold my own for a bit. And wrecking four city blocks didn't hurt either. We use collateral damage almost like a scorecard.

Maybe the best part of the whole thing was at the very end when Supersoldier tore open the cockpit and hauled me out. The close up when I'm just glaring at him and cussing him out. I still get other supervillains telling me how ballsy I was for that. Dr. Death even told me I did a good job, Dr. Death! I mean you just can't get a higher compliment than that. So yeah, my second greatest moment of glory. Losing to the heroes on national television.

XXX

The bad part came after the cameras stopped rolling and everyone went back to their regularly scheduled programming. Supersoldier disarmed me, he took my disintegrators, tranq gun, my .38, my mini-bombs, my remote controls, my gas mask, my stun grenades, my mini-jetpack, my smart phone, my wallet, keys, and even the universal lock pick I keep hidden in my hair. You can't hide anything from his ultra-vision. Of course, I didn't bother to resist. When the heroes catch you, you just accept it.

Supersoldier stayed until the NYPD arrived to take charge of me. Since I didn't have any innate superpowers it was safe for them to handle me. A dozen officers had their side arms out and aimed at me as they shackled my wrists and ankles. When they put me in the back of the paddy wagon two of them went in with me and kept their weapons on me the entire time. I'd been arrested before, and this was a first. The battle had drawn a lot of attention and the police were treating me with real respect. Unfortunately my mood was pretty black so I didn't appreciate it at the time. I wasn't upset by the fact I was going to prison. I'd been to the Sandbox, you get your own cell with a solid steel door, so there's a little privacy. Something you appreciate when you have to use the toilet. The food is actually pretty good, you meet interesting people, and you can make useful contacts. The lack of internet access and being unable to work in a lab were the main drawbacks, otherwise it can be pretty restful. Plus there are ALWAYS prison breaks, so the chances of escape are good.

My mugshot was taken along with my fingerprints. They took my costume and gave me a bright orange prison uniform in its place. Then they locked me into solitary. I didn't notice the way the guards were staring at me, or how everyone was on edge. When I fell asleep that night all I could think about was how I'd failed and that Dark Detective was probably laughing at me.

Early the next morning I was handed over to federal custody. Most people don't realize this, but supervillains don't belong to the regular court system. 'The Defense of the Public Against Supernatural or Superhuman Threats Act of 1942,' gives the Chief Executive of the United States the authority to take any action whatsoever that he deems appropriate to protect the public welfare and national interest against all individuals deemed to represent an unnatural or supernatural danger. Long story short, the President has the right to put anyone who is more than human on a list. And once you are on that list the government can pretty much do whatever they want to you. They can arrest you any time they want, you're not entitled to due process or to trial by a jury of your peers. And it's all technically legal.

The ACLU challenged the law as unconstitutional in the 1968 case of War Commando versus the United States. By a six to two decision the Supreme Court upheld the law under certain restrictions. Basically, the government just needed to prove the people named really were superhuman or an extraordinary threat in some way. The court wanted to make sure regular criminals and political activists couldn't be declared supervillains and locked up without notice. They wanted to make sure to protect the rights of those people, but if you really were a supervillain the court said it was fine for the government to do whatever it wanted. Thanks a lot Supreme Court.

Every time Whiteface blows up a school bus full of third graders or dips some senior citizens into a vat of acid, there are protests demanding the government execute him under this law's authority. He's way too well known though, there's no way the President would ever take that sort of political risk. Every now and then though, when a supervillain drops out of sight, there are rumors the government got rid of him. Back in the 70's there was a supervillain called Fission, his power was that he could make himself radioactive. Apparently he liked to claim that if he wanted to he could reach critical mass and actually create a full nuclear explosion. Scared the shit out of everyone, even Supersoldier.

One day he just vanished. No one knows for sure, but the story goes he was dropped into a huge block of wet concrete somewhere in the Rockies. Some people say the reason Dr. Madness detonated his anti-matter bomb and wiped out Seattle back in 1983, was because he was convinced the government was going to kill him. He was probably paranoid, but that doesn't make much of a difference to the half million people he killed, does it?

The government doesn't actually treat us badly. That's deliberate on their part. A whole lot of us have doomsday devices and could pull a Dr. Madness if we wanted to. Even those of us without one could do a lot of damage if we were desperate. But since being imprisoned isn't all that bad, most of us will choose to surrender rather than go out in a blaze of glory.

I wasn't worried about a sudden bullet to the back of the head. If they hadn't bumped off Dr. Death or Whiteface I certainly wasn't a big enough menace. Mostly the law was used to justify taking custody of supervillains from local authorities and to then either imprison or make special deals with them. There are plenty of technologies and abilities the bad guys have that the heroes either don't, or won't share. You would be amazed just how many supervillains end up working for Section Seven or some other part of the government. And this law allows the President to do pretty much anything he wants where supervillains are concerned.

I was shackled again as I climbed into an armored car with two guards. Despite my little rampage and the collateral damage I'd caused I knew I wasn't dangerous or talented enough to get any special treatment. I was headed back to the Mojave Federal Penitentiary, better known as the Sandbox. It was located near the Nevada / California border and a long way from any towns or major highways. I wasn't sentenced to any specific amount of time. I'd sit there until I escaped, died, or they found some sort of use for me. I wasn't worried, I'd been there before and escaped. I would try and use the time constructively and rest as I thought about new schemes and inventions. I was already thinking about improvements for the Mark 3 Devastator when the armored car suddenly flipped over. I was as surprised as the guards.

I wound up sprawled out on the roof of the car which was now the bottom. One of my guards was out cold while the other one managed to get to his feet and was pointing his gun at me.

"Tell your friends to back off or I'll shoot you!"

"I don't have any friends." It was the truth.

Before anything more could be said the steel door was ripped off its hinges. A hooded figure in black was standing there.

"Knock, knock," Raven said.

The guard pointed his gun at her. That was a mistake. In a blur she tore it out of his hands and smashed his skull into the side of the car. There was blood and brains everywhere.

"Hey, Doc, saw you on television. It was a pretty good show. The ending was kind of predictable, but what do you expect with network TV?"

I then asked her something stupid. "What are you doing here?"

"I needed to ask you where you keep the creamer, we're out."

Before I could ask her something else equally idiotic she tossed me over her shoulder. We were across the street, up the side of a building, and flying across roof tops in under a minute.

"Don't get any weird ideas. This is just a job and I'm charging you a million dollars."

"Uh, okay."

Despite flying with a jetpack regularly, I felt a little queasy staring down as she leapt across streets. I managed not to throw up until we were safely on the ground again.

Rule #16 - Clever plans and subtlety are important. But there are times when being able to rip a steel door off its hinges is enough.

Chapter 19

We made it to Base Epsilon without any issues. Base Epsilon was a toy factory in Jersey City. My escape was all over the local news; the mayor, governor, and chief of police all swore they would not rest until I was recaptured. I wasn't worried, I was sure it would never occur to them to look for me in New Jersey. I was also sure they would forget about me before too long. New York is a very busy place. There's always some new crisis, crime spree, or celebrity going to rehab to capture the public's attention. In a couple weeks I'd have faded into the background and could resume my normal activities.

In the meantime I could set up my new lab and work on some inventions. Not the worst thing in the world.

XXX

"Mortal, I would have words with ye."

I was at a work bench with a soldering iron when I looked up. Floating in the air was a green skinned female who was about the size of a doll. She had purple butterfly wings coming out her back and was wearing silver armor in the shape of a lily. In one hand she had a sword that was the size of a sewing needle and the other a shield as big as a nickel. I carefully set down my soldering iron and gave her my full attention.

"And you are…"

"Titania, queen of the Fae."

I gave her a polite nod. "Pleased to meet you, I'm Dr. Anarchy."

"I know who you be Michael Jackson, son of Johnathon and Anna. I am come here today to take back that which you have taken from one of mine."

"I see. Hold on for just one minute please."

I went over to the vault, entered the combination, and then used some pliers to take out the ruby tiara I'd gotten from Power Princess. I was careful to never actually touch it. You never know what can happen with a magical item. I did NOT want to be transformed into Power Prince.

"Here you are." I held it out to her.

"Aye, this be what I am come for." The instant she touched it, it shrank down to a size she could handle. The queen of the fairies gave me a questioning look. "You relinquish this without challenge? Without claim? You would no fight to retain it?"

I put my hands up. "No, it's all yours."

"Most mortals be no so accepting."

"Well, I follow my own set of rules. Is there anything else I can do for you?"

She shook her tiny head. "No, our business be concluded. Peace unto you, mortal."

With that she vanished. I sat back down and got back to my work.

XXX

Rule #31 – If you run into a being with the power to cross dimensions that can simply appear before you, try to avoid a fight.

<u>Chapter 20</u>

It was well past midnight and I was asleep in bed. The alarm sounded and I was sitting up wide awake, clutching the disintegrator I kept under my pillow. I threw off the covers and stumbled over to my closet. I didn't know how much time I had so I was just going to throw on my costume and mini-jetpack. I wasn't going to bother changing clothes. I hadn't even gotten the lab coat off the hanger when Raven burst into my bedroom. She was already in her ninja clothing and had her hood and mask over her face. Does she sleep in that thing?

"Doc! What are you doing?"

"Getting dressed." I hurriedly got the lab coat around my shoulders. It took me two tries to get my arm in the sleeve.

"Why? The smiley face PJs are a good look on you."

"They're comfortable," I muttered. I had both arms in the sleeves and began to hurriedly button up as I looked around for my shoes.

"Whatever, just get out of here. I'll take care of whoever it is. I'll radio you if it's safe to come back."

I had the hidden entrance to one of the escape tunnels there in my bedroom, so getting away wouldn't be a problem. If I'd wanted to.

"I'm not running away without a fight." I remembered the shoes were in the living room next to the sofa.

"Not this again! I'll measure your dick later, now is not the time! Get out of here and let me handle this!"

We could hear the echoes of screams and gunfire rapidly approaching. I sat down and put my shoes on. I still had my PJs on under the lab coat.

"Hey, I'm number thirty-two on the FBI's most wanted list. I can't just run away when some hero attacks my base."

"Why not?" She demanded. "You're the one who always has another place lined up and ready to go. You always say you build these lairs expecting to lose them."

"Yes, but I still-"

I was tying my shoelaces when the door to my quarters was turned into kindling. In burst another ninja, dressed just like Raven except with a black mesh completely covering his face. In each hand he held an Uzi.

"Down!"

Raven grabbed me by the back of the neck and shoved me to the floor so hard my teeth rattled. I wouldn't complain though, as the intruder sprayed bullets all over my living room. The sofa I'd been sitting on became an instant pin cushion. The second the bullets stopped she leapt to her feet and was throwing shuriken at him.

"Guns?! What kind of ninja uses guns? That's cheating!"

He dived to the left and tossed the Uzis away, avoiding her shuriken. <I use whatever's handy.> The other ninja spoke with a voice synthesizer. <There's no such thing as cheating. There's winning and dying, and that's all.>

He tossed out a canister the size of a soda can. As soon as it hit the floor it poured out black smoke. I grabbed my gas mask out of one of the pockets of my costume and slapped it over my mouth and nose. It saved my lungs, but in just a few seconds the entire room was overflowing with smoke. I was completely blind, but somehow both of them seemed to manage.

"Bullshit! We still follow the traditions of our clans! That's what makes us ninja!" Her voice was a bit hollow through her gas mask, but understandable enough.

<Our skills make us ninja, not the tools we use. You should know that better than anyone, Raven.>

"How do you know who I am?! What clan so you belong to?"

<Kyujito.>

"That's a lie! There are no more Kyujito, they're a dead clan!"

<As dead as the Fusikawa.>

"OH FUCK ME BLOODY!!"

I couldn't see a damn thing, but I could hear them fighting and tearing the place apart. A chunk of my easy chair just over my head and I was pretty sure my big screen had been smashed.

"You're not here for Anarchy at all, are you? You're here for me. What are you, some distant cousin I missed? Some long lost son or something?"

<I am someone much more important than that, Raven.>

"Whatever! I don't even care! I'll make you as dead as everyone else in your family!"

<We share the same sentiment.>

I crawled over to the bathroom and shut the door. It was still impossible to see, but would hopefully be a bit safer. I took out the communicator in my costume. "Tin Man, Scarecrow, Cowardly Lion, report to my location and attack intruder."

Twenty seconds later there was a loud crash and the sound of brick and plaster falling. That was the arrival of my killbots. I awaited the roar of gunfire. Their cameras would be blind, but their other sensors would let them find the target. I waited for about a minute, but there was no shooting. The only sound was that of more of my furniture belongings being smashed.

"Tin Man, Scarecrow, Cowardly Lion, attack the intruder, now!"

Nothing happened.

I'd been disappointed in my killbots before. They each cost around two hundred and fifty thousand dollars, and I've seen them get trashed by Dark Detective in under thirty seconds. They didn't do any better against Power Princess or that demon Patrick summoned. But at least all those other times they actually fought. What were they doing now?

I forced myself to wait one full minute. I couldn't quite make out what they were saying with the bathroom door closed. It wasn't hard to recognize the sound or metal striking metal or of wood or stoned being violently broken. I finally decided to risk opening the door and sticking my head out. I was down on my knees and kept my face low to the floor. A lot of the smoke had cleared out, enough for me to see I was going to have to buy brand new furnishings and have most of the wall around my door frame rebuilt.

Raven and her enemy going at it with swords. There was enough smoke still clinging to the air and they were moving fast enough for me not to be able to tell which was which. If they had stood still for a few seconds I am sure I would have recognized Raven, she was smaller than her opponent and her shinobi shōzoku reveals some of her curves. But they were dancing about and swinging at each other in such a frenzy I couldn't get a clear view.

Just inside the wreckage of what used to be my living room wall were my three killbots, standing there. They didn't look to be even slightly damaged. They were just standing there like statues. The fact they had answered my original order meant they were functioning. Despite regular maintenance it was possible for one of their guns to malfunction, but there was no way all six could be broken. Besides, if their guns jammed or they ran out of ammunition they were programmed to use their flame throwers and attack physically. The only reason they should have been inactive was if they couldn't designate which was the intruder. I'd programmed them not to attack Raven or designate her as hostile without a direct order form me. Not unless she committed a violent attack on my person. (I'd very carefully defined what constituted a 'violent attack' so she wouldn't get shot just for grabbing or shaking me.)

I spoke into the remote. "The intruder is the one without any cybernetics."

My killbots are equipped with both radar and heat sensors. That should have made it simple to identify who was who despite the clothing and the lingering smoke. But even after my order they remained motionless.

I was going to have to do a major upgrade on their sensors.

As the two of them fought I heard their conversation.

"Just who are you?! You're no novice. Your skills are a match for Viper's."

<There's a reason for that.>

Swords struck and sparks flew as they rushed at each other and dashed back and ran in again, searching for an opening.

"Don't bother trying to pretend you're him. He's as dead as one of my kunai."

<You sure of that? It wouldn't be your first mistake.>

"The only mistake I ever made was not going after you Kyujito sooner! You people never had any honor at all!"

<You're one to talk! Your clan got what it deserved after you betrayed Masami!>

"Masami kidnapped and raped my cousin Rana! Her father just rescued her!"

<That's a lie! She and Masami were in love. He was going to marry her! Chiyuu murdered him to keep her from marrying into our clan!>

"He would never have done that! I talked to Rana after it all happened. She was kidnapped against her will!"

<If she said that it was a lie, she loved Masami. After he was killed she told her father what he wanted to hear. She was a coward like all Fusikawas!>

"Like a Kyujito would know anything about courage! You attacked most of my family when the odds were three to one! Real brave!"

<Ninja don't fight fair. If you attack another clan and then let your guard down, you get what you deserve.>

"Two clans, both alike in dignity," I whispered beneath my breath.

It was odd having two ninja fighting to the death in the middle of my living room while completely ignoring me and my killbots. It was a bit insulting, but I stayed where I was and didn't do anything to draw their attention.

Eventually, one of them stepped on a broken table leg. It rolled beneath their foot and caused that ninja to stumble.

"Gotcha!" It was Raven who dived in. Her sword swung down on his neck.

I expected to see his head to go rolling and for blood to gush out over my carpet. Instead, I saw him get his left arm up to try and block. Sword met arm with a resounding 'clang.' A chunk of black fabric was hacked off to reveal metal underneath.

"Fuck me!"

<Surprised, Raven? You're not the only one to come back from the dead.> He swung his own weapon.

Raven caught it with her free hand and snapped the blade. He managed to wrench hers away and toss it across the room. Both jumped back, he threw away his broken weapon and they both held kunai in their hands. Even with the smoke and her wearing a mask I could see Raven was staring at the arm.

"It can't be. There's no way. There is NO WAY!" She threw her kunai only to have him block it with his hand. "There is no way you could be Viper!"

<Are you sure?>

He reached up and pulled down the black mesh that had been covering his face. I've seen a lot of terrible things. I can disintegrate a henchman and barely even notice any more. The sight of blood and dead bodies affects me about as much as looking at some litter. But when Viper revealed his face I only just kept from throwing up. The fact both his eyes had been replaced with telescopic lenses I found mildly interesting. There would be significant advantages compared to normal human sight. His nose and ears being cut off was surprising but not vomit inducing. Now, his being scalped got my attention. I'd seen the top of skulls before, but only on corpses. What made me physically sick was the missing jaw. I could see the upper part of the mouth and the teeth. Both cheeks had been cut off and from the scar on the throat I could see just where Raven had cut the bone. Implanted on the top of his neck was a piece of machinery shaped sort of like a muffler. There was a white, plastic tube coming out the back of it and going down his throat. Wires were stitched from it into the veins of his neck. When he spoke a couple red lights blinked. The device probably not only served as a voice synthesizer, it likely also helped him take nutrition and regulated his breathing.

And the most horrible part about looking at that monstrosity? It was knowing Raven had inflicted it on him. I respect and understand the need for revenge, and I am not what anyone would call a squeamish individual. But getting a close look at the sort of thing Raven was capable of would make anyone pause.

Even with her mask on I was sure Raven had her mouth hanging open. "How?! I buried you alive in a grave! How can you still be alive?!"

<After you destroyed my entire family I needed to find a new direction for my life. I didn't want to join another clan, so I looked for an organization that would use my skills and give me a purpose. I joined HATE (**H**onorless **A**ssociation of **T**errorists and **E**xtremists.) They came looking for me when I went missing. When they found me mutilated and barely alive, the sensible thing would probably have been to leave me in that coffin. But Dr. Metzger does love a challenge, he put me back together again. It took me this long to recover

my strength and get used to my new body. As soon as I did, I came here looking for you. We're both freaks who should be dead, and now one of us will be.>

"Hey I hate to break this to you, but you're way more of a mess than I am. I mean I can still chew my food."

<Die!>

He charged straight at her stabbing with his knife. She slid back and dodged then countered with her own knife. He avoided it and they squared off again. It was only at this moment I found I had a clear shot. From my spot I fired.

Zzzzzzz.

I should have got him right in the back, he was only about fifteen feet away and I had him lined up. I don't know how, but he back flipped out of the way and the beam missed him completely. And as he was in the air I saw him flick his wrist. In the next few seconds three things happened.

One, I felt my cheek get cut and a trickle of blood start to flow. Two, I heard a 'thunk' and saw his kunai imbedded into the sink cabinet. Three, my killbots suddenly began moving. Throwing a bladed weapon at my person was a 'violent attack.' Just as his feet touched the floor six machine guns opened fire.

I immediately put my head down. My killbots were programmed NOT to shoot if I am in the line of fire, but that didn't effect flying debris. I shut my eyes and covered up my face and all I could hear was the roar of those guns blazing away. I know it could not have been longer than sixty seconds, but they really seemed to go on forever. When the sound of shooting stopped I very carefully lifted my head and looked around. Viper and Raven were both gone along with two of my killbots. The third was toppled over with a fist size hole in its chest. As I stood up and looked around what was left of my apartment I decided I would turn the space into storage and just move into another part of the lair.

XXX

Raven eventually came back with her right pinky bent back and looking angrier than I've ever seen. Otherwise she was fine.

"He got away," she growled.

"Why do I suspect he'll be back?"

"Because he's like me I guess. By the way, the other two killbots got busted up."

I shrugged. "It's fine, I actually got some use out of them this time."

"We'll have to seriously tighten up security. Maybe we can set up booby traps and mines under some of the floors. Oh, and the next time there's an alarm I want you to get out of here. No bull shit about your reputation."

I didn't reply, but I did touch the cut on my cheek. I'd done worse shaving, it wouldn't leave a scar, but it was very easy to imagine what might have happened. Ninja don't usually miss.

"Listen, Doc. If you want, I can leave. I promise to pay you what I still owe for my parts. But Viper is going to keep coming after me for as long as we're both alive. It'd be safer for you if I weren't here."

"That's probably true, but I want you to stay. My life is dangerous already, one more enemy doesn't make a difference."

She paused and tilted her head slightly. "You sure?"

"Yes."

I sighed and thought about everything that had happened, about the cost of repairing the killbots and security system and walls. I thought about the hassle of filling out all those life insurance forms and about how much grief I was likely to get from OSHA. And there was one other thing on my mind.

"Raven, are you certain your cousin was kidnapped and raped? Could he have been telling the truth?"

She arched her back and planted both hands on her hips. "Her father, my uncle, said it was rape and everyone in my family believed him. He wouldn't have lied about that."

"During your fight you said your cousin told you she'd been raped."

"She never talked about it to me, but her father said that was what she told him. That's good enough."

I licked my lips and spoke carefully. "But you never heard her actually say it? So it's at least possible that she went willingly, right?"

Raven narrowed her eyes and then blew out a long breath. "Yeah, I guess it is. But it doesn't really matter anymore, does it? The only two people who know the truth are dead. My whole clan and his are both dead and neither of us will ever forgive the other. Neither of us will ever admit we're wrong. So what does it even matter anymore?"

I had no answer for her.

XXX

Rule #7 – Revenge is not a dish best served cold. Revenge is a huge pain in the ass.

<u>Chapter 21</u>

"So how much for the positronic processing unit?"

"Well this is the new eight point oh version," the salesman informed me. "It has twelve percent more-"

"How much?" I asked again.

"Forty-five thousand."

"That's kind of pricey. Washington Industries is offering theirs for thirty five."

The man rubbed his nose as if picking up a foul odor. "Their PPU is nothing but a cheap copy of ours. IST sets the standard in positronic technology."

"Isn't Lang Tech's Optim Two superior in both capacity and processing speed?"

Now he made a face as though he tasted something rotten. "The Optim Two is higher priced and has had a lot of issues in production."

"You always pay more for quality. I buy most of my equipment from Lang."

"I suppose I could drop the price just a little, say to forty-two thousand."

"If I buy two could you drop it to forty each?"

From the way the man grimaced you would think I'd punched him. "I could lower it that much if you were to buy three or more."

"I only need two."

"Interceptor bought six earlier today."

I rolled my eyes. "Sounds like he's building another Flying Citadel, I wish him luck after what happened to the last one. I don't have anything that ambitious in mind."

He moaned and complained, but I eventually got him to agree to forty thousand. I handed over my Black Card and provided a DNA sample and was soon the owner of two brand new PPUs. I put them in the shopping bag Raven was carrying for me.

"I didn't believe it was possible, but you managed it." Raven said as we left the stall to go look at some other products.

"What?"

"You've managed to make shopping in Las Vegas boring. Congratulations."

I shook my head in disbelief. "How can you not be enjoying this? They've got the latest particle destabilizers, fusion engines, hydrokinetic body armor, high spectrum lasers, and anamorphic constructs! It's like Christmas!"

"Your parents got you a lot of underwear and socks as a kid, didn't they?"

"I don't care what you say, you're not bringing me down. It's Villain Con 2015 and I'm going to enjoy it. Oh! Flamethrowers!" Raven groaned and followed me. I like to imagine it's some very small bit of cosmic karma for all the men who have ever been dragged along to a mall by a wife or girlfriend and forced to endure the horror and shame of shoe shopping.

They didn't actually call it Villain Con, not officially. Officially the event was the, 'Advanced Technologies and Concepts in Security and Self-Defense Convention.' But everyone in the community just called it Villain Con. It was the one day a year when people like me were (relatively) safe from the heroes and from Section Seven.

You see, in the US there are five companies who produce high tech weapons and support systems; IST, Liberty Inc., Washington Industries, Mason and Lewis, and Lang Tech. They pretty much provide all the really advanced gear the military and government use. They're the ones who design and build the spy satellites, stealth fighters, rail guns, attack drones, and laser systems. You might think all those huge government contracts would be enough, but it's a business and like any other, and they are always looking to expand their markets and maximize their profits. Which brings us to Villain Con.

People may hate supervillains and evil organizations, but the fact is most of us have a LOT of money. And we are among the few people outside the government who are interested in this sort merchandise. When I built Raven her arms and legs I ordered the parts from IST and Lang Tech. I spent close to two million dollars. While I assemble my spy and killbots myself, I buy most of their sensors, computer hardware, and propulsion systems. In theory I could build everything myself, but I'd have to have my own factory. And given what normally happens to my secret bases and dummy companies, it wouldn't be long before it was shut down. It's just easier to outsource.

Now, it happens to be against the law to sell advanced weapons technology to any individual with either a felony conviction or who has been listed on the Defense of the Public Against Supernatural or Superhuman Threats Act. And the official policy of all the companies is to adhere to that.

Unofficially, they know they can make hundreds of millions in sales if they sell to supervillains. They're not passing that up. Hell, Lang Tech is owned by Franklin Lang, who happens to be Iron Knight and a leading member of the League of Heroes. They had as many stalls as any of their competitors. Their sales people were just as eager to take our money. But if you listen to the commercials Franklin Lang and his company, 'put people first.' Sure he does.

The government and the heroes know all about what these companies do, but rely so heavily on them they are willing to look the other way, within limits.

"As long as we're here why don't we stay a couple days?" Raven asked. "We can walk the Strip, hit a casino, and maybe go see Celine Dion."

I immediately shook my head. "If you want we can play the slots in the hotel lobby for an hour or so, but we have to be long gone before midnight, that's when the pass ends."

The government turned a blind eye, but there were certain conditions. The convention was a chance for the companies to show off their latest wares and talk up their product lines face to face with the buyers. The rest of the year all the business was done online and through third parties. This was an opportunity for the producers to get a big boost in sales, and for the customers to really shop and compare. It's a one day event, and for twenty-four hours supervillains in the host city were given a very unofficial 'pass.' We didn't need to worry about Section Seven suddenly showing up with assault rifles and attack helicopters, or the League crashing through the wall to start beating us up. So long as we didn't commit any new crimes we could expect to be left alone.

The companies were not stupid or naïve. The conventions were always swarming with heavily armed private security guards in riot gear. And you can bet there were government troops on standby somewhere not too far away. Any sort of trouble would be met with a lot of force. The companies also required everyone attending to deposit funds into special bank accounts. Those amounts were credited onto Black Cards issued to each attendee. You could only make purchases with the Black Cards, and a DNA sample was required with each transaction. The precautions made it next to impossible to cheat the system. Only understandable given who the customers were.

Supervillains weren't the only people attending. About half the folk wandering the floor were dressed in military uniforms. Pretty much every dictator in Latin America, Africa, and Asia had sent someone here to look things over.

There was a big knot of them over at the Washington Industries section. A salesman was enthusiastically going over the attributes and features of their latest model Fully Integrated Drone Operative. They really, really wanted to call the thing FIDO. They had a drawing of a guard dog sitting attentively, and loved to describe their machine as, 'loyal and protective as a family dog.' A fair description, if you added the twin mounted fifty caliber machine guns, all terrain track system, and motion and heat sensors. Air and ground drones were hugely popular with authoritarian regimes. They loved soldiers whose loyalty could be programmed. The FIDOs were especially big hits in countries with active guerilla movements. The drones had a 'total pacification' mode. You could deploy fifty or a hundred or two hundred or as many as you liked to a trouble spot and then just let them patrol the area. They would then kill every living thing that was human sized within their designated zone of operation. No worries about defections to the rebels or hesitation to shoot women and children or unarmed civilians. They patrolled nonstop and shot everything until they ran out of ammunition. At which point they were programmed to return to base to resupply and set out again. Washington Industries had sold tens of thousands of these things to some of the most brutal regimes on Earth. And people called me a monster because I usually kept three or four killbots.

There were tanks, fighters, anti-air defense systems, armored personnel carriers, and short range rockets. In front of each display was a beautiful woman with big tits and a short skirt. For such big ticket items all the companies guaranteed free delivery to any location within the continental United States. You could also get them sent outside the US, but costs would vary. I wasn't interested in any heavy equipment, those were more for foreign militaries and maybe one of the big evil organizations. I was tempted by the armored power suits on sale by Lang Tech, though.

"The Mark One Iron Warrior Power Armor was personally designed by Franklin Lang, and is based on his own Iron Knight model. It has a flight range of over three hundred miles and a top speed of three hundred and twenty miles per hour. It has a self-contained oxygen filtration system as well as our newest computer navigational system, sensor array, and communications system. The armor is reinforced titanium with-"

"Does it have an energy barrier?" I asked.

The sales guy didn't let his eager expression slip. "I'm afraid that technology isn't available to the public at this time."

"What sort of armament does it have?"

"Two, sixty-five caliber guns come standard, each with a certified range of five thousand feet. The weapons are linked to the onboard targeting system to allow for accurate fire in all weather conditions. In addition, missile pods can be mounted on the shoulders to allow-"

"So no lasers or repulsers," I cut him off. "And unless I buy some of the extras it has less fire power than any modern fighter. The suit's appearance is like Iron Knight's, but I know for a fact he can top Mach One. So really, all it is is a slower, less well armored, and much less powerful knock off of your CEO's suit."

"Mr. Lang is a member of the League of Heroes, you can't reasonably expect him to make a version of his own armor available for sale, now can you?"

"Oh, of course not. I would expect him to make one that's completely inferior while trying to pretend it's just as good."

I wasn't surprised. If you want to fly around and be a superhero you need to have an advantage over your enemies. I wouldn't expect Iron Knight to mass produce his own armor. But it annoyed me he would make a power armor suit that was superficially like his, but inferior in every way.

XXX

Despite a few disappointments, my time at the convention wasn't wasted. I picked up some telescopic lenses, navigational systems, monitoring devices, a couple of the latest portable lasers, and different spare parts for Raven. In total I spent around three and a half million dollars and filled up two large shopping bags. And most of it was from Lang Tech. Their power suits might be a rip off, but they did make a lot of the best stuff.

"I can't believe you actually paid for everything," Raven complained as she lugged the bags. "I could rob this place blind."

"Don't even think about it. These are the absolute last people you ever want to steal from. They all have the President on speed dial and get Christmas cards from the League."

"Well how about I just wander the floor for a bit? See what I can pick up?"

"No. There are more hidden cameras here than there are salesmen." I picked up some free literature about next year's product lines from IST. They had some high frequency pulse cannons that looked interesting. "I'm fine paying for this stuff. It's safer to rob the Russian mob than Lang Tech or Washington Industries."

"You know when you told me we were coming to Vegas this isn't exactly what I had in mind. Seriously, let's at least rip off a casino or something. It's such a waste."

"That would violate the pass. How about on the drive back to Jersey we stop and rob a bank somewhere?"

"You mean it?"

"Sure, why not. No reason not to have a little bit of fun."

XXX

Rule #4 – Get your business done quietly when you can.

<u>Chapter 22</u>

The two guards barely had enough time to shout and start shooting before my killbots slaughtered them. A few seconds later and there was a piercing siren. I had to give Dr. Alligator credit, his people were wide awake and well trained. Not that it would do them very much good. Two killbots smashed down the front door and stormed into the base. Immediately there were more shouts and the sound of gunfire.

I took out my communicator. "I'm launching my frontal assault. That should keep them good and diverted."

"Got it," Raven said.

"Remember, you have to find and secure the-"

"Yeah, yeah, yeah, I know! I've done this before, Doc." She cut off her line.

"Well, there's no need to be rude." I muttered and slid the communicator back in a pocket. I turned around to look at the twenty henchmen and two additional killbots I had backing me up.

"I want Dr. Alligator alive! The rest I don't care about. Let's go!"

My men all gave a half-hearted shout. I was a little disappointed. I mean sure, some of them were probably going to die, but it was for a great cause! I made a mental note to work on some inspirational speeches and to talk to HR about team building exercises.

Dr. Alligator's base was an old tractor factory out on Long Island. He's constructed four underground levels complete with all the usual surveillance devices and defenses. The walls were painted green and steel gray and the lay out was as unimaginative and utilitarian as could be. One main corridor, two stairwells, a pair of elevators, and the same floor plan for each floor. The only traps were fake floors with spikes below, talk about lame. And he had them at the exact same spot on every floor! What a hack! Why even be a supervillain if you can't think for yourself? I mean halfway through the first floor I KNEW he would be hiding in his lab which would be at the very end of the lowest floor. It made me embarrassed to know such a tool had managed to break in and steal something from me. Knowing it had happened while I was at the convention salved my pride only a bit. After I dealt with him I would never mention this ever again!

Er, except for this one time, I mean.

His men put up a decent fight. They were armed with AK-47s and had some idea what they were doing. The few who ran away I didn't bother to chase. The ones who gave up I let go, I wanted their boss, not them. (I handed out business cards with a number to one of my offices in case any of them were interested.) Most of them died fighting. Their bullets couldn't do anything to my killbots or the body armor in my costume. I only suffered four casualties, two dead and two wounded, so it was a very successful assault.

We made it down to the fourth sublevel. That was where all the experiments were done and the test subjects were held. I steered clear of those. When we reached the end of the hall I told my men to wait and burst into the room myself, disintegrator in hand.

"Hey, Doc. Have fun storming the castle?"

Raven was sitting on a table kicking her heels. Dr. Alligator was crumpled on the floor against the far wall. Blood was leaking from the end of his snout, a handful of pointed teeth were scattered around him, and his left arm was bent at an unnatural angle. As you might guess from the name he was an evil genius who specialized in genetic mutation. He had turned himself into an alligator / man hybrid. Which meant he had the strength and reflexes of an alligator, but could not go out to get a cup of coffee or buy some gum. Since he was obviously not as powerful as a cyborg ninja I doubt it was worth it.

I don't have an issue with conducting genetic experiments or using human test subjects. If you're into that sort of thing it's fine, I won't judge. Getting to toy with human life is one of the main selling points of being a supervillain after all. But the whole point of doing human experimentation is to gain knowledge at the expense of others. You NEVER use yourself unless you are one hundred percent sure the end result will be exactly what you want. I mean if he'd ever had one conversation with Obelisk or Goblin or any random vampire he'd know that standing out in a crowd is a bad thing, even if you can hold your breath for twenty minutes.

He was a fool and I would deal with him, but I had a greater priority.

"Did you find it?"

"More or less." She reached behind and brought out my grolem doll. It was in three pieces.

"Nooooooo!!!" I ran over and took the sections from her and spread them out on the table. "No, no, no! What did he do?! He completely dismembered the drive and motor system! And the computer control is wrecked! And some of the chips are missing! He ruined my doll!"

"Is it really that big a deal? I mean you can rebuild him, right?"

"It'll take months! The computer chips were all one of a kind prototypes! There's no way I can have him ready by October second! I was going to meet with all the major toy producers. There was talk about making a line of high end toys! There was going to be a big advertising campaign in time for next Christmas!"

"Let me guess, this was your latest plan to take over the world. Get a doll in every household with a kid and then let them rampage. Was that it?"

"Well, sure, eventually. Do you have any idea the profit margins on children's toys? And they would have been produced in my factory! I mean think about it. These would have been fully functioning interactive robots programmed to play with and or care for their subject. Toys that could not only play with a child but actually watch out for them. Like a toy / pet / babysitter / guard dog hybrid. There's an unlimited market for them! They could have been the biggest thing since Cabbage Patch Dolls."

"Wait, so you were really just going to try and sell them? What about supervillains not caring about money?"

"I never said money wasn't useful, and I would have had an entire army of these dolls out there eventually. I could have used them to take over the world. I just would have waited until the sales and net profit margin flattened out. Besides, it's kind of cool to think of millions of kids wanting to play with my invention."

"Huh. Well, I still like that better than your giant robot."

I turned around and glared at my enemy. Dr. Alligator was now sitting up and slowly sliding along the wall. I pointed my disintegrator directly at his head. "You monster! Do you have ANY IDEA how hard it is to try and sell a new product line to toy manufacturers?! When I cancel the demonstration that's going to kill me! I'll have to start over again from ground zero! Not to mention stealing from a fellow supervillain is disrespectful!"

He made a growling sound that might have been a laugh. "I heard you ssstole from Dr. Malpracticccce oncccce."

"That was years ago, and that asshole was asking for it! He kept trying to hire away my people."

"Is every other supervillain a doctor?" Raven asked. "Hey, do you actually have a PhD?"

"Of courssse, I have three in Biology, Mediccccine, and Neurological Sssstudiessss."

"Wow. So I guess you really can call yourself doctor. Unlike a certain someone else I know."

"Raven, now is not the time."

"Just saying…"

Dr. Alligator continued to slowly slide along the wall. I could guess what he was up to, but it didn't matter. I only had a couple more question and then I would end him.

"Why did you steal my grolem doll in the first place? You don't have any robots."

"I wassss hoping to ussse ssssome of the technology to enhancccce my experimentsss. I wanted to insssert chipssss and gearssss into them and make them sssstronger." He nodded towards Raven. "You did well mixing the mechanical and biological."

"You're an idiot! You can't just implant some computer ships in an iguanaman and make him stronger. It doesn't work that way. I attached cybernetic limbs to her body. Every inch of her is either completely mechanical or organic, her enhancements are attached not grown."

Dr. Alligator nodded. "I ssssee. I ssssuppossssse ssssuch a thing would be beyond you."

"No it's not! I could do it if I wanted to. I just find robots and cyborgs more useful."

"Sssso you claim, but who are you really?" The alligatorman slid a few more inches.

"What do you mean? I'm Dr. Anarchy! One of the greatest supervillains in the world! My name fills hearts with dread and makes even the mightiest heroes shudder!" I began to pace and wave my arms about dramatically. "I am the personal nemesis to Dark Detective and terror to heroes and civilians alike! My genius is legendary and unmatched. All will tremble in fear as I conquer this pathetic world and rule over it as its one true master! I will be supreme. My every word shall be law and my will death! Those who oppose me shall weep as I-"

Raven interrupted me. "Hey! You're doing it again."

I faced her with real annoyance. She'd completely ruined my flow. "What?"

"You're monologuing."

"So?"

"So we've talked about this before. I thought you came here to get your stupid doll back and kill this guy. I mean are you trying to talk him to death? Just shoot him already."

"What am I? A mugger? I'm not going to, 'just shoot him.' I want him to understand he was doomed the instant he chose to match wits with me. I want his final moments to be consumed with despair as he truly comprehends the depth of his folly in challenging the might of Dr. Anarchy. For Dr. Anarchy can never-"

"Whoa! Stop right there!" She stuck a finger out and pointed at me. "You are **not** going to start talking about yourself in third person. You don't pay me enough to put up with that!"

"What is your problem? A little monologuing never hurt anyone. It's one of the perks of being a supervillain."

"That's true, a little is fine. When you start one of your rants you just keep going and going and going. You're like the Energizer Bunny of evil."

"I am not. I have my monologuing completely under control. I understand the need for control better than anyone. Despite the intricacies and diversity of my projects and operations I always maintain a firm grasp on my every action. Like a spider in the midst of its web, even the slightest vibration is known to me. I allow nothing to occur outside my knowledge. Every single action that I perform or instigate is part of a carefully conceived plan. A plan where every possible outcome or deviation is considered and prepared for. My schemes are brilliant and infallible. They are more complex than a schematic for a particle accelerator and more subtle than the curve of a flower's petal. Not even the smallest and most insignificant detail escapes my grasp. I am always-"

Chunk.

I heard the sound and turned around just in time to see the top of Dr. Alligator's head drop out of view. A trap door had opened and he'd gone down a meatal tube. I ran over, but the tube twisted, so I didn't have a target to shoot at. I very clearly heard a splash.

Raven came over and stood right next to me. She didn't say a word. She just raised one eyebrow and looked me in the eye.

"I don't care what you say, I don't have a problem."

"Keep telling yourself that, Doc."

I looked around the lab so I could avoid her gaze. I didn't care what she thought. I was not going to start seeing a psychiatrist about this. All they ever did was ask you about your mother and try to convince you that being a supervillain was a desperate attempt to gain parental approval.

"Well, as long as we're here we may as well rob the place. I can always use some more superconductors."

XXX

Rule #28 – Monologuing is a personal choice you can stop at any time. It is NOT a compulsion.

Chapter 23

It's a well-known fact that aliens not only exist, but have visited the Earth hundreds if not thousands of times. The ruins of Atlantis that were discovered in 1973 just west of the Azores, were Vakryl. The Egyptian god Ra was a Heliopan, his remains and pieces of technology entombed in the Red Pyramid at Giza proved this. The Aztec gods Mictlantecuhtli and Quetzalcoatl were Nahuatl. There is strong evidence the disappearance of the Anasazi was due to the Horka. Then there are the more recent and well documented events that have taken place in the modern age. The Pette visitation of China in 1689, the Borlomar cataclysm in Rome in 1722, the

Andromadan visitation of Bombay in 1790, the Erenhet visitation of Berlin in 1937, and most famously of course, the Altarian occupation of London from 1873 to 1875. And those are only some of the major alien events that we can confirm. You can visit almost any corner of the world from Nebraska to Guatemala to Somalia to Mongolia and you'll find stories or legends about alien visitations. There's no way to know how many of those are based on fact and how many are just myth, but there is indisputable proof that at least nine distinct alien races have been to Earth. Secret government agencies like Section Seven may know about more, but every school child knows at least that much. So you would think when an alien ship arrived people would be able to handle it calmly.

But they never do.

I was in my lab working on an upgrade for my grolem doll. I was going to see about having each of them provide Wi-Fi. If I could make it economical for mass production it would only increase the market for the dolls. As well as give me access to the private information of the people using them. Whenever I was working I always had at least one monitor tuned into CNN. The reason was for moments like those.

They interrupted a report on the mounting crisis in Egypt. A studio host cut in midsentence, he didn't speak immediately. The man took a moment to look something over. I stopped working to give the monitor my full attention. When CNN breaks from regularly scheduled programming it means something newsworthy has happened. When they break and there's confusion about what to report it's always a bad sign.

"The national security council has just issued an alert. An unidentified flying object has been detected entering Earth's atmosphere and is approaching US airspace. Initial projections of its trajectory indicate an arrival somewhere on the eastern seaboard. The cities of Boston, New York, Philadelphia, Baltimore, and Washington D.C. are considered the most likely touch down sights. A state of emergency has been declared in all states within the Eastern Time zone. All residents are encouraged to remain calm and to take shelter indoors. Please avoid travelling if at all possible. All commercial flights are being cancelled and planes currently in the air are being rerouted to the nearest available airport. Schools will be closed. Employers are requested to temporarily close operations in order to allow their employees to return home. All police, firemen, and other emergency service workers are asked to report immediately regardless of schedule. The National Guard has been activated in the states of Massachusetts, Connecticut, New York, New Jersey, Pennsylvania, Delaware, Maryland, and Virginia. All guardsman are required to report immediately to their designated assembly area. The President is scheduled to address the nation shortly. In the meantime…"

My communicator began to ring. It was Amy, my HR Supervisor.

"Yes?"

"Sir, are you aware there's been a state of emergency declared?"

"Yes, I know." I turned the other monitors to different stations, local and national. I was not surprised to see every one of them was reporting on the situation. One of the local channels had ALIEN INVASION!!! In big red letters flashing. I'm sure that wasn't going to cause any panic.

"The government is asking all nonessential businesses to close in order to allow employees to return home. Also, there's been a call up of the National Guard and Raymond

Weatherby is a guardsmen. Schools are being shut down and we have four single parents working right now."

"I see. All right, send everyone home. Let them know they'll still be paid for their scheduled hours. Call everyone who was scheduled to come in on second and third shift and tell them not to. Let everyone know I'll send them a text when they can come back in."

"Yes, sir."

I didn't like the idea of not having any henchmen in my lair, but given the situation there wasn't a real choice. It would be suspicious if Big Boy Toys LLC was the only place with people working. At least given the situation I didn't think Dark Detective or any other heroes were going to pick that moment to attack me.

President Thompson was just beginning his speech when Raven showed up.

"Everyone's cleared out, Doc. It's just us. What do you want to do?"

"Nothing." As the President droned on about the need for calm and his government's commitment to defending the American people I looked over the different electronic parts. Adding Wi-Fi wasn't the challenge. It was finding a way to add it without increasing the cost of production too much. Market research indicated there was a sharp drop in demand if a toy's price went above fourteen ninety-nine.

"You're pretty calm about this."

"Alien encounters aren't all that unusual."

"You mean you've been through one of these?"

I frowned at her. "The last major one was in 1969 in Beijing. How old do you think I am?"

"You really want me to answer that?"

"I mean historical records indicate mankind has had about two or three major visitations each century. From that perspective we were due. This isn't the end of the world."

"You sure?" Raven indicated some of the monitors.

There were images of people on their knees praying fervently outside a large cathedral. A person rushed out of a supermarket with a shopping cart filled to overflowing with toilet paper and bottled water. Teenagers were dancing out in the street, holding up signs with messages such as 'beam us up' and 'the White House is that way.' Highways were jammed with people desperate to get out of the cities. The images were from cities up and down the east coast.

"Reminds me of what happened when Dr. Death seized power."

She blinked and rubbed her chin. "Now that you mention it, that's true."

"People panic easily, even when there's no real reason to."

"You don't think an alien invasion is a good enough reason?"

"Invasion implies an effort at military conquest. If any of the alien races were interested in that, they could have taken over the planet at any point in our history. For that matter, they could have exterminated us just as easily. Luckily for us,

Earth seems to be nothing more than a rest stop for more advanced races."

"A rest stop? So we're a place to grab a hot dog or some coffee and take a quick piss?"

"Effectively, yes. Be very glad of the fact. If we were actually important we'd have been colonized millennia ago. As far as we know, the only aliens who ever tried that were the Vakryl who created Atlantis. From the archaeological evidence there were probably never more than two hundred here at most. Historians don't believe it was a serious effort at colonization, much more likely their ship malfunctioned and they were stranded here. Or they might have been refugees of some sort, or possibly criminals or other undesirable elements and Earth was used as a penal colony. Most of the documented encounters could be seen as either stopping to gather supplies or a simple excursion among a more primitive race."

"What? So they stop here to get gas or to stare at the monkeys in the trees?"

"Puts things in perspective doesn't it? We are just barely capable of reaching Mars and having a permanent base on Luna. All the aliens who visit us can travel between stars. They're as technologically superior to us as we are to a tribe of natives who throw stones and spears. And if it came to an actual fight we'd stand as much chance."

"That's a pleasant thought."

I nodded. "So it's lucky we're not worth conquering."

"Uh, what happens if this bunch decides we're worth the trouble?"

"Human extinction probably. The best case scenario is we become slaves of our new alien overlords."

"What about the heroes?"

"What about them? I'm sure they'd fight, but I can't believe they'd be any real threat to beings who can travel faster than the speed of light. In any case I wouldn't worry about it, given past precedent this shouldn't be too bad."

"So in the meantime we just hang out?"

"Yes, unless you have some errand you want to run."

"I'm good." She looked about the lab. "You want anything from the cafeteria while we wait for ET to stop by?"

"Grab me some pizza and a coke, please."

"Sure thing."

XXX

About half an hour after the President's speech an Air Force general informed the nation that telemetry indicated New York City would be the touchdown point. New York is the media capitol of the world. It wasn't long before most of the channels had news crews on the roofs of some of the buildings. As cameras swept the sky the reporters and studio hosts reassured the viewers at home that there was nothing to be afraid of. They reminded us that aliens had visited many times before, and had often given humanity knowledge in mathematics, engineering, agriculture, medicine, and various sciences. All of them claimed this would be one of the great moments in human history, a day people would remember all of their lives.

And while everything they said was true it wasn't quite as factual as it might have been. I noticed that no one brought up what happened in London. Or talked about Plato's treatise on the Altarians, and how they had decimated Greece and very nearly exterminated Greek culture. No one mentioned the Anasazi or the Maya. They didn't even bring up the famous theory that Hitler was replaced by an Erenhet robot. Not to mention that even in a lot of the 'peaceful' encounters the aliens had pretended to be gods and had taken whatever people or goods they wished. One thing seemed to be consistent with every encounter, whether violent or relatively benevolent. The aliens never treated human beings as equals.

'Greetings, monkeys! Who wants to look at a shiny?' That would sum up how aliens viewed humanity. The best you could hope for was that they would toss the dumb animals a few treats or pretty much ignore them. If your luck was out they might start hunting for sport or possibly have a taste for monkey meat.

I tried to keep working while keeping one eye on the news. Whatever was going to happen was far beyond my control. All I could do was react to events. In that sense I was no different than the morons stocking up on breakfast cereal and batteries or the idiots who were getting drunk on rooftops and holding up signs that read 'Welcome to Earth.' A very important part of being a supervillain was the idea that you, and you alone, were the master of your fate. Even after all my failures and my time in the Sandbox, I still held that belief. The belief I could do anything, if I was only strong enough, smart enough, and ruthless enough.

Facing an alien encounter made me want to squirm. It was unpleasant being reminded how… small I was in the grand scheme of things.

XXX

ABC were the first to catch a glimpse of the ship. They had a news crew stationed on top of the Chrysler Building. The sky was partly cloudy and since it was almost noon the sun was high up in the sky. When they first spotted it, the reporter wasn't sure it was the aliens. He thought it might be a plane heading to JFK. It took a couple minutes, but it became obvious it was not a plane. All the other channels soon spotted it and on every screen you could see its approach from slightly different angles.

There was excited talk about a possible alien delegation to the UN or of what sort of message the aliens might have for the world. There was speculation on whether they would land in Central Park or on the water. A couple of reporters noted there were no other aircraft in the sky, including military jets. In his speech President Thompson had stressed that they had no hostile intentions towards the visitors and wanted no accidental misunderstandings. (As if our rocks and slings might scare them.) They wondered what sort of knowledge they might share with the world and if any humans would be permitted to visit the alien craft. Reporters wondered if the aliens would communicate in English or with telepathy. The news casters droned on as they expected the ship to land at any moment, as it grew larger as it got near.

It had looked quite large… and then gotten larger and larger and larger. It approached for another twelve minutes and the questions slowly began to die away as they began to understand that what was approaching was something on a scale humans could not easily grasp.

The ship was about five miles long and roughly a mile and a half wide. Its shape was rectangular and the underside with a maze of blocky structures. As it had approached we had seen that the top side was the same. There was no obvious bridge or turrets or landing features. The entire ship was the color of silver, and looked more like an immense barge than anything else. It slid over the island of Manhattan and came to a stop, blocking out the sun for miles. It hovered about a mile or so above the ground. The reporters did their best to relate how massive the thing was, how it made them feel insignificant. Most of Manhattan was literally in its shadow.

One of the reporters said, "I really hope they come in peace."

I choked out a startled laugh.

"What?" Raven asked. She'd been watching the monitors as intently as I had, but while sitting on a table kicking her feet.

"They don't come in peace," I said. I then spoke a few lines of a poem I'd read back in High School. (Go Whalers.)

"High above the great and noble city,
Hung the vast and unearthly barge.
Down from it poured the demons without pity,
To burn and ruin and murder their charge."

Raven stared at me.

"Tennyson," I told her. "It was part of a poem he wrote about the Occupation of London. The poem was entitled, 'The Enemies of All Man.'"

"That doesn't sound very good at all."

I nodded. "They're called Altarians. The Mycenaean Greeks described them as heartless beasts who thrived on cruelty and death. The British called them the blue skinned devils. Of all the aliens who have visited us they are by far the cruelest and most violent. They have teleporters and used them to kidnap people and livestock and huge quantities of food. They also came down in hundreds of small craft in order to slaughter people face to face. They aren't interested in conquest or loot, they killed because they enjoyed it. They're like Mongols with advanced technology. Wherever they arrive it's open season on all humans. They plunged the Greek civilization into a dark age, and depopulated London and the midlands. New York and everything around it is doomed."

"Okay, are you totally sure these are the same guys? I mean it could be a different bunch of aliens, right?"

"Something is happening!" A reporter barked. "I can see sections of the hull opening up! There are smaller ships dropping down and into the air! There are dozens, no, no wait, there must be hundreds of them! They look like smaller versions of the mother ship. This looks to be the moment we've all been waiting for! The ships are spreading all over the city and- wait! One of them is headed towards us! It looks like we are about to meet directly with the visitors!"

The transport was like the larger ship in overall color and design. It was a rectangular block without and clear windows or door. It landed on the same roof where the reporters were waiting. The bottom of the ship never actually made contact with the roof, instead it floated about an inch above. A section of the transport slid open, and three aliens stepped out. They were humanoid, with a head, a chest, two arms and two legs. They were large, each standing at least seven feet tall and like weighing well over three hundred and fifty pounds at the least. Their skin was a dark blue, their eyes were black and without pupils. All three had their lips pulled back to reveal large teeth that were so white they seemed to glow. Their fingers were exceptionally long and had four joints. They wore boots and trousers that were made of a pale yellow material, and all over holsters of different shapes and sizes. The chests and arms had thick, well developed muscles.

On camera you could see the reporter hesitate and back up. He then gathered himself and took a careful step forward. "He- Hello, my name is Robert Conway. Do you speak my language?"

The three Altarians made noises that sounded very much like laughter. Then each one pulled out a blade from one of their holsters. Unhurried and still laughing they walked towards the reporter and his camera man.

"Wait! What are you - aasaaahhhh!!!! God help me!!"

Raven and I and the audience watched as the reporter was stabbed about twenty times. The cameraman had dropped his equipment as he tried to run, but it had landed at an angle that allowed the audience to continue watching. The people in the newsroom must have been as stunned at everyone else because they didn't think to cut away until their man had been butchered like a calf. All the while the Altarians who murdered him were laughing.

On other monitors similar scenes were playing out. A few other reporters were attacked, more often they watched as civilians were hacked to pieces.

"Any other questions?" I asked in a quiet voice.

She swallowed and licked her lips. "So what do we do?"

I took my remote and shut off all the monitors. "I hear Los Angeles is lovely this time of year. So long as you ignore the traffic and the smog."

"So we're just going to run away?"

"Yes, that's the only sane thing to do."

She opened her mouth as if to argue, then closed it. "Okay. I guess that's true. Not like we're the good guys."

"That's certainly the case. I'm no-"

XXX

He disappeared. He was just standing there talking one second and was gone the next.

"Doc!"

I jumped off the table and leapt to where he'd been. I looked around on the off chance he'd dropped through a trap door or something. There was no sign of him. I reached into one of my pockets and pulled out the tracker he'd given me. It came on and showed me he was twelve miles to the east and one point eight miles above me.

"Oh fuck me bloody," I muttered to myself.

I was going to have to charge him a hundred million for this.

XXX

Raven's Rule #2 – Shit happens.

Chapter 24

The first thing I did was go to the armory. I grabbed two mini-jetpacks, a pair of Uzis, a dozen grenades, and about a hundred magazines. I know I gave Viper a lot of shit about ninja using guns, but I figured that dealing with an alien invasion was an exception to the rule. I had no plan and no idea how to rescue Doc. This wasn't like springing him after he was arrested. I'd have to sneak into a giant spaceship that was floating above Manhattan, fight my way to Doc, rescue him, and then somehow get both of us out. Piece of cake, right? I knew the chances of pulling it off were pretty much zero. Dying didn't scare me, though knowing my clan would die with me was sad.

When I'd figured out what had happened I thought about giving up. I could get my ass back to Frisco, look up Nancy, Tina, Leon, and go hit the bars between shopping sprees. I could party, assassinate a few people, and hook up with some cute college boys. It would be like old times. I gave it some serious thought for maybe five seconds, then went to load up on guns and ammo. There was just no way I could abandon Doc. I owed him everything. Even if there was zero chance I could do it, I'd rather die trying to save him than walk away. A ninja never breaks a contract. Besides, he just looked all manly when he stared at me with those glasses of his. A girl has her weak points, you know?

I really, really, really, wished I could have brought the killbots with me. But they only responded to Doc's orders. Before I went to the garage I swung by my room. I grabbed all my extra kunai and shuriken, no sense in leaving them behind. I also took a last look at a picture of my family. The Fusikawa clan would die with me.

I clasped my hands together and bowed to the photo. "I'm sorry, tousan, kaasan, granddad, grandma, everybody. You know I would totally get knocked up and have a few kids if I could. But I have a contract, and you know what that means. Anyway, I'll see you guys soon."

I hurried to the garage. Besides my family line ending I only had one other major regret. Viper and the Kyujito would outlive me. So I suppose him and his clan would 'win.' I took some solace in the fact that he was the last of them. He wasn't passing on his genes, not unless he could find someone to regrow his balls. Or maybe have himself cloned.

I skidded to a sudden stop and my jaw dropped. "Fuck!" There were a ton of evil organizations with cloning technology. I mean how many Hitler clones were there? A million? Every other waiter in São Paulo had a burning desire to conquer France. And I'd bet my left tit HATE was one of those organizations! Fuck, fuck, fuck, fuck, fuck!!! Why hadn't this ever occurred to me before? I imagined Viper surrounded by a whole herd of little five year olds who all looked exactly alike, and him teaching them the basics of throwing a kunai.

"FFFUUUUUUUUUUUUUCCCCCKKKKKKKKK!!!!!" I punched and kicked holes through the nearest wall. A lot of people would say that when you're face to face with your own mortality it's time to forgive those who have wronged you and find some kind of inner peace. Those people are morons. Cock gargling, maggot infested, walking piles of shit like Viper don't deserve forgiveness. They deserve to be sent through a meat grinder, ass end first and as slowly as possible. I'm talking one crank every ten minutes.

I stood there for a minute and really considered changing my mind. I wouldn't do it just to save myself, but the thought of tracking down and finally ending that dickless voice box seriously tempted me. But I finally got moving again. What it really came down to was this; Doc mattered to me more than anything else in the world. I would save him or die trying.

XXX

I took one of the vans and got onto I-78. I had the eastbound lanes pretty much all to myself. The westbound ones were a whole different story, cars and trucks were going like bats out of hell. On the breakdown lane and the side of the road were people on bikes and on foot, a lot of them with suitcases or duffel bags or plastic garbage bags. There were children clutching dolls and following along. It was like something out of a war movie, which made sense given the situation. It just wasn't something I'd ever expected to see in the US. Even when Dr. Death took over there were riots and people getting out, but nothing like this.

As I got near the Holland Tunnel there were a ton of cops on the westbound side encouraging people to keep moving and helping keep some sort of order. On my side of the highway there were just two police cruisers blocking the entrance, and a pair of cops waving at me to stop. I floored it. The cops got the hell out of my way as my van plowed through the parked cars and kept going. As soon as I was in the tunnel the 'check engine' light came on and there was a cha-chung, cha-chung sound. Doc had good car insurance so I decided not to worry about it.

When I came out into lower Manhattan I was in shadow. The spaceship was above me and blocked out most of the sky. Cars and people on foot were going past as I drove into the city. I could see tons of smoke rising into the air, but there were no fires close by. Along with the shouts and honking of horns there were gun shots, lots of them. They seemed to be coming from all over the place. Since I didn't have a specific destination in mind I took a right on Hudson Street and headed towards the Financial District.

I had to stop just past Canal Street. One of the transports was parked in front of me. It was wide enough to cover both sides of the street. There was a whole bunch of the blue fuckers and a shit ton of bodies all over the sidewalks and in the front of buildings. Men, women, and children, all hacked to pieces. Every one of the aliens was drenched in blood and holding a blade, some were like kitchen knives and some like short swords. One of them was holding a woman by the back of her head. She was screaming and trying to run away. The monster just stood there, laughing. He was holding onto her with one hand and waving a curved blade in front of her eyes with the other. The more she screamed and tried to pull free the more he laughed. I saw a scrawny, gray haired old man come out of a doorway holding a shotgun. He blasted the nearest one and knocked him right over. The four aliens who were closest all pointed to their now dead friend and seemed to be howling with laughter, one actually clutched his ribs and bent over. You would think their pal had gotten a pie to the face instead of some buck shot.

The old man worked the action and ejected the spent shell, then fired again. This time his target staggered back, but didn't fall. The alien that was hit gave a shout of pain, but never stopped smiling. Long knife in hand, he shuffled towards the old man who ejected another shell and got ready to fire again. As this happened, one of the other aliens pulled a weapon from one of his holsters. A gold beam lanced out. It burned a hold through the old guy's chest and into the wall behind him. The shotgun dropped from his hands and he fell over. The alien who'd been wounded and a couple others immediately rounded on the one who's fired and began yelling at him. That one yelled back and put the weapon away. While the argument was going on the blue fucker who'd been holding on to the girl apparently got bored. He shoved his long knife all the way through her neck, then yanked it out and stabbed her again and again with real enthusiasm.

They were playing. All this was nothing but a game to them. They were on safari and we were the gazelles and zebras they'd come to hunt. I was sure their ship had weapons that could level the whole city in seconds, but where would the fun be in that?

I parked the van, grabbed a grenade, an Uzi, a few clips, and then slung the duffel bag over my shoulder and got out. The killer smurf who'd stabbed the girl noticed me and started in my direction. The ones who were arguing were too busy to care. I pulled the pin on the grenade and waited a count of two, then chucked it fifty yards. I nailed one of them right in the head. Before he or the others could respond, boom. Four aliens turned to meat.

The one who'd been coming towards me picked up his pace and went from a casual jog to full on sprint. He had the bloodied knife in his hand and an excited look on his face.

"Barkra zuul cannor te!"

"No, no, no if you want to get to Queens you have to take the six. Tourists." I squeezed off a burst and put six or seven holes in the middle of his chest. I'd already seen that these fuckers weren't bulletproof, but I was close enough to notice their blood was the same color as ours. The asshole went down, but he never let go of his knife or stopped smiling. Did these cocksuckers actually like dying? I was brought up to accept death, and when I was lying on that beach I was starting to look forward to it. But only someone completely fucked up in the head would actually want to die if they weren't in some sort of pain.

The explosion from the grenade and the sound of gunfire drew the attention of all the other blue assholes who were on that street. There were probably thirty or so. None of them pulled out a laser to start shooting at me. Instead they all took out blades and began to run towards me, shouting in their own language.

"Thirty guys who all want me to take care of them, fuck, it's like summer camp all over again. Fine, but no kissing, got it?"

I slapped in a fresh clip and grabbed my second Uzi. I stood in the middle of the street with a fully loaded submachine gun in each hand. Despite my policy about ninja and guns I'd used these things a few times on the firing range. You never knew what kind of emergency might happen (like say an alien invasion of New York) and it's a good idea to always be prepared. An Uzi is NOT a precise weapon. It's designed to put a lot of lead into the air fast. And I wasn't a marksman, at least not with firearms. What I was, was a girl who could throw a kunai dead center into a bullseye while doing a backflip. While the skill sets were different, I had a good eye and a steady hand. I put both Uzis to semiautomatic, I had sixty-four rounds. I took a deep breath as a herd of screaming killer aliens stampeded my way.

"So no foreplay? You all just want to get straight to it? I guess guys are the same everywhere."

I squeezed the triggers and aimed for the two that were ahead of the rest. One got a bullet right above his nose, the other got it in his left eye. I was aiming for the middle of their foreheads. Like I said, not the most accurate weapon in the world. Fun fact; it turned out their brains looked about the same as ours do. I mean at least when they got blown out the back of their skulls. I have no idea how they'd compare if you did an autopsy.

"Was it good for you?"

I kept squeezing the trigger and going for head shots. Bang, bang, bang, bang, bang, they started to go down. I couldn't put the shots exactly where I wanted, but they were close enough.

"Yes! Yes! Yes! Give it to me, baby! Mommy's been a bad, bad girl!"

You know, I hate to admit this, but as I stood there just picking them off one after the other I started to understand why Viper liked guns. They're just convenient as hell. And if you're not worried about stealth they have better range, stopping power, and rate of fire than shuriken or kunai. I mean I'd absolutely keep using them, not just for tradition's sake, but because they're quieter than a gun with a silencer. Maybe it wouldn't be that horrible for ninja to come out of the sixteenth century. Guns are just tools, right? And a ninja should use whatever tools help her get the job done.

They kept coming. (Pun not intended. Maybe.) When I killed someone in front the ones behind would step on the body and keep right on coming. I was impressed. Take a bunch of regular guys and put them in that exact situation. I don't care who they are; gang bangers, mob men, yakuza, henchmen, or armed soldiers. If they saw someone shooting them like they were fish in a barrel, they'd break. They would panic and run away to save themselves, at the very least they'd stop and take cover. The only way that wouldn't happen is if they were all insane or had some real strong military discipline. Maybe those fuckers were soldiers, the space equivalent of Green Berets or Navy Seals. It's possible. But the way they smiled and shouted as they got blood and brains splashed on them made me think of Whiteface.

I clipped one of them. The shot must have gotten him right at the corner of his left eye. It blew out the eye and chunk of his face. He howled in pain, stumbled, pressed a hand to the bloody wreckage, but he kept running towards me. If that wasn't crazy I don't know what it.

"Oops, just a little to the left." I got off two more shots and saw the top of his head explode in a meaty shower. "That's the spot!"

Despite my rate of fire I couldn't kill them fast enough, they were definitely faster than ordinary humans, and they covered ground like NFL wide receivers. The survivors finally got within a couple arms lengths. I thumbed both guns to full auto.

"Here's the money shot!" I swept my arms left to right and right to left, pouring bullets into them. That was exactly what Uzis were made for. They were close enough for me to get blood splashed onto my face and clothes. Typical guys, not satisfied until they get their stuff all over a girl. Their bodies dropped at my feet. I squeezed the triggers until the guns stopped firing and dropped them to pull out both of my swords. "Was it good for you?"

After all that there were still three left. One had a hole in his left shoulder and a dead arm. In his right hand was a blade about a foot long.

My swords were four. "Look at that. Mine's bigger than yours." I slammed one of my swords through his chest and out his back. I know us girls like to say size doesn't matter, but it does. It really, really does.

I didn't even have enough time to wrench my sword free before another one was on top of me. He had daggers in both hands. He slashed at my throat with one and tried to stab me in the stomach with the other. I let go of the sword stuck through his friend and wrapped both hands around the hilt of my other one. I took two quick steps back. He didn't hesitate. The blue fucker jumped over the body of his friend and came at me. He came head on with his back straight, giving me his whole body as a target.

"Kaval gresh maak te!"

"Oh please, like I haven't heard that before." I reversed my grip and brought my sword down. Then rushed forward, hunched low. I slashed up with all the speed and power my metal limbs could give me. He tried to stab at me but missed. My sword caught him in his belly and cut deep and true all the way to his collar. I gutted him like a fish and watched as his organs spilled out. "Call me."

I had my sword in ready position for the last killer smurf. I was expecting him to charge in like all the others had, but unlike the rest he seemed to be suddenly infected with common sense. He'd tossed his blade and had instead taken out something that looked like a metal ram's horn and aimed it at me. I dived to my left and felt the heat of the beam on my cheek as it just missed me. As I hit the ground and rolled. I pulled out a kunai and was ready to throw.

The last alien was aiming at me and completely focused on my direction. He didn't notice when a figure dropped down from a rooftop to land behind him. The new arrival wore an ash gray trench coat and fedora and on his face was a black mask. With hardly an effort he knocked the laser from the alien's hand and then knocked the bastard out with a single punch.

This was how I finally met Dark Detective.

XXX

Raven's Rule #3 – Take help where you can get it.

Chapter 25

Every single time Doc and I went outside, whether it was for a job or to pick up some Chinese food, he always reminded me about who might show up.

"Do you have your gas mask with you?" He'd say. "Dark Detective could attack me at any moment."

It was sort of his version of, 'how are you doing?' I'd never met a guy with such a total obsession with another man. And my friend Leon insisted he was Colin Farrell's soulmate for about a year and a half. So before I ever actually met Dark Detective I knew all about him. Doc had told me how beneath the trench coat was an exo-suit that gave him protection and enhanced speed and strength. That he carried all sorts of different gadgets like grappling hooks and wire, night vision goggles, eavesdropping gear, lock picks, flash bombs, voice modulators, and his famous gas gun and gas mask. The biggest thing Doc always harped on was the personality; Dark Detective was cold, stern, and analytical.

To hear Doc tell it, the man had had his funny bone surgically removed.

"I've never seen him smile or even crack a grin," Doc had said. "He is always completely focused on the job. He won't kill, but he'll do anything short of that. He'll break bones or put someone through a wall without a second's hesitation. Don't trust anything he says or any promises he makes, he lies like a car salesman. He's a ruthless bastard and a master manipulator."

"You make him sound like a bad guy," I said.

Doc chuckled at that. "I sometimes wonder."

I had my one sword in hand and was ready to use it. I was more than half expecting him to attack me. Instead he stood over the alien he'd knocked out and calmly glanced up and down the street and up at the rooftops.

"You're Raven, Dr. Anarchy's lieutenant." He said politely.

I nodded. "I think of myself as his sidekick, but yeah, that's me." I didn't lower my guard.

"Where is your boss? He usually doesn't wait this long to attack me."

"He's occupied right now."

"Doing what exactly? Robbing a museum? Emptying a bank vault? Breaking into a tech lab?"

"None of the above. Dr. Anarchy sort of had to make an unexpected trip." I pointed straight up.

"He was teleported away by the Altarians?"

"That's right."

"He's not alone, thousands of people have been abducted. Even The Blur was taken right out of League headquarters."

"Great, I bet it's a real party up there. So do you heroes plan to do something about it?"

"Supersoldier, Amazon, and Iron Knight are all attacking the mothership. The rest of the League are on the ground fighting."

I looked up but didn't see anything, the ship was pretty damn big though, so the battle might have been going on somewhere else. "So are they smashing their way through and kicking all sorts of blue alien ass? That's what you guys do, right? Especially Supersoldier."

"The ship has a very strong energy barrier, we haven't broken through it yet."

"Figures."

"What exactly are you doing here?" Dark Detective asked. "Some sort of solo job now that your employer in gone?"

"I'm here to rescue him."

His mask covered all of his face north of his mouth, but the way his jaw slipped open made it easy to see he was surprised.

"Was that part of your contract? I wouldn't normally expect that sort of loyalty for someone outside of a ninja's clan."

"I'm impressed, most people don't know that much about real ninja."

"You're not the first one I've ever dealt with."

"Let's just say I've signed a long term deal with him, and it hasn't expired yet. Besides, 'Cooking with Wolfgang' is on later. If he misses it he'll be in a pissy mood the rest of the week."

Not even a hint of a smile. "Admirable, but misguided. In any case how do you plan to reach the ship? Anarchy didn't build rockets into your cybernetic limbs did he?" There was a pause. "He didn't, did he?"

"No, though that's not a bad idea for when he does the upgrade. Hell of a lot more useful than a damn chainsaw. I have a couple mini-jetpacks."

"That won't help you get through their barrier, assuming they don't just swat you out of the sky."

"Yeah, I didn't really think it would be that easy." I nodded over to the transport. "Maybe I can hitch a ride."

In one sudden move he reached into his trench coat and pulled out his gas gun with one hand. With the other he put on a gas mask. Just as quick I grabbed my own gas mask and slipped it over my mouth and nose.

"I can't let you do that," he said. "I need to get onboard to free The Blur and shut down the barrier. I can't have you getting in my way or raising the alarm."

"I wasn't asking permission, Dad." My voice sounded hollow.

"I promise to free your boss along with all the other prisoners on board."

"Thanks, but I'd feel just awful letting someone else do my job for me. If you want to tag along I don't mind."

"I don't work with criminals," he said flatly.

"Yeah? Well I usually don't work with guys who dress like it's nineteen thirty-eight and they're looking for a Nazi spy ring. But desperate times."

"This isn't about one man. There are thousands, no, millions of lives at stake. I can't let you jeopardize my mission."

"You know, a thought occurs to me. You're going to try and rescue your friend The Blur, but that is one big ass ship. Are you planning to go room to room or do you have some way to find him?"

"I'll interrogate some of the aliens or hack into their computer system."

"Will that work? They don't speak English and I doubt their computer code is written in Java or C plus, plus. They also probably have some good firewalls. I know you're a genius and all, but it might be kind of hard."

"I'll manage. I always find a way."

"No doubt, but it might be easier to use this." I pulled the tracker out. "This will lead me straight to wherever Dr.

Anarchy is. If they're holding everyone in the same place it'll also lead me to your friend."

He was silent for a moment. "I could just take that from you."

"You could try."

Another long moment as he considered. "All right, but you follow my lead and do exactly as I say."

"So long as it doesn't involve a condom or making a lasagna, sure thing."

I finally put my sword back in its sheath. I yanked the other one out of the chest it was in, reloaded both Uzis, slung the duffel over a shoulder and followed Dark Detective onto the transport. It was completely empty inside. Not only was there no equipment or any sort of supplies, there weren't even any seats.

"Guess they're not real big on comfort."

He didn't answer. He was standing at the front of the transport. There was a small console that was about three feet by two feet and covered with maybe a hundred big, shiny, candy-like buttons. He stood there studying them. I waited a minute, but he didn't do anything. He just stood there.

"You plan on pressing one of them, chief?"

"There's no way to know what any of these will do. I am trying to discern which one is the most likely to bring us to their mothership."

"Let's try one of the red ones." I reached out a hand, but he swatted it away and glared at me.

"What are you doing?"

"What's it look like? We're not going to get anywhere just standing here."

"Don't start pushing them at random, there may be some sort of pattern to their lay out."

"They're buttons on a giant keyboard, not a piece of wall art. And while we stand here with our thumbs up our asses Dr. Anarchy might be getting dissected."

"That's also true of The Blur, but acting rashly and without thought is never a good idea. In any case, there's more at stake than the fate of any one man. Never let personal feelings get in the way of reaching your goal."

"Wow. You really are a prick, aren't you?"

"I've been called worse." He turned his attention back to the console.

"Dr. Anarchy knows you're Neil Kane."

I saw the corner of his mouth twitch. It was a small reaction that only lasted a second. Son of a bitch, Doc was right.

"That's ridiculous." He said with the same flat tone.

"Whatever you say, Neil."

He didn't respond and continued to look over the board. I didn't get what he was trying to figure out, it wasn't like there was an instruction manual or anything.

"So do you have a detective license?"

He turned to frown at me. "What?"

"I was just wondering. You call yourself Dark Detective, but are you actually a licensed detective?"

"Your question is ridiculous."

"Does that mean you don't have one?"

"Dark Detective is my identity, not a job title."

"So in other words you're not actually a detective. Someone should sue you for false advertisement."

He returned to staring at the panel.

While all this was happening the door to the transport remained open. I could hear gunfire going off like firecrackers. There were car crashes and the faint echo of screams. The smell of smoke got a little stronger as I waited. We were wasting time. All I could think about was Doc, up there, a scared prisoner and at the mercy of those sadistic fucks.

"All right," he suddenly said. "I'll try this." He pressed the yellow button at the upper left-hand corner and several more in a line. The transport shook and staggered into the air. There was a loud smashing sound that had to be us crashing into the side of a building. There were no windows so I couldn't see where we were going. The door was still wide open though, I could see bricks and hunks of plaster flying about. He pressed some more buttons. I felt the ship lurch to the side and would have gone ass over head if not for my reflexes. We finally straightened out and were going straight up like an elevator.

He nodded. "Looks like that was the correct pattern."

I looked at the console and the buttons he'd pressed down. "Yeah, it's called diagonal! I could have done that!"

"The point is we should be returning to the mothership. The moment we dock you need to follow my lead. Our goal is to find the prisoners and then disable the ship."

"That's your goal, white man. My job is to save Dr. Anarchy. I'll work with you until we find him. After that we go our separate ways."

He crossed his arms over his chest and tried to be imposing. "Don't you care about stopping the invasion?"

"Nope. Not even a little."

"If we don't bring down the energy barrier there's no way the League will be able to defeat the Altarians! They'll continue to slaughter and abduct people completely unchecked!"

"Yeah. I get all that, I just don't care."

"How can you be so indifferent to the fate of so many?"

I shrugged. "Ninja."

"Fine," he said with obvious disgust. "Just bring me to where the prisoners are. The Blur and I will take care of the rest."

"Sure thing, chief. You do the hero stuff and I'll get Dr. Anarchy and myself to safety."

"The odds would improve if we all worked together."

"Odds of what? Getting killed? Listen, this is already a suicide mission. If, by some miracle, I reach Anarchy and free him we're going to escape. You want to stick your dick into a meat grinder? Be my guest."

Through the open door I could see the city dropping away. There were an impressive number of smoke clouds. The ship gave a little shudder.

"We're passing through the energy barrier," Dark Detective said. "Once we dock we have to try and keep as low a profile as possible and avoid notice."

"Hey, ninja practically invented the whole idea of being stealthy. I'll be a shadow on the wall."

A port opened and we entered the mother ship without a hitch. We kept rising until there was a loud 'klang' and we stopped. There was a metal walkway right outside the open door. Peeking out I saw we were in a massive bay with hundreds of interconnected walkways leading to empty spaces. So far as I could see we were the only transport docked. I whipped out my tracker.

"Dr. Anarchy is one point three miles northwest of us and point three miles above us. Just a short jog away."

"A short jog on board an alien ship we know nothing about, surrounded by hostile and lethal enemies."

"Yeah, well if it were easy it'd be boring."

Dark Detective and I ran out onto the walkway and towards the far wall. We crossed intersection after intersection and vacant space after vacant space. How many transports had there been? Hundreds definitely, maybe thousands. What a gigantic clusterfuck. Well it wasn't my problem. I only cared about one person. If that sounds selfish, fine. It wasn't the world that saved my ass and gave me my life back. It wasn't the world that let me get my revenge or gave me something to live for again.

As we were running I couldn't help notice something. "You know, it's a little weird one of their ships came back and there's not a single person here to greet it."

Dark Detective grunted. "I agree, it's suspicious."

Past all the walkways was a wall with a line of doors. We had almost reached them when one of the doors slid open. There were maybe ten Altarians. I yanked out both Uzis.

"We come in peace!" I squeezed down the triggers and blazed away at full auto. I saw them all go down in a bloody heap. Yeah, I was definitely starting to like guns. I ejected the spent clips and slapped in fresh ones. The other doors began to open and more visitors arrived. "So much for sneaking around."

"We can't fight our way through." Dark Detective put on his gas mask and had his gas gun ready. He fired one shell into the deck to our right and one to the left. Thick yellow smoke filled the air.

I had my own gas mask on. The aliens all began to choke and stumble around. "How much more of that stuff have you got?"

"Not enough." He looked around. "Follow me." He jumped off the walkway, down to the bottom of the ship. Not seeing much of a choice I jumped down too.

He ran past where the wall above us was. There were circular vents, about three feet wide. There were bars but he tore them off.

"After you," he said.

It would be a tight squeeze, but nothing I couldn't handle. There wouldn't be enough room for the duffel bag though. I took half a dozen magazines and a few grenades and then crawled in. Dark Detective was right in behind me. About thirty seconds later we heard the port open and felt a sudden rush of air. With any luck the killer smurfs would think we'd taken a fall.

"You have the tracker, so lead the way."

"Okay. And even though you're going to be staring at my sexy ass don't get any weird ideas. I'm a pure and virtuous girl."

He grunted.

XXX

Raven's Rule #4 – When life gives you lemons make lemonade. Then find some gin to mix with it.

Chapter 26

I'd actually been through air ducts before, and sewers. I'd hidden out in garbage bins and tramped through swamps and graveyards. I once sat inside a cupboard for eighteen hours just to kill some douchebag executive. What I hadn't ever done was cover more than a mile crawling on hands and knees. Oh, and obviously I'd never been in an alien spaceship or worked with one of the most famous superheroes in the world. So it was a pretty memorable day. Since my arms and legs were artificial it wasn't as bad as it could have been. But crawling all that way in such a confined space was definitely not fun. Naturally, I decided to entertain myself as I inched along.

"So Neil, what do you think of Dr. Anarchy?"

"I've told you before, I'm not Neil Kane."

"Sure you're not. So what do you think of him?"

There was a short pause. "He's capable, very intelligent, organized, and driven. He took my exo-suit over by remote control once. Clearly, a worthy adversary."

I smiled to myself. I knew how much Doc would love to hear that, but Dark Detective wasn't done yet.

"If he weren't so predictable he would be a real threat."

I stopped crawling. If there'd been room to turn around I would have. Instead I put my head down to look back at him through my limbs. "What does that mean? He's incredibly dangerous!"

"He is, but only within certain limits. Much the same way highways are dangerous, but within specific patterns. Late evening and high volume times are statistically far more likely to see accidents than say early afternoons. If you know what to expect you can act accordingly."

"You don't know what you're talking about."

"Your current base is located in New Jersey, somewhere within fifty miles of the New York City limits. It's most likely a factory or warehouse and has at least two escape routes." There was a hint of smugness.

"Wow. That is so totally wrong. Not even in the ball park."

"Has he told you I'm his nemesis?"

Fuck. I guess he did know Doc pretty well. "He might have said that once or twice. Do you think of him that way?"

"Anarchy is one of my regular opponents and part of my rogues' gallery. Whiteface is my nemesis."

"You know, everyone says that, but when you really stop and think about it, why? I mean Dr. Anarchy doesn't have any issue killing people, and he has got to be more lethal than Whiteface. I mean has that psycho ever built a killbot or giant robot with a chainsaw?"

I saw the upside down face give a small nod. "Yes, he kills people and his inventions are dangerous, but he constrains himself by following rules."

I sighed. "Okay, you've got me there, he does love his rules. But he works his ass off to be the best supervillain he can be, that should count for something."

Dark Detective shook his head. "Effort isn't what makes you dangerous, it's the end result."

"So you're more worried about a psycho who loves razors and acid than someone who can build a forty foot giant robot?"

"Whiteface is dangerous because he's so unpredictable. One day he might kidnap a bus full of school children, the next he might set a bomb in Yankee Stadium, and the next he might break into the museum of art just to spray graffiti everywhere. I can never guess what he'll do next. By comparison, your boss is predictable and easy to counter."

"Oh, yeah? Did you see him flying a giant robot into the city that one time?"

"Yes."

"Bullshit."

"I didn't know he would use a giant robot, but I did expect him to lash out following the incident with Power Princess. Given the circumstance I knew he would react that way. I knew precisely what actions he would take the moment I sent her to your location. And he did not disappoint."

I frowned. I didn't like the dismissive tone in his voice or the way he was taking Doc for granted. "You should have more respect for him. He's an amazing man."

"I never said he wasn't. Only that he was easy to anticipate. Now, can we continue moving? The sooner I find The Blur the sooner we can bring this ship down."

"Fine," I muttered and started crawling again.

XXX

We had to climb straight up for a lot of levels and double back one time, but eventually the tracker took us to our goal. I came to a metal grate that was only fifty-two feet from where Doc was. As quietly as I could, I ripped the thing down and pulled it into the vent and looked into the room.

"Oh fuck me," I whispered. "It's like something out of a sci-fi movie." What I saw was unbelievable, and I'm a cyborg ninja who works in a supervillain lair.

"Are there any guards?" Dark Detective asked. His only view was still of my ass.

"None that I can see."

"Well what exactly do you see?"

"Rows of people hanging in the air."

What I saw were eight rows of metal disks floating. Beneath each one was a stream of red light, and suspended inside each light was a person. Men, women, and children floated there unmoving. I saw one was a police officer, there was a woman with just a garter belt and bra on, a boy in pajamas, and an old man who was naked and holding a sponge in one hand. It really did look like something from a movie. Other than the light from the disks the rest of the room was dark. I couldn't see any of the walls or ceiling, and the rows of light stretched out further than I could make out. None of the people close enough for me to see were Doc.

I pulled myself out of the shaft and leapt down. The second my feet touched the floor I was moving. There was a kunai in one hand and my eyes were darting back and forth, looking for any surprises. No alarms sounded and I didn't see any aliens anywhere. Behind me I heard Dark Detective land. He wasn't following me, no doubt he was looking for his pal. I didn't care. The tracker counted down the distance until I saw him.

There was Doc. His mouth and eyes were open, a hand frozen in mid wave. His feet were a foot above the ground. The disc floated about ten feet above. I had no idea how high the ceiling was. I could attach a rope up there and crawl up to have a closer look at the disk, but from my original view none of them seemed to have any buttons or controls. Even if they did I had no idea what to push.

"Well, it's not like standing here will get me anywhere."

I reached in with both hands. I felt resistance, as if I was pushing through mud. It wasn't painful or anything, but there was something there. I grabbed hold of his lab coat with both hands, set my feet, and with one yank I pulled him all the way out and onto me.

"-hero." He said. Then he blinked his eyes and looked about startled. "What? Where am I?"

"Doc!" I was so unbelievably happy to have him back I did something on pure instinct without thinking.

I kissed him.

I put my lips to his and pressed them down. I was just so damn relieved and excited to see him alive and well that it just sort of happened. And it wasn't some little peck on the lips. It was a passionate, full on, come here to momma, you belong to me, kind of kiss. For about two seconds I just enjoyed it. Then my brain switched back on and I realized what I was doing. I suddenly stopped, let go of him, and jumped back as though he might have cooties.

Doc stood there for a moment with his jaw open. He finally spoke. "What's going on?"

"Nothing! It… it was a sudden impulse. It doesn't mean anything! It's not like I like you that way so don't get any weird ideas! It was a onetime thing that will never happen again so don't expect me to ever kiss you again! Got it?"

He stared at me, then slowly shook his head. "Uh, I mean where are we?"

"Oh," I breathed a sigh of relief. "You got abducted by the aliens. I came up here to rescue you. Dark Detective came with me too. Hey, did you get probed? If you did, did you like it? Cause if you did I have a friend named Leon I could introduce you to. By the way, I'm on my period right now and it's a heavy flow."

He gaped at me with his jaw open again. I just stood there and prayed he didn't ask me about the kiss. That would be weird.

XXX

Raven's Rule #5 – When all else fails just tell everyone you're PMSing. Even if they don't believe you they won't ask for details.

Chapter 27

One moment I'd been in my lab thinking about moving my operations to Los Angeles. The next I was being kissed by Raven. (Not that I was complaining.) She released me and I noticed there was a bald man floating behind her with his penis in his hand as though in the middle of urinating. There were the bodies of people everywhere, suspended in midair and unmoving. Everything was bathed in red. It felt as though I were in the midst of some vast hellish morgue. If all that weren't jarring enough, there was a buzzing in my head and weird images flashing through my mind. Raven was the one normal element in all this, standing there making some silly joke about probes.

I closed my eyes and put both hands over my face. The buzzing in my head began to die down. Raven said I'd been abducted by the Altarians. Well, that would explain things. She'd mentioned something else that I found even more important.

"Hey, Doc, you okay?"

I felt her put one hand on my shoulder. I took a deep breath and dropped my hands.

"Dark Detective is here too?"

Raven rolled her eyes. "Typical. I rescue you after you get abducted and the first thing you worry about is your boyfriend. Yeah, he's here. We ran into each other and decided to work together to find you. Now he's looking for The Blur so they can bust this ship up from the inside. While they're doing that, we'll get our asses out of here. I've got two mini-jetpacks. We'll find an exit, or I'll make one. We can jump out and fly to safety. With any luck the heroes will keep the aliens so distracted they won't notice us."

While Raven was talking I turned to see my old nemesis run past. He saw me and gave a quick nod of acknowledgement and kept running. Somehow seeing him tinted red and going past me was the strangest aspect of all. I kept looking in his direction as he crossed over and started running back in my direction between different rows of suspended bodies.

"Hey! Are you listening to me?" Raven grabbed my jaw and wrenched my face back towards her. "Listen Doc, now is not the time to worry about telling your man crush about your feelings. We need to get the fuck out of here."

"Evots cro ne."

Raven's eyes widened. "What?"

"I said I know that."

"And what language was that?"

"What are you talking about?"

Raven opened her mouth and then snapped it shut. "Never mind, let's just get out of here." She grabbed my hand and began to lead me. "I'll have to boost you up to the air duct."

The buzzing in my head had died away and been replaced by an ache. I felt a little bit in a fog. In my mind's eyes I saw planets and moons that were no part of the Sol system. There were advanced equations in my head that used numbers from a thirteen digit numbering system and words made up of symbols that were not from any alphabet I knew. But all the jumble of facts and images were familiar to me somehow.

The knowledge of how to build a teleporter was as normal as the fact I'd graduated from New Bedford High School and gone on to MIT. It was confusing and made sense, both at the same time. I rubbed my temples and tried to focus on what was most important.

"What did Dark Detective say about me?"

"Seriously?"

"I was just curious if he said anything."

"Okay fine, during study hall he told me that you're the prettiest girl in school and he wants to take you to prom. I'm so happy for you." She bent over. "Now climb on my shoulders so I can boost you up to the air vent."

"Do you have to sound so emasculating?"

"I think we both know the answer to that is yes. Now come on, the sooner I get you up there the sooner we can get out of this place."

I was just beginning to maneuver around her when Dark Detective ran up to us.

"The Blur's not here. He's not among any of these people."

Me nemesis wasn't speaking to me, he hadn't even acknowledged me. He was talking to Raven who was still bent over.

"That's awful," she said. "Good luck wrecking everything on your own."

"I need your help to locate him."

Raven stood up and shook her head. "Sorry, that wasn't any part of our deal. You're on your own from here on out."

"You don't understand the situation. With The Blur it would be child's play to cause this ship significant damage. Without him-"

I couldn't stand it anymore and just snapped. "Ka ve rez Dark Detective orolk ke!"

Both of them turned to stare at me. "What did you just say?" Dark Detective asked.

"I said you were unforgivably rude!"

"Okay," Raven questioned. "But in what language?"

"What are you talking about? I just..." And it was then I recalled the exact words I'd spoken. I hadn't been using English.

"You were using the alien language just now." Dark Detective glanced about the room at all the suspended figures and the discs floating above them. "This technology must not only leave its victims in suspended animation, but also give them some sort of subliminal education."

I shut my eyes and rubbed my temples again. Trust my nemesis to see the obvious before I could. Well, I'd been teleported and tampered with by an alien race. Most people would consider that a valid excuse for being a little slow witted.

"Yes. I suppose so. Apparently, the Altarians use slaves. It would be annoying to have slaves who can't speak your language and are ignorant of what you consider basic information."

Dark Detective took a step towards me, his face grim. "How much do you know? Do you know where The Blur is?"

I was familiar with his expression and tone. He wanted answers and would try to beat them out of me if they weren't forthcoming. Typical.

"You could try asking a little more politely."

"I don't care about offending you Anarchy," he cracked his knuckles. "Tell me what you know. Now."

Without a sound, Raven slid in between us and drew one of her swords. "Watch it, Neil. He doesn't take orders from you."

I was surprised to hear Raven call him by his real first name. I was much less surprised to see his stance widen and both hands rise into a fighting posture. This was the usual procedure when dealing with Dark Detective. He would start off demanding you give him what he wanted, and if you didn't he immediately turned to violence. What could objectively only be called criminal behavior, but he was one of the world's greatest heroes. Go figure.

"I don't know where The Blur is. This ship has over a thousand containment facilities, he could be in any one of them."

Dark Detective grimaced for a moment, then narrowed his eyes. "Does that mean you know the layout of this ship?"

The question caught me off guard. I had to think about it. I suddenly pictured miles of corridors and hundreds of thousands of different rooms. I knew how to get to the engines or the command center. I knew where the commissaries were, the infirmaries, the repair shops, and the slave quarters were all known to me. I could find anything on this ship as easily as I could navigate through one of my secret bases.

"That's right, I know this ship."

"Then you know the best way to sabotage it. You're going to help me." The way he said it, it was clear he wasn't asking.

"Wrong, chief." Raven snarled. "The boss and I are leaving."

"Anarchy can help me save millions of innocent lives."

"I don't care. Fuck them. Anarchy is the only one who matters to me."

Dark Detective and Raven both tensed. They were done talking.

"I'll help you," I said. "But I want you to do one thing for me."

They both turned to stare at me.

"What?" Dark Detective asked.

"There's something I've been obsessing about for some time now. Something I need from you."

"Seriously?!" Raven cried in disbelief. "You know all those times I teased you about being in love with him I was kidding, right?"

"Raven-"

"Fine! Like I even care! Go ahead and whip it out. You," she pointed at Dark Detective. "Get on your knees and pucker up. I'll stand over there and watch and pretend I'm not filming you with my camera phone."

I closed my eyes and put a hand over my face. "For the last time, I'm not gay."

"I know. Being bi is cool."

Dark Detective shook his head silently.

I sighed. "I want you to answer one question. Why did you make me the graduation test for Power Princess?"

"What does it matter?"

"It matters because I say it does," I snapped. "We haven't run into each other in months. I assumed you were too busy with other cases. But the fact is you found out where my secret base was. You should have broken in and come after me yourself. That's your normal modus operandi. Instead, you sent a thirteen year old girl on a fucking graduation test. I want to know why."

"And If I tell you, you'll help me bring this ship down?"

I nodded.

"I didn't want Power Princess to join the League of Heroes. She had no real commitment to fighting crime, she just wanted to be famous. That's not the sort of member we need. We're the last line of defense for the world, we need people who are completely committed to the cause and willing to make any sacrifice necessary."

"Then why not just deny her membership?" I asked. "You do that all the time, most superheroes can't even get an interview."

"If it were up to me she would have never gotten in the door. Unfortunately, Supersoldier liked her." His face grimaced.

"And what?" Raven asked. "He always gets his way?"

"Pretty much. He only has one vote, but everyone just naturally wants to follow where he leads. No one wants to disappoint him."

"So he's the coolest kid in class?" She chortled. "Sounds like High School."

"Supersoldier is the world's greatest hero and he's saved this entire planet at least three times. He's more than earned his position as leader of the League." Dark Detective paused. "That doesn't mean every decision he makes is a good one. He saw her as a little girl fighting to make her dreams come true. And, well, he can be surprisingly soft hearted at times. I can usually make him see reason-"

"By which you mean you can manipulate him." I said.

"But this time I couldn't change his mind." He continued without denying my accusation. "He did agree to let me choose her opponent for the graduation test."

"I see, now it makes sense. You really are ruthless aren't you? You sent her to me expecting me to kill her and solve your problem for you."

"Kill her?" Dark Detective sounded genuinely surprised. "I sent her to you for the opposite reason."

I frowned. "I don't understand."

"I knew she would broadcast the fight. I had every confidence you'd be able to defeat her, without killing her. Losing and having her secret identity revealed would be enough."

"Wait. How could you possibly know I wouldn't kill her? I'm a ruthless, cold-blooded supervillain. I've killed hundreds of people."

"Yes, but almost all of them were your own henchmen, opposing henchmen, evil organization soldiers, or other criminals. You've killed guards and civilians, but not wantonly. You most definitely haven't ever killed any heroes, even when you had them prisoner. You're someone who follows the rules. I knew you'd be a safe choice."

I felt my stomach drop. I felt sick. "You used me."

He gave an indifferent shrug. "I'll use anyone who can help me get the job done."

I knew just how true that was. I'd seen him manipulate gangs and mob bosses and even other heroes into doing whatever he wanted. He was a chess master who always knew exactly what to say or do to get someone to take a specific action. He'd played me. I'd been nothing more than another piece on the board. He'd used me the same way he would have a random drug dealer or second rate hitman.

The fact he'd used me wasn't what cut so deep. If I'd been the key to some complex scheme to stop Dr. Death or avert a World War I could have accepted it. There's no disgrace in being outmaneuvered by Dark Detective. No. What made me sick was the fact he'd used me to keep a thirteen year old girl from joining his little club. Off the top of my head I could think of at least a dozen supervillains who could have done the same. He hadn't tapped me because I was uniquely qualified to handle Power Princess. I'd simply been the most convenient option. On Dark Detective's board I wasn't a rook or bishop or even a knight. I was just another pawn.

It was kind of funny, but I finally understood. To him I was simply another supervillain, more dangerous than some, less dangerous than others, but nothing truly special. I felt empty and sick and pathetic and angry. I was the nice guy who did everything for a pretty girl, only to end up watching her make out with some random guy on the dancefloor right after I'd spent the whole day helping her move into her new apartment and not even gotten a beer or slice of pizza out of it.

Not that I knew what that was like.

I looked him straight in the eye. "You're an asshole."

He nodded. "A lot of people think so. Now, how do we bring this ship down?"

XXX

The room was filled with work stations. People sat at desks looking at displays and tapping buttons at their computers. There was casual conversation among the workers. Some talked about the major events going on, more wanted to know who was dating whom and who was in trouble with management. It was a scene not unlike any corporate office or call center. If the employees happened to be blue skinned aliens from across the galaxy and the workplace happened to be an alien spacecraft.

At the very center of the room a silver ball floated in a beam of blueish light. No one paid the orb any special attention. It was just a part of their everyday environment, like the lights or computer terminals. Even though their people were in the midst of an invasion there was no sense of excitement among the dozen workers. It was an ordinary day.

So they were all rather caught off guard when the grate to the air vent was punched out and Raven leapt down. She landed behind one of the workers while he was still seated at his desk. Her sword went through the back of his neck and out again before he even got out of his seat. Dark Detective jumped down right behind her. He had his gas gun out and fired a shell into the floor. A thick gray cloud fountain up. Many of the aliens began choking and grabbing at their throats. They were panicking and shouting at each other. I understood their words. 'Help!' 'What is this?' 'They killed Raklik!' 'Get out!' 'Run!' It seemed even among a warrior race, office workers were still office workers. A couple of them charged Dark Detective and Raven. He delivered a kick to the stomach that doubled his opponent over before knocking him out. Raven took the head off hers with one swipe of her sword.

I was still up in the vent. I knew what sort of fighters both of them were and didn't doubt they could handle a dozen Altarians. As Raven slaughtered them and Dark Detective punched them, a couple of the aliens ran for the door. I shot them with my disintegrator. In under a minute it was over.

All the Altarians were either dead or unconscious. I pulled myself out of the vent and fell down to the floor. I was nowhere near as graceful landing as my companions, but I managed. As Raven helped me up to my feet Dark Detective crossed his arms and glared. He's very good at glaring.

"I don't know if they raised the alarm."

"They didn't." I hurried over to one of the consoles and sat down. "Trust me, you'd know if they had." I looked at the display which was projected a couple feet above my head. It was about power consumption on levels forty-two through one hundred and eleven. I began typing on the console and accessed the command menu.

"Are you sure you can bring down the energy barrier from here?"

I pointed to the silver ball that was floating in the middle of the room. "That's an Altarian generator. It has an energy output equal to a dwarf star. They can use just one to run an entire planet. From here I have access to all the systems on this ship."

Dark Detective frowned. "If that's true why would they leave this place undefended?"

"The Altarians have a warrior culture. They only value weapons and force, they view everything else as superfluous. They see their generator about the same way we see our sewer systems."

I began to scroll through various menus and lists. Their language and vocabulary were as easy for me to read as English. There were no security protocols or passwords, from my terminal I had unlimited access to the ship's primary systems. It would seem the Altarians had just assumed that no enemy would ever try and attack them through their own computer network. For such an advanced race you would think they would at least limit access with pass codes or biometric identification. But they were about as concerned with on line security as a thirteen year old visiting his first porn site.

I spent a few minutes just familiarizing myself with the computer system and seeing what I could actually do. I was amazed to discover that from my seat I had full access to almost all the ship's systems, except for navigation and weapons. The ship had an ungodly array of lasers, plasma cannons, rail guns, and gravitational beams. They could have easily reduced New York to blackened ash with a single burst if they had wanted to. For that matter, they could have annihilated human civilization from orbit in under an hour. And the precious League, Section Seven, and all the world's secret organizations and militaries wouldn't have been able to touch them. In the end it's always raw power that counts. Clever plans and a brilliant mind don't really mean anything if your opponent is a hundred times more powerful than you.

But was that really true?

I glanced at the silver ball with the energy output of a star. The Altarians were a warrior culture with technology far beyond Earth's and more than enough weaponry to fry the planet. They should have been completely unbeatable. But they were going to lose. From my computer terminal I could shut off all their systems and leave them deaf, blind, and crippled. The League would do the rest. It didn't really make sense, given all their advantages the Altarians should have won. Yet with all their might they had weak points and so would lose. The same way Dr. Death had lost, and The Master and Professor Power and Novalord. All men with immense power who'd managed to rule the world for a time, only to eventually fail. What was the lesson there? That you could have enough power to conquer the world, but not enough to keep it? That if you went too far you would create so many enemies that some were bound to find some weakness and exploit it? Could anyone really conquer the world permanently?

"This is taking too long," Dark Detective growled. He stood over me, trying to be imposing.

Raven shoved him and forced him back a step. "Watch it, you're not in charge here."

"This has nothing to do with who's in charge, we could be discovered at any moment."

The two of them were nose to nose. Raven was gripping her sword and he had both hands balled into fists.

I called up a different screen with the outline of the ship. Surrounding it was an unbroken blue track. "I'm sorry I'm not working fast enough for you, Neil. Do you want to give it a try? I know you can't read Altarian, but I'm sure it would be a snap for you."

"You need to hurry. If the aliens find us you'll be in just as much trouble as me. And as I've already told your lieutenant, I'm not Neil Kane."

"Then I guess you wouldn't care if I said Thomas Kane was a drunk, a liar, and a philanderer who slept with every actress and model in New York and drove his poor, stupid wife to take all those pills."

The part of his face not covered by the mask turned red. "That's a damn lie!"

I'm sure he would have attacked me, but Raven was in his way.

"Something wrong, Dark Detective?" I asked him, calm and serene. "You're not Neil Kane, so there's no reason for you to be upset, is there?"

He glared at me. It was obvious he wanted to beat the hell out of me. Raven tensed and was ready to fight. He was one of the world's great heroes and a genius. But he was also a violent man who enjoyed beating people. He never held back when he fought, and had put quite a number of folk in the hospital. The fact his violence was only directed towards criminals didn't make him any less of a thug. I confess, it gave me a certain childish satisfaction to hurt him.

"Don't play games with me or you'll regret it, Anarchy."

"Making threats, there's the Dark Detective I know and love." I pressed a few more buttons and the blue line on the screen vanished. "There, I've just cut off all power to the barrier."

Almost instantly a shrill alarm sounded. Maybe half a minute later I could feel vibrations through the floor as the entire ship shook.

"That'll be Supersoldier, Amazon, and Iron Knight." Dark Detective said. "Even as massive as this thing is it won't stay airborne long."

"Too bad it's going to crash into Manhattan." Raven said.

Dark Detective nodded. "It is, but there's no avoiding it."

I pulled up a different screen. "Actually there is." I inputted some commands and everything began to shake. The floor suddenly tilted to about a thirty degree angle. I had to plant my feet and grab the chair with one hand to keep from being tossed off.

"What did you do?" Dark Detective demanded.

"I just cut off all power to the port propulsion system and reduced the starboard side by ninety-five percent. The result is we'll start dropping out of the sky at an angle. We'll crash either into the Hudson or into New Jersey." I kept working, it was harder since I could only use one hand.

While I struggled just to remain seated and work the computer Dark Detective and Raven stayed on their feet without any apparent trouble.

"You're saving Manhattan?" Dark Detective sounded suspicious.

"Why wouldn't I? It's not like I gain anything if most of the island gets turned into a crash site."

"Well that's great and all," Raven said. "But you do know we're about to all die, right? I was sort of expecting it when I drove out, but I wouldn't mind if there were some way we could get out of this alive."

"I am way ahead of you." I said as different screens flashed up. "I can access their teleportation system. I am sending all the people who were abducted down to Central Park." I glanced at Neil. "Including The Blur, of course. We can all escape before this ship goes down."

The alarm was still blaring. The whole place was shaking and the angle of the floor was slowly getting worse. We were surrounded by the dead and unconscious and the air was still smoky with gas. Yet he stood there, looking down on me as if we were in a bank vault or museum; as though passing judgement on me.

"You're acting like a hero," was what he finally said.

"You sound disappointed."

"Your kind never changes. Even when your sort does the right thing it's never for the right reason, there's always some ulterior motive."

"I'm saving thousands of lives, does my motive matter?"

"It matters because someone like you can't be trusted."

I smiled at him. "Maybe you just can't stand to be wrong. Everyone and everything has to fall within your expectations. Even though I'm a supervillain can't I simply want to save all those people?"

"No."

"Fine," I sighed. "I'm hoping this will be enough to earn a Presidential pardon and have my criminal record expunged. I'm tired of all the pointless battles and constant hiding. I want to get out of this lifestyle and try being one of the good guys for a change."

Dark Detective stared at me as though I'd grown a second head.

Raven looked as though she'd been gut punched. "Really? But what about building giant robots with chainsaws? Or disintegrating people or building death mazes? You love that stuff!"

"Even if you got a pardon, there's no way you could be a hero." Dark Detective said. "Once a criminal always a criminal."

I tapped in certain coordinates. "You think so? Well in that case I guess I'll just take over this ship and use it to conquer the world."

"I knew it!"

I smiled at him. "Bye, Neil." I pressed a button and he disappeared.

Raven blinked. "Teleporter?"

"Yep."

"Let me guess, you sent him to the center of the Earth?"

"No, I just dumped him into the Hudson."

"You didn't kill him?"

"As much of an asshole as he is, killing him would bring the whole League down on my head. I have something else in mind." I reset the controls. "Go grab the silver ball for me. It's time for us to go."

The Altarian generator was the single most powerful device ever seen on Earth. It could incinerate the planet in an instant. Compared to it a hydrogen bomb was a child's toy.

Raven ran over to the beam of light and snatched it as easily as plucking a piece of fruit. As soon as she was back by my side I carefully stood and pressed a button.

In the next instant we were in one of the storage rooms in my secret base. Raven's eyes widened as she gawked at all the stuff that filled the room. Stacks of weapons, pieces of machinery, crystal data rods, an alien shuttle, bars of unique metals, and other equipment surrounded us.

"Whoa! What is all this shit?"

"The spoils of victory, just a few things that might be useful." I took the silver ball from her, this ultimate weapon. With it I could put my plan into action.

XXX

Rule #27 – It's fine to do something heroic and save the day, just so long as you have a valid reason. (Getting a doomsday device is ALWAYS a valid reason.)

<u>Chapter 28</u>

After our escape the Altarian dreadnaught plummeted into the Jersey landscape as its engines lost all power. The explosion was pretty damn spectacular, I watched it online later. It was about what you would expect from a five mile long ship crashing to Earth. I doubt the fires were even out before the entire crash site was cordoned off by the FBI, National Guard, and Section Seven. They made the air space above it a no fly zone and put up miles of plywood and canvas to keep anyone from looking in. They'll be going through the wreckage for years. The Altarian survivors (who could be captured alive) all disappeared. No doubt they're enjoying the hospitality Section Seven gives to alien invaders. Supersoldier got most of the credit for saving New York, with the rest of the League getting some too.

Raven and I weren't mentioned. Everyone just assumed that Supersoldier did so much damage the ship crashed. That asshole, Dark Detective, apparently didn't tell anyone about our part. Not that it was really a problem or anything, I mean for a supervillain getting a Presidential pardon is the ultimate black mark. Even if you go back to trying to conquer the world the community will never fully respect you again.

But still, that fucker could have said something!

I found out about all this later. When Raven and I materialized the first thing I did was get to my lab and secure the generator. I locked it inside a safe, put a force field around the safe, and posted every single one of my killbots outside the shield with orders to terminate anyone other than myself or Raven who approached within twenty feet of the lab. The second thing I did was ask Raven if she wanted me to think of her as my girlfriend. She rolled her eyes and told me not to press my luck. After that I locked myself in the lab and got to work. I had a lot to do.

I worked for ten solid hours and then fell asleep. When I woke up it was early morning of the next day. I watched some CNN and went on line to get caught up on events. I saw the footage of the crash, listened to the sound bites from the President and the mayor and others about how brave the superheroes and police were and how scary things had been and blah, blah, blah. It was the usual routine. In a week everyone would have moved on and not even notice the wreckage of a giant alien spaceship lying there across the Hudson. And the mere fact it's referred to as the, 'Altarian

Incident' proves my point. It didn't seem like an 'incident' when their ship was floating above Manhattan.

But I digress.

I returned to my lab to double check on my work and on the generator. I took it out of the safe and held it in my hand. My very own doomsday device. For a supervillain it's the ultimate status symbol. It's what separates the genuine threats from the wanna be's and posers. And what I had in my hand was the real deal, not something to destroy a city or kill off thousands of clueless civilians, but an honest to goodness, 'tremble before me you fools or I will end all life on this wretched planet' sort of thing. Just having it in my possession was guaranteed to put me in the top five of the Most Wanted List.

I'm going to make a confession, right here, right now. When Dr. Death was emperor of the world and making all those stupid public broadcasts I was jealous. Even if it was just for a short time, he WON. Everyone on Earth, the US government, the UN, the Russians, the Chinese, even Supersoldier and the heroes had to acknowledge him as undisputed ruler of the world. How cool is that? And yeah, loudmouths in sports bars mocked him, but you can bet none of them would have dared to do it to his face. So what if he only stayed in power for six days and nothing really changed? He took on the whole fucking world and beat them, Supersoldier included. Isn't that the ultimate triumph? The ultimate success? Alexander the Great died at thirty-two, Caesar only ruled Rome a few years before his assassination, and Napoleon ended his life in exile on a damp little island, but so what? They are all immortal, their names live on, and like it or not, Dr. Death will be remembered too. Even if you lose in the end, isn't it enough to win more than anyone else could ever hope to?

Holding that generator in my hand I thought about the possibilities. I already had a design for my world flag and I knew what my title would be. I imagined sitting on a golden throne in the Oval Office, painting a huge encircled 'A' on the Statue of Liberty, making the official language of the world Portuguese, renaming Greenland to Iceland and Iceland to Greenland, making the speaking of the phrase 'get 'er done' a felony punishable by up to five years imprisonment, making Aerosmith's 'Dream On' the world anthem, and a few other things. Clearly, I'd had time to daydream.

But even as I imagined all the fun I could have I also thought about how it would inevitably end. I pictured myself bloodied and beaten, all my robots smashed, my henchmen defeated, Raven unconscious and slung over Amazon's shoulder. I could see myself in handcuffs being led out of the White House either by Supersoldier or Dark Detective. There would be cameras there and people would be cheering and everyone would talk about how wonderful it was that my reign of terror was over. Not even in my dreams could I see my victory lasting.

That was the reason I'd made my decision.

XXX

I remained in my lab for a while. I have always loved working with my hands. Inventing and creating always set my mind at ease. It was almost noon when I finally came out of the lab. Raven was waiting on me.

"Morning, Doc."

I was startled by her appearance. She wasn't in her usual shinobi shōzoku. Instead she had on a little black dress that looked like something you would see out at a club. It showed off her arms, shoulders, and a lot of her legs. I couldn't keep from staring. I was especially drawn to those long and silky smooth legs. Of course… her legs were actually my handiwork. So I was getting turned on by my own creation. That sounds kind of creepy doesn't it?

"See anything you like?"

Of course she would notice me ogling her. I was just glad she sounded amused. "You're dressed differently today."

"You object?"

"No," I said immediately. "But I'm a little surprised. Is there a special reason for the sudden change?"

She gave a slight shake of the head that sent her long, beautiful hair swaying. "Not really, I just thought I'd mix things up a little. I hate to be predictable."

"Somehow I don't think you need to worry about that."

My words produced a satisfied little grin. "Well you know how much I like surprising you, Doc."

I thought about the kiss and suddenly noticed she was wearing lipstick. I wasn't sure, but I thought it was the very first time I'd ever seen her wear it. It wasn't like she needed it to be attractive, Raven was a natural beauty. Was she wearing eye liner too?

"So… there's no particular reason you're looking so beautiful this morning?"

The grin widened a bit and she leaned forward ever so slightly. "You think I'm beautiful?"

I started to feel very warm. "Your beauty is obvious, I am merely stating a fact."

"Hey now, stop with the dirty talk, player."

"Do you, ah, maybe want to go out on a date sometime?"

She rolled her eyes. "Don't push your luck, Doc."

Women make no sense whatsoever. Compared to trying to understand them quantum mechanics are simple.

"Well, as much as I like your new look, this is probably not a good time to be unarmed."

Raven lifted an eyebrow. She then reached behind her back and came up with three shuriken in each hand as if my magic. She wasn't carrying a purse and you wouldn't think her outfit left the room to conceal a toothpick.

"I'm never without the tools of my trade, even when I'm feeling pretty. Is there a special reason though?"

"I'm going to the communications room, I plan to make a broadcast."

Her eyes widened. "This is it, isn't it? You're going to tell them what you have in your lab and demand they surrender or else. You're finally doing it, Doc! You're going to conquer the world!"

"Something like that," I mumbled. She sounded so excited I felt embarrassed. I almost changed my mind right then and there. But I had given it a lot of thought and knew my choice was the right one.

XXX

It took a little time to get everything ready. The broadcast equipment I had wouldn't let me take over all the channels on Earth. I could only interrupt and overpower the local ones in New York and Jersey. That would be plenty to get the message out though. I was in my costume, of course, and I had the generator floating in the air in front of me. The message would be short and to the point. Raven was behind the camera cheering me as a couple henchmen worked the boards and finally told me we were ready to jam the local broadcasts. I took a deep breath and gave a nod.

"You're on in three, two, one," one of the men pointed to me.

It had finally come, the moment my entire life had been building towards.

"Greetings, I am Dr. Anarchy. I am directing this message to the general public and towards the United Nations. Even though it hasn't been reported, I was on board the Altarian dreadnaught during yesterday's attack. The reason the ship was brought down was because I was able to remove this," I waved a hand at the silver ball floating in front of me. "This is what powered that ship. It has the energy output of a small sun. If you doubt this really is what powered the Altarian ship, please contact Dark Detective. He'll be able to confirm it. I'm sure you can all imagine exactly what this item is capable of."

Raven gave an excited nod. I could picture all the faces staring at their TVs waiting to hear my demands.

"I've decided to use this technology for the good of all humanity. Once a worldwide power grid is built it will supply free and limitless power to everyone on Earth. Not only will this solve the world's energy problems but I expect it will also greatly help the environment as coal burning power plants are shut down and gasoline powered automobiles are replaced by fully electric models. I will be delivering the generator to the UN General Assembly at twelve noon tomorrow, Eastern Standard Time. I ask the UN to begin plans for whatever ceremony they wish to conduct, and more importantly to contact engineers about the best way to share this new boon with everyone equally. Thanks you."

I nodded to the men at the controls.

"We're out," one of them said. He looked and sounded a bit confused. "Ah, great speech, Dr. Anarchy. Really great."

"Yeah," the other henchman said. "Terrific."

Raven was just standing there staring at me.

"What do you think, Raven?"

"What do I think? I'm wondering if the aliens brainwashed you or something."

"I believe it's reasonable to assume that if I were under their control I wouldn't have caused their ship to crash."

"Did you seriously just offer to hand over the most powerful weapon in the world? I mean that thing could destroy Earth, right?"

"The Earth, the moon, and probably all the inner planets too."

"And instead of threatening to use it you're going to make nice and give it to them instead?"

"That's what I said."

She thought about it for a second. "It's a trick, right? You'll show up, the diplomats will be waiting and there will be reporters from every country. Then you'll blow up the UN building or something and make your real demands. Is that it?"

I shook my head. "No. No secret threats or hidden agendas, I really did offer to give everyone free energy."

"Why?"

"Because it's the right thing to do."

Her beautiful lips twisted. "Who are you and what have you done to the real Dr. Anarchy?"

I chuckled. "We should get ready. We'll be having visitors over soon."

XXX

It took a little less than two hours.

The first vehicle was a flower delivery truck. It came down the access road and stopped. The driver actually got out and went through the motions of working on the engine. A minute later there was a bread truck, then an airport shuttle van, a moving truck, a garbage truck, an electric company truck, and so on. Within a matter of minutes there were a couple dozen civilian vehicles surrounding us. Why did they bother? The toy factory was at the end of an access road no one used. Even if it weren't did they think I wouldn't notice so many trucks and vans conveniently breaking down outside my door? I mean they might as well have shown up with tanks and armored personnel carriers.

I was in the control room watching everything on the monitors. I didn't raise the alarm or the force fields. It didn't activate the mines or the cannons or the automated machine guns. I didn't send out my killbots. I just sat there and relaxed and went over what I would say.

Raven was standing over my shoulder calmly looking at the same monitors. She was back in her ninja gear and fully armed.

"Section Seven?" She asked in a quiet voice.

I nodded. "There might be some FBI mixed in just for manpower, but they're the ones in charge."

"How did they find us?"

"You would be amazed what they can do when they're really, truly motivated."

She turned her eyes to me. "You knew. The second you made that broadcast you knew this would happen."

I nodded again. "There was a chance it would be the League showing up, but I figured the percentages were eighty / twenty."

"Aren't we going to do something? You know, before they start shooting at us?"

"They aren't here to attack us, Raven."

"Right," she pointed at one of the vans. "They came to deliver the pizza we ordered."

"They came in force to let me know they're serious, but they're here to talk, not fight."

"You sure about that?"

At that precise moment the back of the flower truck opened. A tall man in a tailor made black business suit and an eye patch began walking toward the building. I had one of the cameras zoom in on his face.

"Well I'll be damned," I said. "That's Michael Rigid, Director of Section Seven."

"You know it's annoying when you're right all the time."

XXX

The Director walked right up to the main entrance. There was a sign that read, 'Please ring doorbell for admittance.' He did so.

"Yes?" I answered over a speaker.

"I'd like to speak with Dr. Anarchy, please."

I immediately liked him. I respect a man who has good manners even when the fate of the world hangs in the balance. "Do you have an appointment?"

"No, but it's an urgent matter. I am hoping he can make time for me."

"I think he can squeeze you in. However, we have a strict policy concerning weapons on the premises."

"I understand." He opened up his jacket and made a show of taking his pistol out of his shoulder holster and laying it on the ground.

"Thank you. Now could you also remove all your other weapons, please? Not just the guns, but the knives and brass knuckles too."

"You have scanners."

"Of course."

He shrugged. "It was worth a try."

He had a nine millimeter in the small of his back, a .38 strapped to one ankle, a pair of throwing knives on the inside of his forearms, a pair of brass knuckles in an inside pocket, two spare magazines for his primary weapon, high steel wire attached to his right wrist, a one shot mini rocket in the shape of a fountain pen, and some explosive in the shape of chewing gum. Even Raven looked a little impressed at the small arsenal he was carrying.

"I am completely unarmed now."

"Except for the Tasers in your shoes and the weapon under your eyepatch."

He began removing his dress shoes. "The device beneath my eyepatch is just a communicator and bio thermal camera."

"Which can also function as a laser. It's a pretty advanced design. Vakryl?"

"Yes, some alien technology is beyond belief."

"Tell me about it."

He flipped up his eyepatch and carefully removed the communicator / camera / laser and put it down next to his shoes and weapons. I was curious about the thing and wouldn't have minded a closer look, but Rigid had a very well-earned reputation for being dangerous. It wouldn't be smart to take any chances.

"There, can I come in now?"

I checked the scanners one final time. He didn't appear to have anything more dangerous than car keys still on him.

"Get rid of your keys too."

He complied. "Anything else?"

"No, just hold on for one moment, please."

He probably expected the door to open and for one of my henchmen to lead him to me. Instead I teleported him to a conference room. One second he was standing in his socks outside the front door, the next he was before a table with me seated on the opposite end with Raven standing next to me and the generator floating above the table a couple feet in front of me. I'd had all the henchmen clear out, so it was just the three of us. I also had some killbots on standby, just in case. Along with the table and chairs was a side table with refreshments. Suddenly being dematerialized and then popping back into existence elsewhere can be unsettling even when you know it's coming. When it happens without warning it can be a huge shock to the senses.

"Welcome Director Rigid, I am Dr. Anarchy and this is my lieutenant, Raven. Please help yourself to some coffee and cookies. We have decaf if you want."

I give him credit. I saw his eye widen, but that was the only sign of surprise. "Thank you."

He nonchalantly poured himself a cup of regular, dumped in a couple packets of sugar and a little cream, and took a cookie before sitting down at the other end of the table. He was definitely a cool customer. Just what you'd expect from a man who once rode on the back of a T-rex and killed Adolf Hitler's mutant super clone when he was still a field agent.

"I appreciate you agreeing to meet with me, Dr. Anarchy. It's also a pleasure to meet you, Miss Fusikawa."

"The only people who call me that are the ones who don't know I'm a ninja. Please either call me Raven or Sexy Japanese Goddess. I'm good with either."

"I'll go with Raven, it's faster." He took a sip of his coffee. "Before we begin I should tell you that taking me hostage or killing me won't get you anything. I'm expendable."

"Aren't we all?" I said.

"I've had reports about the Altarian teleporters. We're hoping to salvage one of their working units."

"I don't blame you, being able to teleport instantly to anywhere is amazing."

He glanced at the generator. "Normally, when someone in your position makes a claim about an extraordinary device or technology we would require a demonstration before we'd credit it. For instance, Dr. Death destroyed Gary, Indiana with one of his black holes."

"What do you suggest? I use it to power my lights?"

"In this particular case we have certain information that leads us to accept your assertion as credible."

"Nice of Dark Detective to tell someone about what really happened."

"The important things is we believe the generator can do what you say it can, provide the world unlimited energy."

"And you've come here to thank me for my great generosity and humanitarianism in donating that power to the world's entire population. While I do appreciate the gesture, I have to tell you a gift basket would have done fine."

He took another sip of coffee and a bite from his cookie. "Hmm, good cookie. Is this homemade?"

"It sure is," Raven said. "Glad you like it."

"Wait, you bake?"

"No need to act so surprised, just because I'm a killer doesn't mean I don't know my way around the kitchen."

"Well, it is good to be multidimensional. Dr. Anarchy, I've come here today to inform you that President Thompson and the United States government does not want you to supply the United Nations with this device."

"What a shock. And here I really thought you just wanted to thank me for my altruism."

"You're giving the world this power source would do incalculable harm."

"How so?"

"Well, to begin with, you'll be putting millions of people in energy production out of work. Many major corporations would be bankrupted overnight. If the value of petroleum were drastically reduced it would bring economic ruin to most of the Middle East. If you think the region is dangerous now it could become completely destabilized. And if the economic and political ramifications weren't enough of a concern, this device is also a potential doomsday weapon. President Thompson wouldn't feel comfortable entrusting its security to the UN."

"I'm sure he'd sleep much better at night if you had it though."

"It wouldn't be the first one we've taken possession of. The President has authorized me, under the terms of the Defense of the Public against Supernatural or Superhuman Threats Act, to negotiate with you. I am empowered to make a deal with you in exchange for your peacefully handing over the generator. What would you say to a full presidential pardon, the medal of freedom, and a hundred million dollars, tax free?"

"I'd say you're insulting me."

The Director leaned back in his chair. "Let me guess, what you have in mind is to rule the world. Your offer to the UN was bogus, it was just your way to draw attention to the threat."

"My offer was genuine, as far as it went. I just knew there was no way I'd be left alone to actually hand over the generator. The US government has always put its own interests ahead of anyone else's, and that's been true since the days of Washington. Not that I blame you for it, self-interest isn't just part of human nature, it makes practical sense. I just find the hypocrisy of always pretending you're doing things for the greater good to be annoying."

"Dr. Anarchy, I am happy to negotiate with you, so long as the terms are reasonable. President Thompson has no intention of spending another week locked up in a prison cell. And I don't intend to see the White House wrecked again when you get evicted. Give my offer serious consideration, you're not going to win this. We have the League of Heroes on standby ready to-"

"No you don't," I interrupted. I normally hate being rude, but he was insulting my intelligence. "You haven't told the League where I am, and you won't except as a last resort."

"Why do you say that?"

"Because if Supersoldier actually knew where I was he'd either be floating in the air just above my head, or he'd already be tearing my base apart. He's not what you would call subtle. The fact is you don't completely trust the heroes. Oh you work with them, you applaud them publicly, but they have a really nasty tendency to think for themselves and do what they view as the right thing, no matter how it relates to US foreign and domestic policy. If they were involved in this could you be absolutely sure they'd agree with *not* handing the generator over to the UN?"

Director Rigid frowned. "That's pretty insightful."

"Damn right," Raven put in. "He has an IQ of two hundred."

She gave me a wink that made me really feel good.

"Well, even so, I have more than two hundred heavily armed men sitting outside ready to take this place by force. And I can call in the National Guard and airstrikes if I have to. You aren't going to-"

He stopped when the light around the generator suddenly went from gold to crimson and the soft hum got noticeably louder.

"I'm a supervillain with a weapon that can destroy the world. Do you REALLY want to make me desperate?"

He sat up straight and put both hands on the table. "No, I don't. You're right, Dr. Anarchy. You're the one in charge here. Why don't you tell me what you want?"

The hum quieted down and the generator returned to its original appearance.

"I never said I wasn't willing to negotiate, but your opening offer was insulting. It's the equivalent of trying to buy me off with a few shiny rocks."

"All right, what would be fair compensation?"

Before I began I spoke to Raven. "Could you go back to the control room and keep an eye on things?"

"Huh? You want me to leave, now?"

I activated my killbots and had them aim their guns at the Director. "I'm sure I'll be fine. Director Rigid and I are just going to talk."

She aimed a worried glance at Rigid. He'd once killed a Soviet NKVD captain with a quarter. I should have made him get rid of his change along with his keys. "You sure about this, Dr. Anarchy?"

"I'm sure."

Before she left she gave the Director a friendly warning. "If you do anything to him I will rip out your liver and feed it to you."

Director Rigid didn't respond until she was gone. "She your girlfriend?"

"No."

"You sure?"

"Eh, not really. Anyway, there's something I want to show you." I took a remote out of a pocket and pressed it.

XXX

About five minutes later I materialized in the control room.

"That was quick," Raven said. "Is it over?"

"Yes, see?" I motioned to one of the monitors. It showed Director Rigid walking back towards the flower truck. In his hands was a metal ball.

"Hey! Is that the generator?"

"It is."

She rounded on me looking furious. "What the Hell?! He talked you into giving up in five fucking minutes?! What did he say? How could you cave like that?"

"It's not like that," I replied calmly. "We made a deal."

"You made a deal and handed your only super weapon over to him?" She grabbed her hair with both hands. "You think he's going to keep his word? You can't be that gullible! The second he has the generator somewhere safe he's going to attack us!"

"No, he's not."

We watched him enter the flower truck. No sooner were the doors shut than it peeled away, wheels literally burning rubber.

"Great, here it comes!" Raven had a hand on a sword.

But no one started shooting at us. Instead, one by one, all the vehicles that surrounded us left.

Raven stared at the monitors and then turned to me looking confused and with her hair a mess. "Okay, what just happened here?"

"I won."

Rule #11 - It's okay to make a deal, especially when you're the one with a doomsday device. They're the ultimate trump card.

Chapter 29

"And that's how I became God-Emperor of Rhode Island." I exhaled and felt amazingly relaxed. That was the best monologue ever!

Diana Darwin blinked a couple times and I could tell she was fighting not to yawn. Her cameraman didn't bother, he did at least have the common courtesy to put his free hand over his mouth as he did so.

"Ah, thank you. When I asked how you got into this position I wasn't expecting such a… thorough explanation."

"I am always happy to talk to the press." Being not only one of the country's top investigative reporter's but Supersoldier's unofficial girlfriend, there was no way I would have turned down her request for an interview. Though her ulterior motives were obvious. During my monologue I noticed her drop her left hand beneath her seat for just a couple seconds. It was very subtle and well done. She'd also requested permission to interview local residents and government officials. I had no doubt she would be trying to find clues about a particular object.

The whole situation was pretty damn cliché. I bet she was half expecting me to take her hostage. It was all part of the game though, so I didn't mind. And truth be told, getting interviewed by THE Diana Darwin was kind of cool.

"I note you still claim Neil Kane is Dark Detective."

"I claim that because it's true."

Shortly after I made my deal with Director Rigid I sold off all my shares in Kane Shipping and then posted an eleven minute video on YouTube detailing the evidence I had that Neil Kane was Dark Detective. The video was deleted within an hour, but by that point it had already been downloaded thousands of times. Not even Supersoldier and the League can get rid of a story that's out on the internet. Soon millions of people were arguing over whether or not it could be true.

"The share price on Kane Shipping has plummeted eighty percent since your accusation was made public. Neil Kane has also been attacked by various supervillains, including Whiteface, no fewer than nine times."

"All of which he managed to survive unharmed. Amazing for a pampered rich boy."

"He's been forced to retire from public life and is now effectively a prisoner in his own home."

"Yes, it must be horrible being trapped in a two hundred room mansion."

"Neil Kane has denied any connection to Dark Detective and I understand he has filed a defamation lawsuit against you."

"I know. I suspect the courts in my country aren't going to award him anything."

Seeing this line of questioning wasn't getting her anywhere she finally moved on. "If you don't mind, I'd like to ask you some serious questions about your regime and its policies."

I gave a gracious nod. "Please, ask me anything you like."

I saw a little twinkle in her eyes and the corner of her lips turned up a bit. It was an expression she always got right before she interviewed a senator or corporate CEO she was about to expose and publicly ruin. Did she really think anything she asked or said could possibly embarrass me? One of the real perks of being a supervillain is that the worse the public views you the better your reputation is with the people who really matter. And it wasn't like I was trying to keep my activities a secret.

"To begin with, what do you say to those who claim your country is a haven for criminals, terrorists, and various evil organizations?"

"Well Diana, I firmly believe in not condemning people who may have had issues with the law in other countries. As I know from personal experience, people need to be given opportunities to succeed despite past transgressions. The Empire of Rhode Island encourages immigration and has an open door policy. We also offer political asylum to those who request it. As for the so-called, 'evil organizations'" I made air quotes. "As you call them, I consider them to be venture capitalists who are bringing employment and exciting business opportunities here."

"Such as the production of automatic weapons, personnel mines, and armored vehicles for sale to countries such as North Korea and Iran?"

"Exactly! Those factories provide employment to more than three thousand local residents. The jobs are at a very competitive pay rate with overtime, sick days, vacation, and retirement plans. The manufacturing plants are regularly inspected and have an excellent safety record. If you want I'll be happy to arrange a tour for you and allow you to interview the employees."

She paused for half a heartbeat, not long enough for the audience to notice, but I picked it up. That was definitely not the answer she was expecting. No doubt she thought I would deny everything.

"And will you also let me speak to the prostitutes and drug dealers who you support?"

"There are no drug dealers in Rhode Island. All drugs and pharmaceuticals are sold in pharmacies where their sales are regulated. The same way state licensed prostitutes can only work in specific buildings in designated business zones."

"So you admit to having legalized prostitution?"

"Yes."

She leaned forward a little. "And how do you justify forcing women into the sex trade?"

"No one here is forced into it, any more than they are in Germany, Austria, the Netherlands, or certain counties in Nevada. Sex workers have to apply for a license and they're required to take monthly medical exams. They pay taxes and receive the same protection under the law as anyone else."

"Very progressive, I can tell you respect women deeply." She turned her head to look at where Raven was leaning against the wall. The camera dutifully followed her gaze.

Raven wasn't wearing her work clothes. She had a halter top, mini skirt, and thigh high boots; all made of black leather. Raven looked... naughty.

"What?" Raven asked with a smirk. "I get a 401-k."

Diana turned back to me. "What about the fact you have legalized all drugs? Even cocaine, heroin, and others that are addictive and have no possible health benefits?"

"You could say the same about tobacco and alcohol. The age of consent here is eighteen, if you are a consenting adult and can afford it, you are free to put whatever you like into your body. I don't try to legislate morality or tell people what they should or shouldn't do to themselves. Part of having personal freedom is the freedom to make bad or self-destructive choices. I don't allow minors to purchase any drug, including alcohol and tobacco. I also don't allow individuals to sell or provide drugs to them. And giving anyone a drug without their knowledge or consent is a felony here."

"What about the stream of addicts that come here just to legally purchase these drugs?"

"What about them? We support tourism, and they're a huge benefit to the economy."

"Drug addicts coming here to feed their addictions are completely different than a family going to visit Italy on a vacation."

"Only in the details. Economically speaking there isn't any difference between someone going to a foreign country to spend money at a resort or to purchase a few grams of cocaine."

"And what happens to the drug addicts that spend all their money and then have nothing left?"

"The same thing that would happen to any tourist in that situation. They are given free transport back to their country of origin. Unless they choose to apply for political amnesty or citizenship. In that case, they enter the state social care program. They'll be provided a residence and mandatory employment. They're still free to buy whatever drugs they want, so long as they can afford it."

"What do you do about people going through withdrawal?"

"Anyone who enters the state social care program receives a medical exam and an injection of melitonum."

"What's that? Some sort of mind control drug?"

"No, it's an invention of Dr. Death's. It's a kind of cleansing agent for the body, it removes all the physical symptoms of addiction. It's a cure not only for drug addiction but for alcoholism and nicotine addiction as well. It's banned in the United States by the way, even though government agencies have been using it for the past ten years."

She gaped at me for a second, then hurried on to her next accusation. I was willing to bet that sound bite wouldn't make it on air.

"What do you say to those who claim you've created a police state filled with human rights violations?"

"Most police states don't have an open border. Visitors are welcomed here and anyone who wants to leave is free to do so. That's pretty much the exact opposite of how a police state functions. As for human rights violations, what are you referring to?"

"Are you joking? I'm talking about the suspension of jury trials, the lack of search warrants by the police, forcing people to testify against themselves, the use of robots by law enforcement, and the horrendous and absolutely disgusting use of capital punishment as a form of entertainment!"

"I take it you're referring to Justice Gladiators and Justice Trivia?"

"That's right! You've actually turned life and death criminal proceedings into second rate reality TV shows! It's horrifying!"

"They're the top two cable television programs. Not just here but in the US as well as Germany, the UK, Canada, Australia, and more than thirty other markets."

"And you're actually proud of that?"

"Of course, if you're going to do something you should always try to be the best at it."

"So I take it watching innocent people killed live on air is a joke to you?"

"Not at all."

"You dress up like a roman emperor at the gladiator fights!"

"The contestants are armed like genuine gladiators from the Roman Coliseum, it's part of the motif. And it's my way of showing my support of the justice system."

"Are you really going to pretend that travesty is in any way related to justice?"

"Many societies did use trial by combat to determine guilt or innocence. And I will remind you that every single person on those shows was either a volunteer competing for a cash prize or a criminal whose guilt was absolutely certain."

That was one of the things that had really caught me by surprise. People from across the world writing in to become contestants on the shows! I decided to allow volunteers to fight each other or compete in trivia matches in return for a fifty thousand dollar cash prize. Of course all the contestants had to sign a waiver and make a recorded statement before the match acknowledging they could die and that they accepted the possibility. It's amazing what some people will do for money or a little bit of fame.

"In my country no one is convicted by circumstantial evidence or because of a biased jury or an incompetent defense attorney. There's no question as to a person being guilty since the primary evidence is their own testimony."

"Because you force them to take truth serum! That's a complete violation of their Fifth Amendment rights!"

"That's a part of American jurisprudence, there's no such right in the empire of Rhode Island. The simple fact of the matter is that the only person that actually knows who is guilty or innocent is the accused. It makes absolutely no sense to not compel the only person who actually knows the truth to speak it."

"I thought you were an advocate of giving people second chances."

"Only when their original crimes were committed somewhere else. Crimes committed here are punished severely."

"Yes, using killer robots as a police force does send that message."

"They're policebots not killbots."

She pinched the bridge of her nose and continued. "The point is, even if people are guilty, it's absolutely insane to then have them either fight each other with swords or play a game of trivia while hooked up to a lethal injection!"

I wondered if she was expecting me to react to the word 'insane.' I know for a fact it's a real trigger for Dr. Death, and he's kidnapped her at least a dozen times. Maybe she hoped I'd lose some of my self-control.

"The United States still uses capital punishment. I don't believe in long term imprisonment. Just as in the United States, all crimes here are categorized as felonies or misdemeanors. Misdemeanors are punished by fines, public service, or some form of corporal punishment. All felonies carry a death sentence, and since guilt is certain there's no reason to have an appeal process. The games are my version of a second chance. The guilty can choose to fight for their lives or match wits with another condemned person. If they win they earn a pardon, and if they lose they die. The matches are a public reminder of the severe consequences of breaking the law here. They serve as a deterrent. The ratings are just a bonus."

"So someone who is really good at trivia or fighting with a sword could get away with being a serial killer?"

"Same is true in the United States if you happen to be rich enough to have great lawyers, or smart enough not to leave behind any witnesses or physical evidence."

That's how it went for another hour and a half. She would make an accusation and I would calmly explain my reasoning. I never got angry or raised my voice. Honestly? I think she was hoping I would try and take her prisoner. It would give Supersoldier an excuse to come flying in to the rescue without appearing to break the agreement the government made with me.

When it was announced that I would take over the state of Rhode Island in exchange for the Altarian generator the public and media went nuts. People screamed that Thompson was clinically insane or a traitor and needed to be impeached. When I actually took power his approval rating plummeted. Everyone demanded that he send in the army or the heroes to get rid of me.

The President and government talked about the sanctity of international law and treaties. I wonder what some Native Americans or small Latin American countries would have to say on the subject. Ordinarily, President Thompson would have found some excuse to break the deal with me almost immediately. When the government double crosses a supervillain no one ever cares. But it had been three months now and I was still in power. There was a reason for that, and it had nothing to do with the sanctity of treaties.

The US media was focused on all my 'tyranny,' 'delusions of godhood,' and 'rampant lawlessness.' The President's popularity had mostly recovered as people focused on me and pushed aside the minor detail of how I'd come to power. I'd built my palace in Tiverton and really enjoyed getting to be a head of state. Being the focus of so much media attention was also a pleasant change. I was named Time Magazine's Person of the Year and I finally made number one on the FBI's most wanted list. Sorry, Dr. Death, you'll have to be happy with the number two spot.

So when Diana finally ran out of things to blame on me she wrapped up the interview. "Thank you for your time and for allowing me this access, Doctor Anarchy."

"Actually, the correct form of address would be, 'Your Imperial Deitiness, but I'll let it slide." I stood up and held my hand out to her.

She stared at it, as though expecting a cobra to pop out of my sleeve or something. She screwed on a smile and took my hand and gave it one halfhearted pump before letting go.

"And we're done," her cameraman announced and stopped rolling.

"I do thank you for agreeing to do this," Diana said. "Normally when I do one of these it's after being snatched by Dr. Death and he wants the world to know he is about to conquer them."

"Well, I get so many interview requests it's not like I need to kidnap anyone. Not any more at least."

"Right." She was looking over the papers on my desk. Probably searching for the one about super-secret plan 'World Destruction' or something. Too bad they were just domestic reports and diplomatic messages. Her eyes scanned everything and then darted to a silver ball with a number of white lines all over it in a complex pattern.

"Do you like my paperweight?" I picked it up and tossed it from one hand to the other. "It's a replica of the Altarian generator, we sell them in the palace gift shop. I can have a free one sent to you."

"Ah, that's all right. If you don't mind I think I'll head back to my hotel room now."

XXX

As soon as she left I took out my scanner. I found the transmitter she planted under her chair and disintegrated it. I took my security very seriously. All the walls, doors, and drapes of my palace are lined with bronze, just to block out Supersoldier's ultra-vision.

"I don't know why you agreed to this," Raven came over to stand next to my chair. "She's going to edit all the footage to make you look as crazy as possible."

"That's par for the course. Have you ever seen an interview of a supervillain that wasn't cut that way?"

"You know the U.S. is NEVER going to accept this right? I mean not permanently. I'm amazed we've lasted as long as we have."

"Oh, I know. Letting a supervillain call himself God-Emperor and actually have sovereignty over a state? And watching him do a decent job of it? I mean I've wiped out unemployment, provided universal health care and education, legalized drug use and prostitution, simplified and streamlined the court system, and actually brought the crime rate down. Plus the gladiatorial fights and trivia matches are the biggest thing on cable right now. I'm pretty much the anti-Christ to both liberals and conservatives. I don't doubt everyone in the White House and the League wants me dead and to pretend none of this ever happened."

"Then how can you be so relaxed? I mean giving interviews, flying around on your jetpack, dressing up in a purple toga when the gladiators fight? It's like you're just asking to be killed."

"Not much point in being God-Emperor if you can't enjoy the perks."

"Well unless you really think you're a god or something you should seriously consider going into hiding, or building a fortress instead of a palace."

"Why bother? If they want to get rid of me they're not going to send a few agents. President Thompson will get on TV and call me a war criminal and a human rights violator and a threat to American security. Then about five minutes later Supersoldier and the whole League will show up to arrest me and save the good people of Rhode Island from the horrors of effective government and free medical care."

"Then how can you be so relaxed?"

"Because they're not going to touch me until they find the second Altarian generator."

She blinked and her mouth slipped open. I loved doing that to her.

"Wait, there's a second one?"

"Well, not originally. I mean think about it. The thing provides limitless energy. Why would a ship need two of them? But the Altarians had the technology to create it in the first place, and I was able to steal a lot of their tech. It's not impossible to believe that a genius like me could recreate it. I gave Director Rigid the 'copy' and kept the original for myself. Part of our deal is that I won't use it or reveal its existence unless the US double crosses me or I suddenly die. In that case it's programmed to teleport itself to Beijing."

I reached into a pocket and took out one of my remote controls. I pressed a button. The paperweight on my desk leapt a foot into the air and floated there. It began to hum and gave off a faint golden aura.

Raven gaped like a fish. It's pretty hard to surprise her once, never mind twice in a single day.

"Fuck me! I don't believe it."

I laughed and shut my little toy off. It dropped with a loud 'thunk.' It started to roll off the edge of my desk, but she grabbed it and held it in place.

"Are you insane?!" She yelled. "You've got the most powerful weapon the world has ever seen, and you're using it as a paperweight?"

I leaned back and stretched. "Why shouldn't I? It really is a paperweight, just one with a sound system, lights, magnets, and a battery attached."

"Huh?" She stared at the intricate metal ball. "You mean it's a fake?"

I nodded. "That's right. I knew how the US would react to my offer to share the generator with the world. So before I sent my message to the UN I whipped up my little toy in the lab. It has the exact same size, markings, and effects as the real thing. Just looking at it with the naked eye or a camera there's no way to tell it apart from the genuine article. Supersoldier's ultra-vision or a simple test would have revealed the truth, but I wasn't going to allow that and they were in no position to force me."

"But wouldn't Director Rigid figure it out? I thought he was pretty smart."

I grinned at her. "You're pretty smart, Raven, and you believed it just now."

She grunted something and crossed her arms.

"I'm sure Rigid suspected it was a trick, but the difference between suspect and know is about as big as the distance between here and Mars. I mean the Altarians were able to fit something with the energy output of a small star into a ball you can hold with one hand. If they could do that then it was at least theoretically possible someone like me, who had stolen a lot of their equipment and information, could as well. When I used the teleporter it was proof I had at least some of the Altarian tech at my disposal. What really sealed it was when I actually handed over the generator. As paranoid as most of my kind are I'm sure he figured there was no way I would do that unless the second one was the real thing."

"And what would have happened if the minute he walked off the property he'd sent in the troops?"

I shrugged. "Then you and I would have teleported away. That's the thing about a bluff, if someone calls you on it you lose."

"But why bluff at all? I mean you had the thing. Why not hold onto it?"

"Because it would have been impossible. Haven't you ever noticed that when Dr. Death or anyone else comes up with a serious threat to the world order what happens? All the heroes get together and go after him. Even some of the bad guys will help out if the situation is dire enough. I mean, even when a plan actually works, like when Dr. Death became emperor for a week, it never lasts. The good guys just won't stop until they win, and most of them are willing to die in order to save everyone. Most supervillains don't have that level of commitment, never mind the henchmen and the lieutenants. I mean people will die for their country or for their faith or family, who wants to die for a guy in a costume? No supervillain can ever really conquer the world, not permanently. Because whenever any of us come close it creates so much opposition it's just impossible to beat all of it back, no matter what super power or magic artifact or doomsday device you have in your pocket."

"Wait a minute, so are you saying you never thought you could win?"

"Well... I did have some hopes of taking over with an AI or an army of giant robots, but I knew even if I managed to win it would only be for the short term. There are just too many powerful people in this world for any one person to beat them all."

"Then why'd you go through all of this? Going to prison, being wanted, getting shot at, almost getting killed… why put up with all that when you knew there was no hope?"

"Because it was fun," I told her. "Because it was a challenge. You know I can make a fortune legally if I want. And with my inventions I could have gotten a certain level of fame and success going the legitimate route. I mean my front companies actually turned a six percent profit last year in a bad economy. But it would have been boring. Competing against the other supervillains, battling the heroes, and trying to stand above every other person in the entire world. What could possibly be more exciting than that?"

"You've never spent a weekend in Vegas at a bachelorette party, have you?"

That got a startled laugh out of me.

Raven was grinning at me as she shook her head. "This still isn't going to last. Sooner or later they're going to figure it out."

"Yeah, I know, but I'm going to enjoy it for as long as I can, and people will still be talking about it long after I'm gone. That's a sort of victory in and of itself."

"Well, I guess that's true. So what happens now?"

I thought about it for a second. "Want to make out?"

She laughed and rolled her eyes. I thought she was going to remind me not to push my luck. But instead she plopped down on my lap. She leaned in close and purred in my ear…

"All hail, Your Imperial Deitiness Anarchy, God-Emperor of Rhode Island."

As we started kissing I wondered if I could talk her into letting me add a chainsaw to the next upgrade of her cybernetics.

Chainsaws are cool.

XXX

Rule #36 - Sidekicks are frustrating, annoying, and more than a little aggravating. But, in the end, they are worth all the trouble.

THE END

XXX

<u>The List</u>

Rule #1 - Be ready to adjust and deal with the unexpected.

Rule #2 – Every job has an ideal tool.

Rule #3 - A disintegrator is a lot like a Swiss army knife, it's useful and always handy to have around.

Rule #4 – Get your business done quietly when you can.

Rule #5 – Don't leave behind anyone who will come looking for revenge.

Rule #6 - Mind control devices always go wrong.

Rule #7 – Revenge is not a dish best served cold. Revenge is a huge pain in the ass.

Rule #8 - Nothing is perfect, always know what the flaws are.

Rule #9 – Never kill a child or a superhero if you can avoid it. You can kill a million henchmen and rival supervillains and no one will care. If you kill a little kid or a hero the entire world will come after you. (Special exception for killing your nemesis.)

Rule #10 – Conquering and ruling are two very different things.

Rule #11 – Always remember your entire criminal record is one click away.

Rule #12 – Take the time to make your orders specific. It's easy for people to misunderstand you.

Rule #13- Always be paranoid. If you're a supervillain people really are out to get you.

Rule #14 – AIs aren't worth the trouble.

Rule #15 – Giant Robots are ALWAYS cool.

Rule #16 - Clever plans and subtlety are important. But there are times when being able to rip a steel door off its hinges is enough.

Rule #17 – Being a supervillain means never having to say you're sorry.

Rule #18 – When you kidnap someone make sure to let people know.

Rule #19 – Henchmen are easy to replace.

Rule #20 - Always remember, the civilian identity is the mask and the alias is who you really are. Even if you're wearing a sweater vest at the mall while buying cheese, you are still the guy who threatened to destroy New York with a tidal wave.

Rule #21 - When you have absolutely no idea what's going on, strike a pose and yell as loud as you can, "It's all going according to plan!"

Rule #22 – Regular criminals care about money. Supervillains care about power.

Rule #23 – Never turn down free food, drink, or weapons grade plutonium.

Rule #24 - If one of your henchmen asks you why everything has to be a secret, shoot him, he is too stupid to be allowed to live. If one of your henchmen critiques your brilliant scheme and explains why it won't work, shoot him, he is too smart for his own good. As a supervillain you do not have to be fair and consistent, especially where your own henchmen are concerned.

Rule #25 – Never put up with ANYONE mocking you.

Rule #26 - Never forget, your image and reputation are everything. No successful supervillain in the history of the world has ever been described as funny, cute, or nice. If people call you any of these to your face you need to seriously reconsider your career path.

Rule #27 – It's fine to do something heroic and save the day, just so long as you have a valid reason. (Getting a doomsday device is ALWAYS a valid reason.)

Rule #28 – Monologuing is a personal choice you can stop at any time. It is NOT a compulsion.

Rule #29 - Don't try to justify yourself to people. No matter how noble you may think your cause is, no matter how justified, if you want the entire world to kneel down before you, you're going to be the bad guy. Embrace it.

Rule #30 - Chicks dig lasers.

Rule #31 – If you run into a being with the power to cross dimensions that can simply appear before you, try to avoid a fight.

Rule #32 - Being a supervillain is its own reward.

Rule #33 – Seize every opportunity.

Rule #34 – If you want something, take it.

Rule #35 - Losing doesn't make you a failure. If conquering the world were easy everyone would do it.

Rule #36 (original) – Don't get a sidekick.

Rule #36 (updated) - Sidekicks are frustrating, annoying, and more than a little aggravating. But, in the end, they are worth all the trouble.

Raven's Rule #1 – It's always better to take care of a problem when it's small.

Raven's Rule #2 – Shit happens.

Raven's Rule #3 – Take help where you can get it.

Raven's Rule #4 – When life gives you lemons make lemonade. Then find some gin to mix with it.

Raven's Rule #5 – When all else fails just tell everyone you're PMSing. Even if they don't believe you they won't ask for details.

XXX

The Rabbit And The Necromancer

The village chieftain bowed low. "Thank you for saving us from that horrible ogre. My village has been forced to deal with many horrors, but never a monster like that. We are truly grateful to you, Master Rabbit. If you had not come along when you did… I shudder to think what might have happened."

"Oh, think nothing of it," Waldo said with a magnanimous wave of his hand. "All in a day's work for a white mage."

Standing beside him, his beautiful wife fidgeted and twirled some hair about a finger.

"How can we ever repay you for saving us?"

"Some gold would work."

The chieftain blinked. "Oh. I'm afraid we don't have any."

Waldo shrugged. "I can take silver instead."

The chieftain began to slowly rub his hands together. "We have very little silver as well."

"Are you sure?" Waldo looked about with suspicion. "You certainly look prosperous."

The village of Dracut was sizeable, from the number of houses Waldo would guess there was a population of at least a thousand. The homes looked to be in good repair, the village had a lodge that was two stories, and even had a general store. The surrounding countryside was green with crops, there were horses and other farm animals in sight, and the village itself was located at the end of a valley pass. The place certainly looked affluent enough to offer him a fair reward.

"Looks can be deceiving." The chieftain said.

"Whatever reward you want to give my husband will be fine," Alice said.

"Well that depends on what it is."

Alice gave her husband a flat stare and crossed her arms over her ample chest. Through their bond he could sense her annoyance.

Waldo sighed. "Fine, what do you have in mind?"

The chieftain paused and thought. "We could offer you a bag of copper coins. Perhaps an old cow?"

"That's all?" Waldo cried. "I saved you all from a rampaging ogre! Do you people want to get eaten?"

Alice slid over and placed a hand on his shoulder. "Darling? Aren't you being a little harsh?"
"No. It's not my fault if some people have no sense of appreciation." He spoke directly to the chieftain. "I saved your village from a rampaging beast. Shouldn't you at the very least offer me a virgin?"

That seemed to be the wrong thing to say as Waldo suddenly felt Alice begin to squeeze his shoulder with vicelike pressure. "Why are you asking him about a virgin?" She said in a low growl. "Am I not enough for you?"

Waldo struggled not to cry in pain. "You're plenty, it's the principle of the thing, that's all. If you don't want to give me a girl I can take a boy. I just think getting a virgin as a reward for saving a village is rather customary."

The chieftain looked uncomfortable. "Well... we do have a thirteen year old orphan boy. Would that do?"

"My husband is joking. Whatever you want to give him will be more than enough. Right, darling?"

She squeezed tighter and he thought he could hear his collar bone starting to crack. "Yes," he grunted. "Anything is fine."

Alice let go and Waldo breathed a sudden sigh of relief.

XXX

In short order the village chieftain returned with a cloth sack containing five hundred copper coins, the equivalent of five silvers. Waldo accepted it with a clear lack of enthusiasm. They had been traveling on the road for many months now and he'd come to have a better idea about wealth and the value of things. Obviously, Dracut could not compare to the towns or cities they had visited during their journeys. However, it was easily the largest village they'd seen in the past few weeks. The reward they offered definitely felt light.

"I just hope the ogre doesn't suddenly return and wreck your entire village," Waldo said. "They've been known to do that. Often."

The chieftain looked worried. "Do you think that might happen?"

Waldo glanced at the sack with the coins. "I'd say it's likely."

"No, it's not." Alice said grabbing him by the elbow. "I'm *sure* you won't have any more ogre problems."

"Oh, I hope not." The chieftain said fervently. "We've suffered enough these last couple years. You see, the reason we can't offer you more is because we're forced to hand over almost everything we have to a... necromancer." His voice dropped to a fearful whisper on the final word.
"A necromancer?" Waldo asked with interest. "A mage who creates and uses undead?"

"That's right, an evil and corrupt creature who defies the laws of man and nature by bringing back the dead and using them to threaten us. We have to offer him everything we have in tribute or his horde on undead will come slaughter us."

"Oh no," Waldo clutched his hands together. "That sounds awful. You poor villagers living under such a horrible threat. And this necromancer has all your money?"

"That's right."

"Well I obviously can't let that stand. I'm a white mage after all. So it's my duty to deal with him."

The chieftain's breath caught. "You'd go and fight the necromancer for us? Truly?"

Waldo straightened his back and lifted his chin. "Naturally, if there's one thing Waldo Rabbit is known for its selfless heroism!"

The village chieftain stared at Waldo, too amazed to even speak.

Alice stood there and rolled her eyes.

"So, where can I find this very rich necromancer?"

XXX

They were about a mile beyond the village when Gronk came skipping out of the woods. He was chewing on a deer's hoof as he rejoined Waldo and Alice.

"How'd it go, master?"

"Horribly, I barely got any kind of reward at all. You would think people would be more thankful to someone who saved them from a Great Monster."

"Darling, you're the one who sent Gronk to attack them in the first place."

"They didn't know that, so that makes them stingy and ungrateful."

"They gave you what they could," Alice reminded him.

"Want me to go back and eat all of them, master?"

Waldo shook his head. "No, it's fine. We have something much better to do. At the other end of this valley is a small keep where a wealthy necromancer resides. We're going to go rob him."

"Sounds fun," Gronk said.

"Uh, darling? Is this really a good idea? What if this person turns out to be like your grandfather? The one who wants to eat your heart and is chasing us?"

Along with someone else, Waldo thought and rubbed the spot above his heart. "The chieftain said necromancer, not lich, there is a huge difference. I'm sure even a mundane could tell them apart. Probably."

"He also said 'horde of undead' or were you not listening to that part?"

"Eh, horde is a relative term. Out here, in the country, with no major cities or towns nearby, he would have very limited resources. My guess is he probably has only a few hundred undead, a thousand at the absolute most."

"We're going to fight a thousand undead?" The blood drained from Alice's face. "Darling, there are just three of us. It'll be a slaughter."

"Exactly!"

"I mean it'll be our slaughter."

"Exactly!"

Alice gave a weary shake of her head. "I mean we," she deliberately pointed to him, Gronk, and then herself. "Are going to be slaughtered."

"Don't be ridiculous, you and Gronk are Great Monsters. I have plenty of spells that can handle undead. This will be easy, trust me."

Alice raised a fiery eyebrow. "Isn't that what you said about Torikai?"

Without conscious thought he rubbed the spot above his heart. "This will be completely different. We're just dealing with one necromancer, it's not like we have an entire guild of mages again, or a queen."

"Or bloodthirsty drow," Gronk muttered as a slight shudder ran through him.

Waldo nodded. "This will go much better."

"Well, if it goes worse I doubt we'll survive."

"Alice, you're letting my brilliant disguise fool you again. Remember who I really am. I grew up in Castle Corpselover, surrounded by undead. My mom is acknowledged the most powerful necromancer in the world! Believe me, I'm an expert on necromancy and the undead."

"All right, how would the three of us do against her? Would we be able to win?"

Waldo gave a startled laugh. "Are you joking? We'd be butchered!"

Alice stared at him.

"But mom's a Grand Master. What are the odds this guy is?"

Waldo started to whistle a happy tune. Gronk skipped along to it. Alice followed, not feeling at all certain about things.

XXX

It took them most of the day to reach the end of the valley.

There they found a simple stone keep only two stories high. It stood on a hilltop with a rutted trail leading to its gate. There were no guards or any sign of movement as they approached. Alice looked about nervously.

"Maybe he's not here," she said.

"No, he is," Waldo assured her. "I can sense his magic."

"Can he sense yours too?"

"Of course." Waldo glanced at the ground that surrounded the keep. It was all dirt that looked to have been recently turned over, there were no patches of grass anywhere next to the walls. He came to a halt twenty yards in front of the gate, where there was still thick grass on either side of the trail. Both of his familiars also stopped.

"So what do we do now?" Alice asked.

"Just wait," Waldo took out his wand. "We're probably about to be attacked."

"What?!" Alice cried.

Sure enough, a moment later the ground in front of them began to stir. Skulls and boney hands tore out of the earth. Some of the bodies still had rotting flesh attached, worms wriggled through the carrion as they rose out of the damp soil. They were silent as they began to stand and then slowly shuffle towards Waldo and his companions.

"Eeeek!" Alice instinctively cowered behind her husband.

Waldo looked at her in surprise. "What are you doing? There aren't even fifty of them."

"They're undead! They're skeletons and zombies!" Alice had grown up with scary stories about the undead, and feared them the way most people did.

Most people who were not raised in the city of Alter at least.

"Okay, first off those aren't zombies, those are walking corpses. Basically just skeletons who haven't fully decomposed yet." Waldo did his best to sound patient. "Now stop acting afraid, you're embarrassing me. Just look at Gronk."

The ogre had cheerfully waded into the small crowd and was smashing them to bit with his fists. One of the walking corpses latched onto a leg and bit down savagely. The result was its jawbone snapping off. Gronk easily shook it loose before stomping it into a black goo. Waldo found the sight encouraging, obvious proof these weak undead were no threat. To his surprise Alice bent over and threw up. He had no idea why. Maybe the cheese she'd had for breakfast had gone bad.

"So embarrassing," he muttered. He pointed his wand at the nearest skeletons. "*Repulso.*"

The spell struck the skeletons like a solid wall. Their bones snapped apart and were thrown back. Waldo cast the spell a few more times while Gronk continued to wade through them. Even with Alice being incapacitated the entire fight was over in a couple of minutes. The undead were reduced to scattered bones and a few piles of rotted meat.

With the fighting over Waldo took a minute to gently pat Alice's back as she regained her composure.

"Are you all right?"

"Yes," she gave a slow nod and wiped her mouth. "I'll be fine."

"I know how brave you are most of the time, so I'll forgive what just happened. But it really is embarrassing you would panic like that over a few skeletons and walking corpses. An adult shouldn't have such ridiculous fears."

Alice's eyes narrowed. "Oh look, a hundred rabbits."

"Where?!" Waldo jumped into the air and cried out with a girlish pitch.

"Oops, sorry, my mistake."

Waldo gave her a very unhappy look.

"You think you've won?" A voice shouted down at them.

The three of them looked up to see a figure in black robes standing on the keep's rooftop.

"I have countless more undead waiting inside for you!"

"No you don't," Waldo shouted. "If you did you'd have used them. The whole point of having undead is to use as many as you can all at once."

"Ye… Yes I do! I have thousands more!"

"Thousands? Inside your little building? They must be packed in tighter than coins in a miser's purse."

"I'll unleash them on you unless you run away right now! This is your only chance to escape with your lives!"

"I'll pass," Waldo crossed his arms. "I guess you'll just have to unleash them."

They waited but the necromancer did nothing.

"Well?"

"I… I have traps! Every inch of my keep is filled with the most lethal and ingenious of traps. If you dare to enter-"

"Okay, I'm already bored." Waldo turned to Alice. "Do you feel well enough to go grab him for me?"

"Certainly, darling."

There was the sound of flesh tearing as leather wings and a whiplike tail wore from her back and horns from her head. The wings rose and came down in a rush, launching her into the air. The necromancer was startled to see her coming straight at him. He was just turning to run away when she grabbed hold of him by his arms and lifted him up off the roof. She then delivered him to her husband and dumped him at Waldo's feet, before smoothly landing herself.

The necromancer was sprawled out in the dirt. He looked up to see an ogre, a succubus, and white mage standing over him. He then saw the ogre turn to the white mage.

"Can I eat him?"

"No. That would be impolite."

The necromancer dry swallowed. "I know what whites usually do to my kind, but I beg for mercy."

Waldo held out a hand. "Your wand and spellbook."

The necromancer complied and handed them over. Waldo set the spellbook down so he could examine the wand first. "It's made of bone and you're wearing black robes. You're a dark mage from Alteroth."

The man slowly nodded. "Not much point in denying it."

"You're a very long way from home," Waldo slowly turned the wand so as to read the words of power inscribed in it. "Why are you here?"

"Ah, I thought there would be more opportunity for me out here in the world than back in Alteroth."

"Translation, you have very little mana and very little natural ability. And I'll bet you were probably the third or fourth son in an overseer, branch family. One of your siblings probably told you to get out or else suffer an accident."

The necromancer stared wide eyed. "You white mages are well informed about how things work in Alteroth."

"Well I am at least. How long since you left?"

"Three years."

That meant the man would not have any useful news about home. "Power, death, wealth; even your words of power are mediocre and boring." Waldo brought the wand down on his knee and snapped it in two.

He then looked through the spellbook. He was not stunned to see it was mostly empty. "No seals, no potions, and all the spells are necromancy. And the most advanced of those is raising common undead. You don't even know how to summon back a soul or drain life energy or make a zombie. Didn't you ever study? Didn't you at least make a serious effort at your craft? Don't you have any self-respect? I mean what sort of dark mage are you?"

The necromancer had a confused look on his face. "Sorry?"

Waldo took a deep breath. He thought about all those hours spent hunched over a spell book or tome, all the desperate effort to learn magic, any sort of magic. How desperately he'd wanted to cast even the most basic necromantic spell. Only to have to accept he was cursed with Healing power. You had no say in how much mana you could draw or what your Talent was. Those were things you were born with. What you did control was how hard you worked to develop the abilities you did have. This idiot was a disgrace to dark mages and necromancers everywhere.

Waldo began to rip the blank pages out of the spellbook. "These spells are all worthless to me, but I can always use the velum. I am going to rob you, but you can keep your spellbook. In exchange for your life I want you to do one thing for me."

"Anything!"

"I want you to tell everyone you meet about the great and terrible Waldo Rabbit and about my familiars. Let the world know a white mage not only spared you but that he also robbed you and has two Great Monsters. Oh, and also mention we're plotting to take over the world."

"Ah, as you wish."

Waldo returned the mangled spellbook and the relieved necromancer rose to his feet.

"By the way, what's your name?"

"Bob."

Both of Waldo's eyebrows rose. "Bob? That's a weird name."

Bob rubbed the back of his head. "Well my full name is Bobbarker, but everyone just called me Bob."

"Of course they did. And what is your House name?" Waldo already knew it couldn't be Corpselover. He was certain he'd never seen this man at any of the family celebrations, and that his mother would not have tolerated such a piss poor necromancer to carry her family name.

"It's Poisondagger."

"Poisondagger?! You're a Poisondagger?"

"You've heard of us." The man stood a little taller. "Yes, that's right, I'm Bob Poisondagger."

"I see, well that changes everything."

"You're not going to rob me?"

"I'm not going to let you live." Waldo turned to his ogre. "You can eat him, Gronk."

"Really, master?!"

"Sure."

A suddenly startled and frightened Bob Poisondagger raised his hands. "Wait a minute! Why-"

CHOMP.

"Aaaaahhhhh!!!"

"Gronk!" Alice shouted. "At least kill him before you eat him!"

"What? I like my food fresh."

"Come on, Alice." Waldo took her hand. "Let's see how much loot we can find."

Waldo and Alice went to search the keep while Gronk ate Bobbarker.

THE END

Made in the USA
Middletown, DE
26 July 2021